continued . . .

ARMED & MAGICAL

"Fresh, original, and fall-out-of-your-chair funny, Lisa Shearin's *Armed & Magical* combines deft characterization, snarky dialogue, and nonstop action—plus a yummy hint of romance—to create one of the best reads of the year . . . Shearin [is] a definite star on the rise." —Linnea Sinclair, author of *Rebels and Lovers*

"An exciting, catch-me-if-you-can, lightning-fast-paced tale of magic and evil filled with goblins, elves, mages, and a hint of love interest." —*Monsters and Critics*

"Dazzling wit and clever humor. It's gritty, funny, and sexy—a wonderful addition to the urban fantasy genre . . . From now on Lisa Shearin is on my auto-buy list!" —Ilona Andrews

"An enchanting read from the very first page . . . [Shearin is] definitely an author to watch!"
—Anya Bast, *New York Times* bestselling author of *Embrace of the Damned*

MAGIC LOST, TROUBLE FOUND

"Take a witty, kick-ass heroine and put her in a vividly realized fantasy world where the stakes are high, and you've got a fun, page-turning read . . . I can't wait to read more of Raine Benares's adventures." —Shanna Swendson, author of *Kiss and Spell*

"[Shearin] gives us a different kind of urban fantasy . . . Littered with entertaining characters and a protagonist whose self-serving lifestyle is compromised only by her loyalty to her friends, *Magic Lost* is an absolutely enjoyable read."
—C. E. Murphy, author of *Shaman Rises*

"Fun, fascinating, and loaded with excitement! *Magic Lost, Trouble Found* is a top-notch read of magic, mayhem, and some of the most charming elves and goblins I've ever encountered. Enthralling characters and a thrilling plot." —Linnea Sinclair

THE
DRAGON
CONSPIRACY

A SPI Files Novel

LISA SHEARIN

ACE BOOKS, NEW YORK

THE BERKLEY PUBLISHING GROUP
Published by the Penguin Group
Penguin Group (USA) LLC
375 Hudson Street, New York, New York 10014

USA • Canada • UK • Ireland • Australia • New Zealand • India • South Africa • China

penguin.com

A Penguin Random House Company

THE DRAGON CONSPIRACY

An Ace Book / published by arrangement with the author

Ace Books are published by The Berkley Publishing Group.
ACE and the "A" design are trademarks of Penguin Group (USA) LLC.

For information, address: The Berkley Publishing Group,
a division of Penguin Group (USA) LLC,
375 Hudson Street, New York, New York 10014.

ISBN: 978-0-425-26692-2

PUBLISHING HISTORY
Ace mass-market edition / February 2015

PRINTED IN THE UNITED STATES OF AMERICA

10 9 8 7 6 5 4 3 2 1

Cover illustration by Julie Dillon.
Cover design by Judith Lagerman.
Interior text design by Kelly Lipovich.

For Derek

I was working, but if this was work, then sign me up for triple overtime.

This was my kind of Halloween party—cool jazz, a hot date, and a little black dress I'd paid way too much for, but refused to feel guilty about. It was my treat to me. My first Halloween in New York was shaping up to be one to write home about.

The jazz band was playing "That Old Black Magic." I wondered if they knew how appropriate that was.

My hot date was my partner, Ian Byrne. No, not that kind of partner; the kind that works with me battling the forces of evil. He was a senior agent; I was the newbie. But his job title didn't keep him from being the ultimate arm candy.

He was tall, dark, lean, and born to wear a tuxedo.

It was Friday night at the Metropolitan Museum of Art on the night before Halloween and we were posing as a hoity-toity Manhattan couple with an invitation to the season's most antic- ipated opening night at the Met's newest exhibit—Mythos.

Gods and goddesses, beasties and monsters, myths and legends, all safely represented in painting, sculpture, or artifact—all of the thrills with none of the danger.

I say danger, because monsters are real.

My name is Makenna Fraser and I work for SPI—that's Supernatural Protection & Investigations for those in the know. Those in the know consisted of the supernatural community in Manhattan and throughout the outer boroughs.

SPI was headquartered in New York, but had offices and agents worldwide. It was founded by Vivienne Sagadraco in 1647. And no, that wasn't the boss lady's ancestor. It was the boss lady herself. Vivienne Sagadraco was much older than she looked, less human than she appeared, and a lot larger than you could ever imagine.

I imagine there were plenty of people who called their boss a dragon lady and meant it as an insult.

My boss was a real dragon—and a true lady.

Right now, she was . . . Well, "holding court" was about the only way I could describe it.

In her actual form, she'd have cleared the room; every human in the place would have been screaming and stampeding for the nearest exit. But as Vivienne Sagadraco, wealthy socialite and generous philanthropist, she drew a crowd of admirers wherever she went—especially admirers who had a cause or event they needed funded.

A mural of frolicking dryads was currently framing her slim and elegant figure. Whether intentional or not, the mural's jewel-toned tiles of semiprecious stones couldn't have provided a more flattering backdrop for her.

Though I shouldn't have been surprised if she had chosen it on purpose. Not because it made her look good, but because *it* looked good to *her*. Dragons loved their sparklies, and Vivienne Sagadraco was no exception.

In fact, it was her love of shiny things (and uncanny investment skills) that was behind SPI's funding. Monster hunting and protecting humans and supernaturals from one another—and keeping humans in the dark about all of it—took the latest technology, developed and run by the most brilliant minds, and seemingly bottomless financial reserves to pay for all of it. Toss in a financial management staff of scary accurate clairvoyants, and Vivienne Sagadraco's net worth would probably put the treasuries of many first-world countries to shame. Not to mention it made all of us agents warm and fuzzy to know that our 401k accounts were in the best hands.

Ian Byrne and I weren't here on a date.

We were here to prevent a robbery.

When it came to art with supernatural provenance, value wasn't always measured in money. There were a handful of items in the exhibition that could cause a lot of trouble if they fell into the wrong hands.

That's why SPI was involved.

So while we had some idea of what items the thieves were after, we had no earthly clue how anyone could steal any of them, especially tonight.

SPI had received intelligence that there would be a robbery. Tonight. Smack-dab in the middle of a museum gala with hundreds of people in attendance. As to the identity of our potential thief, none of the supernaturals or humans were behaving suspiciously. It looked like a perfectly normal thousand-dollar-a-head museum exhibit opening on a Friday night in New York. People and not-people were out and about, seeing but mostly being seen, looking at ancient art and artifacts, and admiring the pretties and the sparklies from behind velvet ropes and bulletproof glass.

Stealing anything from this exhibition would be humanly impossible.

Inhumans, on the other hand, just might be able to pull it off.

That was where SPI came in.

Or, more to the point, me.

I'm what SPI calls a seer.

Most of the members of my family could see supernatural creatures for what they really were. We could see through any magical veil, ward, shield, or spell any supernatural could come up with as a disguise. I could identify every supernatural present at this little shindig. It wasn't in the least bit surprising that supernaturals were among New York's glitterati. When your life span was measured in centuries, you could accumulate wealth in quantities unimaginable to all but Middle Eastern sheiks, Silicon Valley entrepreneurs, or Kardashian divorce-settlement recipients.

What passed for figments of peoples' overactive imaginations, or things that went bump in the night and day, were SPI's bread and butter.

Fact meets fiction.

Science meets entertainment.

Myths and monsters. If the museum hadn't wanted to tap into that, they wouldn't be officially opening the Mythos exhibition to the public on Halloween.

Most of the supernatural guests were the vampire, elf, and goblin variety. Naturally they were veiled, meaning they had used small magics to conceal their most distinguishing features—or at least those that would be most alarming to humans. That meant fangs for the vamps, upswept ears for the elves, and both of the above plus silvery skin tone for the goblins.

I could see them all, but I'd learned at a young age to keep that knowledge to myself. Most supernaturals didn't want to be seen for what they really were, especially by a human, which many of them viewed as a sub-creature, dinner, or both. I'd always made it a point to avoid being seen as either one.

An unremarkable-looking, middle-aged couple gazed with obvious disdain and quiet, derisive laughter at one of the promotional posters the Met had liberally spread around town on buses, subway stops, and anywhere else people couldn't help but notice them.

The couple were vampires.

In honor of the gala, a few of the more popular posters had been expanded into banners and hung suspended from the ceiling in all their glossy glory. In honor of Halloween, and people's seemingly never-ending fascination with vampires, one banner depicted what the Met's Marketing department knew humans wanted to see if confronted by a vampire—a breathtakingly beautiful, darkly seductive creature, with just a hint of fang visible, and deep bedroom eyes that assured their victim that their primary intent was merely to boff them silly. Yes, there was that tiny, insignificant thing that involved driving those fangs into the side of your neck and essentially ripping your throat out as they drained your blood and left you to die in an alley, darkened park, bathroom in a SoHo nightclub, or wherever they'd found you when the mood to munch took them. But because you'd be so hot and bothered by their sexy selves, you'd enjoy the hell out of the throat ripping while they did it to you.

Though most vamps were discreet in their selection of dining partners, and unless they were feeding for the first time, they didn't need to drain their victims dry. Regardless, it still felt like a pair of nails being hammered into the side of your neck. There was nothing sexy about that; I didn't care what you were into.

I looked again at the banner and had to agree with the vampire couple. The depiction was highly inaccurate. I guess I should just be glad that the damned thing didn't sparkle.

I turned to the man on my arm. "How about a spin around the dance floor? Just one song."

My ever-vigilant partner continued scanning the crowd for any oddity, something out of place that would signal a team of paranormal thieves getting ready to make their collective move. "We're not here to dance."

"No, we're not," I agreed, not about to give up that easily. "But we were told to blend in. A lot of people are dancing, therefore dancing blends in." I had new shoes to go with my new dress, and my new shoes wanted to dance.

"And a lot of people are not dancing," Ian countered. "They're going through the exhibition, which is why we're here, remember?"

How could I forget?

Change of tactics. Ian was always telling me that a good agent is flexible. "Okay, then. Think how many more people you could see from the dance floor." I lowered my voice conspiratorially. "It's raised."

Ian continued his surveillance. "I noticed."

"Of course you did. But I bet even you can't resist that song. It's perfect."

Ian didn't respond, at least not with words.

Quicker than a takedown in one of our hand-to-hand combat lessons, Ian swept me onto the dance floor.

I yelped. Fortunately the music covered it up. "You could warn a girl."

"You asked for it. A good agent is always careful what they ask for—spoken or unspoken." A trace of a grin quirked his lips. "You never know what you're going to get."

Like my normally by-the-book partner being coaxed into mixing a little fun into our business this evening.

"Everything's a teaching opportunity, isn't it." I didn't ask it as a question; I already knew the answer.

"It is until you learn everything."

"Which means my future's gonna be chock-full of teaching."

Even I couldn't deny it. The more I learned, the more I realized I didn't know. My bullets were getting closer to the centers of our shooting range's paper targets, but human silhouettes were only one kind of target that I practiced on. Some of them were so big you'd think I couldn't miss them.

Wrong. In my defense, when multiple targets popped up either at the same time or one right after the other, it was hard to remember where to shoot. Some of the things we came up against didn't have hearts in the same places as humans. Heck, some didn't have hearts at all.

The rest of my training was going even slower, though it'd help if Ian wasn't the ultimate commando-ninja-badass monster fighter. Him being so good made me look even worse. However, if someday I found myself backed into a dead-end alley facing a wendigo with a hankering for a late-night snack, I knew I'd be glad that I'd been taught by the best. Ian hadn't deemed me competent enough to progress past what looked to me like Nerf knives, and I still couldn't last more than fifteen seconds on the sparring mat without Ian pinning me. If he wouldn't throw me quite so hard, at least that part would be fun, though I think that was why he did it; that and to be a constant reminder that any encounter I had on the job with a supernatural critter wasn't going to feel like fun and games.

Ian and I had spent a lot of time together since he'd been assigned as my partner/bodyguard/babysitter. SPI's seers didn't get combat training, but since my three predecessors had met with fatal accidents that might not have been so accidental, SPI's management had taken steps to protect their personnel investment. That would be me. Ian Byrne was that protection. To Ian, a big part of that protection was teaching me to fend for myself. I couldn't have agreed more, and was doing my best to learn everything he had to teach. However, I think Ian was feeling a whole lot like Henry Higgins to my Eliza Doolittle.

During that time, my training had extended to time off the clock. Though it was more like an educational series of "Let's have a beer after work, and I'll tell you how to tell normal sewer sludge from the mucus trail of a giant demon slug." Let me tell you, nothing puts you off your bar-food nachos quicker than a lecture on the color and consistency of slug secretions.

But I'd be lying if I said it wasn't fun, because between the lectures on monster bodily fluids, Ian would tell me about past missions. Purely from an instructional viewpoint, of course. At least that was what Ian wanted me to believe. I could tell he enjoyed the telling as much as I did the hearing. It must have been the Irish storyteller in him.

Ian began maneuvering us toward the center of the dance floor. One spin was so sudden I nearly fell off my heels. Though any heel height was too high for me. I was the only person I knew of who could fall off a pair of flip-flops.

"Easy there, partner. What's the rush?"

Ian lowered his head to my ear while still steering us toward the center, showing his usual impressive coordination. I displayed my usual lack.

"I want you to get a look at Viktor Kain's date," he said. "Human or not human?"

I stiffened, and if Ian's hand hadn't been firmly at the small of my back, I would have stumbled.

Ian knew my reason wasn't due to clumsiness.

"Relax," Ian told me. "He's just dancing."

Well, if Nero had fiddled while Rome had burned, it stood to reason that mass murderers could dance, but that didn't mean I wanted to dance anywhere near one.

Viktor Kain had loaned art to the Met for the exhibit—art that was the main reason we were here—and Ian had spotted him before I had.

Way to be a watchful agent, Mac.

I was glad Ian had seen him first. If my partner had swung me around and I'd suddenly gotten a gander of the Russian, I'd have probably freaked out, which would have blown our cover, at least with Viktor Kain. Though if the people around us had known what the Russian businessman really was, they not only wouldn't have blamed me one bit, they'd have run like hell.

Viktor Kain was a dragon.

That wasn't my problem with him. Far from it. I knew a few dragons. Heck, our boss was a dragon. Once you got past the whole humans-occasionally-on-the-menu thing, dragons could be nice people.

No, my problem with Viktor Kain was that he was the head of an international crime syndicate. He had personally killed hundreds, maybe thousands of people over his long criminal career and even longer life, and he'd ordered the deaths and ruin of even more—and he'd enjoyed every last minute of it.

Ostensibly, the Russian was here in New York because he'd loaned several items to the museum for the exhibition. SPI strongly suspected that wasn't the only reason. Viktor Kain had brought more than art with him; he'd brought trouble, not just for SPI, but for every human on this island and probably beyond.

The Russian's very presence on East Coast soil was a slap in the face to every rule of dragon etiquette, and two skips away from a declaration of supernatural war. No dragon would dare set claw on another's territory without an invitation. I'd put enough agency rumor and innuendo together to know that Vivienne Sagadraco and Viktor Kain had crossed each other's paths in the past, and as a result of those encounters, each barely tolerated the existence of the other on the planet. So if Viktor Kain the dragon wanted to come to New York, he knew better than to ask for an invitation. It wasn't gonna happen, in this century or any other.

Local and federal law enforcement knew that Viktor Kain the Russian mobster was here, but until he broke any laws, watch was all they could do.

We couldn't do anything, either.

Though before the night was over, karma might just kick Viktor Kain in the teeth. In all probability, one of the items he'd brought was the one that was going to be stolen.

The betting had started early among our agents on what the thief would go after. The odds were leaning heavily toward the Dragon Eggs—a massive ruby cut in the shape of a coiled dragon surrounded by seven of the world's rarest, egg-shaped, colored diamonds, all contained in an intricately woven solid-gold nest.

The Dragon Eggs were being shown for the first time outside of Russia since they'd been given to the Empress Alexandra. Yes, that Alexandra. Wife of Tsar Nicholas, and mother to Anastasia, et al. The separate stones had blood-soaked histories that'd turn your hair white, but collectively they were said to be cursed. The curse rumor definitely picked up a couple extra believability points when in July of 1918, only months after the empress received the diamonds, the Bolsheviks wiped out the Russian imperial family. The Dragon Eggs had vanished after the Romanov family was murdered, and the diamonds had only come together again within the past few months in the collection of Viktor Kain.

I wasn't normally the superstitious type, but you couldn't pay me enough to touch the things, let alone own them.

But there were a lot of obscenely wealthy people, or their representatives, here tonight who wanted to do just that—touch and own. They were using tonight's gala as an auction preview. Whether due to the curse or a need for cash, Viktor Kain was selling the Dragon Eggs; however, for a reason known only to him, he'd let it be known that he could be persuaded to sell them separately rather than together. Maybe he thought he could get more money that way.

I got a good look at the white-gowned, willowy blonde in Viktor Kain's arms. I didn't have to look long to determine that she was stunning. The men around her had arrived at the same conclusion, but apparently they felt the need to keep stealing glances at her in case their opinions changed.

While the woman was inhumanly beautiful, human was all that she was.

"Just human," I told Ian. "Though try convincing any guy here that she's not a goddess."

Viktor Kain saw the stir his date was causing, and the oily smile on his face told me that it amused him.

The Russian had a face like the business end of a hatchet, sharp and cold. He was a couple inches taller than Ian, probably pushing six four. His date was only an inch or two shorter, but thanks to the slit in her gown combined with a particularly impressive dance move, I got a look at a pair of what had to be five-inch heels.

Beneath Viktor Kain's human glamour was a monstrous dragon the color of dried blood. While Vivienne Sagadraco was a dragon of incredible beauty with her peacock blue and green iridescent scales, and immaculate wings that held a similar jewel-like glow, many of Viktor Kain's red scales were edged in black as if burnt, or missing altogether, revealing rubbery, bat-like skin below. His wings folded crooked over his back, and had been torn in more than a few places, their healing marked by thickened scar tissue.

The Russian looked like a dragon that'd fought many times, and since he was here, he'd apparently met and defeated every challenger. I knew the boss wouldn't back down from a fight, and I'd seen her in two of them, but she'd either had fewer than Kain, or was so good that she'd never been seriously injured. In a dragon fight, size took a backseat to speed and agility. Viktor Kain was bigger than Vivienne Sagadraco, but I'd seen firsthand how agile the boss was in the air. I got the impression the Russian probably lacked in that area. He looked like more of a use-brute-strength-to-set-an-example kind of guy. Rumor had it he used fire to rid himself of inconvenient business associates. Not with a blowtorch or a flamethrower, but with his own exhaled breath.

Viktor Kain had hidden his true identity over the centuries by assuming a human form; only a small and fanatically devoted circle of associates knew his true nature. I guess he needed a few people to get rid of any crispy critter that used to be an employee whose performance had disappointed him. Though you had to wonder what Viktor's underlings who weren't in his inner circle thought when a live man walked in to see their boss, but a human-shaped charcoal briquette got carried out. Most of them probably didn't want to know how that happened. Keep your head down, don't ask stupid questions, and live to resperate another day.

Our agency briefing had touched on why Viktor Kain had chosen St. Petersburg as his territory. A city of history, palaces, museums, and art. He fancied himself a patron of the arts, and true to his draconic nature, he was an avid collector. He'd been known to pay an astronomical sum to have the Hermitage closed to the public and the alarms turned off so he could walk the galleries alone, admiring and touching the priceless works of art.

A dragon communing with his hoard.

Ian and I stayed on the dance floor for one more song, and then entered the exhibit. I was glad to leave the dragon and his date to their samba.

The art and artifacts were arranged mostly by subject or time period, and what could only be called theater sets had been designed and lit for maximum effect. The exhibit representing the Delphic oracle was located in what looked like a real cave. Hollywood—or since this was New York, a Broadway set designer—couldn't have done a better job.

It was spooky as hell; but I had to admit, it was effective.

There were paintings, sculptures, tapestries, artifacts, armor, weapons, jewelry and huge stained glass windows illustrating dragons, furies, demons, sea monsters, vampires, gryphons, giants, fae, gods, and more fantastical creatures from myth and legend—all perfectly lit to maximize their beauty and impact.

Ian paused by the oracle's cave, getting a report from Edward Laughlin, a security consultant SPI often called upon when the valuables (or the hopeful thief of said valuables) were paranormal in nature. Eddie also had a profitable sideline business as an acquirer of antiquities with a paranormal provenance, making him kind of like Indiana Jones, minus the whip and fedora.

Eddie was also half elf and half goblin, and as such was looked down on by many of both races. Your average elf or goblin on the street was fine with the whole mixed-race thing, but any pure-blood aristocrats of either race here tonight (and there were quite a few) would rather spit on him than look at him. Needless to say, Eddie was rocking a serious glamour this evening that no one short of a mage was gonna see through. And he'd recently added some ubercool sunglasses to his disguise, due to an infection he'd gotten courtesy of an irritated temple-monkey demon that actually *had* managed to spit on him—right in the eyes. Though if you had to get something that was the supernatural second cousin of pink eye, cover it up in style. Between the supersized glamour, the shades, and a thick film over his usual aura courtesy of the nasty magic–infused monkey spit, no one—including myself—could tell what he really was, making it perfectly safe for him to walk around among the upper crust of both of his races.

Ian nodded to me, indicating that I should continue; he'd catch up. I did.

The pieces featured in the exhibit came from a mix of loans from private collections and other museums. I saw a few that I recognized, like the Pre-Raphaelite painting of Pandora by John William Waterhouse. His subject may have been romanticized, but the box she was shown opening was very real. Some of the evils and diseases that had originally escaped from the box had been captured, or contained and re-imprisoned. Agency rumor had it that one of the diseases presently in the box could wipe out the entire human race in a matter of days. Pandora's box and its remaining contents were now securely sealed in a vault deep beneath SPI's Berlin office.

Nearby was a Greek wine jar on loan from the British Museum featuring Perseus having just cut off Medusa's head, with the goddess Athena looking on in approval. Nice lady.

Gold flickered out of the corner of my eye. Vivienne Sagadraco wasn't the only one who liked things that went glitter in the night. I strolled over, and the closer I got, the more familiar it looked. A Viking sword. Not just any Viking sword, but the blade reputed to be the source of the legend of Gram—the sword that the Norse hero Sigurd used to kill the dragon Fafnir.

I chuckled. I had news for the Oslo museum it'd been loaned from: there didn't need to be a source for Gram's legend. The real thing existed, and Sigurd hadn't been a myth, which meant that Fafnir had probably been the real McCoy as well.

I'd seen Gram up close and met Sigurd's descendant personally last New Year's Eve. We'd had a problem with the descendant of another Scandinavian. Grendel. Sigurd's multi-great-grandson was a SPI commando from our Oslo office named Rolf Haagen. He'd brought the sword with him when a team of Nordic monster hunters had jumped across the pond to give us a hand. Rolf killed one of the grendels, but he hadn't used Gram to do it. The crazy Viking had goaded the monster into grabbing him, and then shoved a grenade down the thing's throat.

That'd been messy.

Next to the reputed source for Gram's legend were more swords.

We'd been warned in our pre-mission briefing that there were a few items in the exhibition that were more than what they appeared. The usual arrangement was that people used objects. A couple of the objects in the Mythos exhibition had the reputation of using people.

Between me and the room with the Dragon Eggs was an Egyptian mural of Anubis, a cursed and bloodthirsty Japanese sword that a pair of our agents were keeping a close eye on, gold Incan temple artifacts used in human sacrifices (likewise getting some special SPI protection), and the obligatory statue of St. George and the Dragon. I was betting the boss wouldn't be a fan of that particular piece.

The lighting got even more dramatic with more than its fair share of reds and oranges. Fire. The art in this section depicted evil in its various mythical forms. Everything from a statue of the classic horned representation of the devil, to the black-winged concept of the fallen Lucifer in a more modern—and, quite frankly, hot—painting. I had news: when you caught a real demon, their veils dropped and you got a good look at what you really had on the end of your hook. Kind of like going fishing and coming up with a water moccasin. Believe me, that wasn't something you want sharing an itty-bitty boat with you.

A life-sized painting of Hades had been roped off, not for the safety of the painting, but for the safety of female guests, especially those who resembled the daughter of Demeter. Per Demeter's agreement with the god of the underworld, Persephone was supposed to spend summers with her mom. However, Hades had been known to have occasional bouts of amnesia on that part of the contract. A certain Italian Renaissance artist had traded his soul to Hades for talent with a brush. In return, Hades had added a nifty portal feature to the newly completed painting; a painting that could give you a direct flight straight to Hell. While Hades wanted Persephone, there'd been enough incidents over the centuries of girls disappearing into the painting to prove that any petite blond, blue-eyed beauty with long, shampoo-commercial hair would work in a pinch.

I was petite, but my eyes were green, not blue. And while my hair was blond, it wasn't long. Still, I wasn't taking any chances and gave the painting a wide berth. Even though I wasn't exactly his type, I could swear the painting's eyes followed me.

I guess it didn't make a hill of beans' worth of difference if you were the king of the underworld, or the managing editor of the bottom-of-the-journalistic-barrel tabloid I'd worked for when I'd first come to town; a lecherous sleaze-bag was a lecherous sleazebag.

A hand on my shoulder nearly made me jump out of my skin.

Ian. Not Hades.

"The boss called. She wants us on egg watch," he told me.

Showtime.

2

THE path through the exhibit ended in the Met's Sackler Wing at the Temple of Dendur. It was one of my favorite rooms in the museum; its sloped glass wall gave a marvelous view of Central Park. It was also one of the rooms famous for being used for parties and receptions when wealthy New Yorkers wanted to do it big. Nothing said impressive like having a two-thousand-year-old Egyptian temple as your party's focal point.

The more classically themed pieces of the exhibition were displayed around the temple, including a study in studly featuring Jason—of Jason and the Argonauts fame—wearing nothing but the Golden Fleece. But as the highlight of the Mythos exhibit, the Dragon Eggs had been placed near the entrance to the temple itself. When you had a collection of seven of the world's rarest and most valuable diamonds, they needed a fancy setting. And it didn't get much more imposing than a real Egyptian temple.

The Dragon Eggs were said to be Viktor Kain's prized

possessions. That right there was reason enough to think the Russian was up to no good. And SPI sure as heck wasn't buying the two reasons Kain had given for coming to New York—that he not only wanted to share his treasure with the world by loaning the diamonds to the Met for the exhibition, but he was considering offering the diamonds for sale. One, dragons like Viktor Kain didn't share the prize of their hoard with anyone, let alone everyone. Two, the diamonds in the Dragon Eggs were reputed to be gems of power. The Russian was a gem mage, meaning he could use gems of power to . . . well, do whatever it was that the Dragon Eggs were capable of doing. That was one big unknown in the equation—no one knew what the diamonds were capable of besides giving their owners a lot of bad luck. In the hands of a gem mage like Viktor Kain, it'd take a lot more than a four-leaf clover to counteract whatever he had planned.

The potential for an auction of seven of the world's rarest, and therefore most valuable, diamonds had the likes of Christie's, Sotheby's, and Bonhams salivating at the chance to get the commission off of *that* sale.

Then there was the elf and goblin problem.

Two of the diamonds, the pale blue Eye of Destiny and the pink Queen of Dreams, had been stolen from the elf and goblin royal treasuries about a hundred years ago. And now here was Viktor Kain, about to sell hot rocks that the elves and goblins were chomping at the bit to get back—by any means necessary.

Not to mention, the chance to buy or steal any of the Dragon Eggs was bringing the less savory heavy hitters of the supernatural magic world out from under their collective rocks. Cursed and possessed objects weren't the only reason the boss had deployed agents all over the exhibition. Individuals on SPI's most wanted and most watched lists were lurking among the guests, magically veiled and glamoured like every other supernatural here.

It was going to be a busy night.

From what I could see there was now another reason, other than the pretty windows, why the Sackler Wing was my favorite—that was where they'd set up the food tables and bar. If I was gonna be busy, I needed to keep my strength up.

Ian kept going toward the Dragon Eggs; I made a quick pit stop at the closest table.

Drat. Sushi.

Back home in the North Carolina mountains, raw fish was called bait. I'd tried to learn to like sushi, but I'd always come away with the feeling that it'd taste a lot better breaded and deep fried.

Sushi sure was pretty, though. As was the statue of a trio of harpies close to it.

Like most dragons, Viktor liked sparklies, and it didn't get any more sparkly than the clutch of seven diamonds presently dazzling the eyes of New York's rich and famous from inside a bulletproof and hopefully curse-resistant glass case behind velvet ropes. The case was positioned directly in front of the temple's towering doorway. Two huge men were standing guard on either side of the doorway, with the velvet ropes surrounding the case and its guards on three sides, keeping the guests five feet away from the case on those three sides, the fourth side being the interior of the temple itself.

Those boys seemed to have things well in hand, so I figured it wouldn't hurt to fix myself a quick plate. There was no reason why I couldn't keep my eyes peeled for supernatural shenanigans and eat at the same time. As I got two of the always safe California rolls, I couldn't help but look at the harpies again. I'd say they were closing in on seven feet tall, and they looked like they'd been carved from a single block of stone. Their large eyes reminded me of the hawks that cruised the mountaintop thermals back home. They had cheekbones a supermodel would kill for, and full lips that a socialite was presently snapping a photo of with her phone. She probably wouldn't be the last. I bet some of Midtown's more exclusive plastic surgeons would be getting a flood of client e-mails with that same attachment come Monday morning.

My eyes dropped to the rest of the statue. Make that multiple attachments.

With the exception of their wings, the bird half of their bodies didn't start until below their boobs, which were, like the rest of their human features, enviable. The wings and bird-like lower halves were all feathers, scaled feet, and talons, sharp, sharp talons—all immortalized in a type of stone I couldn't identify.

"Exquisite, aren't they?" purred an all-too-familiar voice from behind me.

I was proud to say that I didn't even turn around, but simply spooned a little wasabi on my plate. "The boobs or the harpies?"

"Yes." His voice was a low seductive purr, like a silvery cat rubbing around your bare legs.

Rake Danescu was a goblin, which made him just about the sexiest creature presently in the Metropolitan Museum of Art, and that included any and all statues or paintings of gods on the premises.

That was saying a lot, but Rake was a lot of hot.

He also knew it—and he wasn't about to let me forget that he knew I knew it.

Though it wasn't like there was any chance of me forgetting the first time we'd met. In addition to owning a few art galleries—and several Manhattan buildings—Rake Danescu owned and ran Bacchanalia, an upscale and very exclusive club that billed itself as the "complete adult enter-tainment experience."

Yep, it was a sex club. One that catered to men *and* women—people who didn't go to simply watch; they went to participate. During my first night on the job at SPI, I'd been part of a bodyguard detail for a leprechaun prince's bachelor party. Fiasco was a nice way to describe how that evening had gone, and one comedy of errors after another had landed us at Rake's club—and landed me in Rake's arms in a backstage dressing room. He'd wanted me to work for him—and no, not as an adult entertainer—as a seer. Appar-ently goblin dark mage owners of sex clubs found them-selves in situations where they needed the services of a seer. Go figure. I'd managed to inhale a lungful of a supernatural recreational drug in Bacchanalia's ladies' room, and as a result, parts of that evening were kinda fuzzy, but the part with Rake in that dressing room had remained crystal clear.

Real goblins were everything you'd been told that they weren't—tall, sleek, and sexy, with enough charisma to make you not only drink the Kool-Aid, but happily stand in line for it.

Tonight, to every human at the Met, Rake looked human.

But he wasn't. No human male looked that perfect.

My seer vision showed me what he really was.

Lean and predatory looking, like a sleek, silvery cat. Combine that with darkly seductive and light-sensitive eyes and you had a race that took sunglasses to the heights of high fashion. Goblins were gorgeous all by their lonesome, but they took their wardrobes and accessories just as seri-ously as their tangled court politics. Goblin politics was a full-contact and often fatal sport chock-full of seduction, deception, and betrayal.

Goblin hair was dark and often worn long. Their skin was pale gray with a silvery sheen, with human-sized ears that ended in a nibbleable point.

And they sported a pair of fangs that weren't for decorative use only.

"Here to do a little window shopping?" I asked. Or casing the joint? I thought.

Rake Danescu held a glass of champagne as he looked me up one side and down the other, taking his sweet time and seemingly enjoying the view. "There are many objects of interest and desire here tonight."

I didn't take Rake seriously—at least I didn't take him saying I was desirable seriously. Goblins were like politicians; they always wanted something, and if they wanted that something from you, they were relentless in getting it. On my first night at SPI he'd tried to hire me as his own personal seer—while his hands smoothly conducted their own job interview all over my body. We'd run into each other a few times since then, though it was more like he kept turning up in places where I was. I wouldn't call it stalking, at least not yet, but it sure as heck wasn't a coincidence. Goblins like Rake Danescu didn't have coincidences; they arranged strategically timed encounters.

"Mr. Kain has acquired an additional escort this evening," Rake noted. "I would almost be jealous except he did it by wealth, not charm. There's no challenge."

Viktor Kain and his now *two* ridiculously beautiful dates had the attention of everyone in the room as they made their way to the Temple of Dendur and the case containing the Dragon Eggs.

"You know anything about Viktor Kain?" I asked Rake.

"I know many things about our Russian friend."

"He may be a friend of yours, but he's not one of mine."

The goblin gave me an indulgent smile. "Is that because dear Vivienne told you he's a stranger you shouldn't take candy from?"

"She only said that about you."

The smile widened to give me a peek of fang. "I've never

offered you candy," he said with the slightest emphasis on the last word.

Time to take a sharp left turn from that topic. "Viktor Kain probably sleeps on a pyramid of gold bullion. You'd think he'd have enough fun money lying around without selling that sparkly handful of pebbles over there. What's he up to?"

Rake glanced casually around the room. I wasn't fooled; goblins didn't do anything casually, and Rake normally avoided large gatherings of supernaturals like the plague— unless there was something in it for him, like the possibility of retrieving a certain stolen goblin diamond.

Rake took a sip of champagne and smiled. "Besides luring the baser elements of our cozy little mage community out this evening to be a pain in the backside of your equally draconic employer?"

"Yes, besides that."

Rake gave an elaborate shrug. "Any move a dragon makes has at least twenty motives. They're delightfully inscrutable. Schemes on top of plots, with intricate maneuvering running underneath." He raised his glass in an admiring salute. "I can only aspire to be as devious."

Typical goblin answer. A lot of pretty dancing around a topic. Except for sex. That was the one thing a goblin would get right to the point about, and keep harping on it until they got what they wanted—their target between the sheets, or against a wall, or on a—

That was when it happened.

I heard a long, low groan. It sounded human, almost. Considering my present train of thought, that was uncanny timing.

Instantly, Rake's attention was on a spot past my right shoulder. He slowly set his glass on the table and held out his hand to me.

"Darling, step away from the harpies. Now."

I'd never seen Rake's eyes as large as they were right now. That was the first and only clue I needed to drop my plate on the table and move my butt.

I spun to face the statue and froze in disbelief, disbelief that quickly spiraled down to "Oh shit."

That statue of three harpies wasn't a statue anymore. What seconds before had been stone was now flesh with wings of bat-like leather. Only the claws looked just as hard, sharp, and deadly as they had before they'd turned.

Turned.

A statue had come to life in the middle of the Metropolitan Museum of Art on a major exhibition's opening night. Hundreds of people were in the Sackler Wing, hundreds of now absolutely silent, regular, normal, everyday people whose eyes were witnessing an event their brains were telling them couldn't possibly be real.

Rake Danescu had hit the nail on the head.

Harpies. Real, honest-to-God harpies. Or, in this case, real honest-to-Hades harpies.

"Finally, the evening gets interesting," Rake said.

3

HUMANS seeing a monster for the first time generally had one of three reactions: scream, run, or faint. This was New York, so while half of the guests were engaged in one or more of the above, the other half had their phones out and were clicking away, camera flashes firing at the harpies like strobes.

The harpies didn't like being treated like paparazzi bait. So, like a married celeb caught coming out of a cheap strip joint, they attacked.

At least two of them did.

The third launched herself into the air and, with two powerful beats of her leathery wings, dive-bombed the two men guarding the Dragon Eggs, clawed hands and feet extended for the attack.

And the kill. A really messy kill.

Any doubt about those harpies being real vanished when the blood and bits started flying. And if that hadn't done the trick, the guards' screams turning to dying shrieks instantly made every human within earshot a believer. Human screams joined the screeches and shrieks, and within two beats of an eye, the Sackler Wing descended into chaos.

We'd come here tonight expecting a robbery, and had come face-to-claw with the very thing Vivienne Sagadraco had founded SPI to prevent—humans finding out the truth that monsters are real, supernaturals exist, and humans share the world with both.

Mythological creatures coming to life in front of hundreds of New Yorkers was bad enough, but entirely too many of them were standing their ground and aiming their phones like those idiots on TV reality shows who see the tiger escape from its cage but who just can't resist taking pictures of the thing right up until the moment when it rips their faces off. It was humanity's way of thinning its own herd.

Right now there was a goodly number of people looking to move to the front of the meet-your-maker line in the next few seconds.

Fortunately for them, the harpies turned their attention to getting the Dragon Eggs out of that case. A case that was supposed to be bulletproof and curse-resistant was no match for three determined harpies. It was a smash-and-grab robbery at its finest.

While one harpy smashed the case to dust, the screeches of the other two were making it abundantly clear what the penalty would be for getting too close to the action. The crumpled and broken bodies of the two guards were a nonliving example to avoid repeating their folly.

People were stampeding to get away. One guy stood still, eyes wide as the panicked crowd pushed around and past him. Tall and gangly with blond curly hair, he looked barely out of his teens, early twenties at the most.

I'd seen shock before, and this wasn't it, at least not

totally. People were either clued in or clueless to the fact that monsters and supernaturals shared the planet with us, and that humans weren't the apex predator.

Judging from his wide, pale blue eyes, mouth open in disbelief, and general appearance of WTF, the safe bet counted him among the clueless.

But in an instant, stunned turned to determined, which signaled either bravery, stupidity, or an unhealthy dose of both. It didn't really matter which one he had; both were going to get him just as dead. The math wasn't in his favor. Three harpies with more razor-tipped talons on their hands and feet than I could count equaled untold chances for evisceration. I didn't care if he was all kinds of lucky and had a pocket packed with rabbit feet; those weren't good odds.

I couldn't stop the harpies, but I could keep this guy from doing something he wouldn't live to regret.

"Rake, I'm gonna need some . . ." I looked behind me. The goblin was gone. Why was I surprised? "Backup," I said to the now empty space. "I need backup. Thanks for nothing."

I couldn't see Ian through the screaming, running, and YouTube-recording masses, so I was on my own.

I was wearing pumps with three-inch heels. Never again. No more cute shoes. Chucks were the new cute. Or hiking boots. Or better still, combat boots.

The guy gave a shout that was at odds with his boyish features and charged the harpies. I kicked off my heels and ran to intercept.

The harpy reached inside the shattered case, flung the ruby dragon aside, and scooped up the eggs in a single swipe of her taloned fingers.

The guy was faster and had longer legs. There was no way I could reach him before he got within gutting range.

He lunged for the harpy and grabbed the claw clutching

the diamonds. At the instant of contact, a blaze of white light exploded from either the guy, the harpy, or the diamonds. Hell, I didn't know. I hadn't seen light that bright since I'd nearly fried my own retinas the first time I'd used my phone's flashlight app. The screams in my immediate vicinity changed from terror-fueled to pain-induced. I think mine might have joined them.

There was something else. A tightening in the air, pulling in toward the core of the light, then releasing in a shock wave of color and heat that felt like it went right through me, popping the hell out of my ears in the process.

The harpy he'd attacked shrieked in outrage, and I knew what was coming next, even though I still couldn't see for crap. That harpy had two hands, both with talons, and the one not holding those diamonds would be coming to slice through that idiot's midsection or take his head off.

Blinking back teared-up eyes, I dove toward where the guy had been before I'd been struck blind.

A male-sounding "Oof" told me I'd latched on to my intended target.

We landed in a heap and tumbled ass over teakettle, off the floor slab of the Temple of Dendur, crashing into a nearby buffet table.

Over the screams came a roar, a roar barely contained in a human throat.

Oh hell.

Viktor Kain.

All we needed was the Russian going dragon and getting medieval on three harpy asses in front of hundreds of witnesses uploading it all to the social media of their choice.

I quickly crawled to the corner of the temple and peeked around.

Kain was fast but his speed was limited by his human form. The Sackler Wing was large enough for him to turn dragon, but he wasn't that desperate.

Yet.

And if he chose to go dragon, there wasn't a damned thing any SPI agent could do about it, except the same thing every human who witnessed it would do—run like hell.

Kain shouted something in Russian, and a trio of men ahead of him ran faster. They must work for him, and knew what would happen if they didn't stop those harpies.

Harpies that had just gone airborne.

The first one crashed through one of the glass panes of the far wall and out into the Central Park night. Her sisters followed, leaving us in the middle of SPI's worst nightmare.

Public evidence of the existence of monsters.

And three harpies on the loose in New York with seven cursed diamonds belonging to a Russian dragon.

Happy Halloween, y'all.

4

I was wearing cocktail sauce. At least I think it was cocktail sauce. It was too thick and too cold to be blood—at least the human variety. I had no clue what harpy blood looked or felt like.

The man was sprawled next to me, half under the buffet table, all the way out cold. At least I thought he was only unconscious. I put two fingers to the side of his throat, checking for a pulse. The guy shifted and groaned, answering my question. What he had running down the side of his face from a cut on his forehead was definitely blood and positively human. It looked like that harpy had clocked him, or since he was still breathing, just grazed him.

He being mostly unconscious gave me the chance to give him a good seer once-over.

There was no sign of a ward, shield, or magical disguise of any kind. He was exactly what he looked like: a human who'd made the monumentally bad choice of tangling with a harpy.

But as a seer, I could also detect the residual traces of magic having been worked.

The man had the aura of a practitioner who'd just engaged in some serious practicing.

He hadn't had the aura before he'd touched that harpy, which meant he'd had more than a little to do with the flash of light that'd temporarily blinded everyone who'd seen it.

He had magical talent. I wasn't familiar with the type, but whatever he had, it was a lot.

I reached up onto the table and grabbed a cloth napkin and a handful of ice from a big bowl of shrimp. I put the ice in the napkin, and the napkin against a goose egg forming entirely too close to the man's temple.

He groaned again and tried to sit up.

"Easy. You need to stay still." I put my hand on his shoulder and gave a little push, not even a push, more like pressure, gently leaning him back against the table leg.

That was a mistake.

A big one.

New personal rule: don't lay hands on a man whose last remembered touch was from a creature Zeus traditionally sent after people who'd pissed him off.

His hand grabbed my forearm. Something like an electrical shock ran up my arm, and the next thing I knew, I was airborne and slamming into the far end of the table, knocking over the bowl I'd just had my hand in, and was now wearing shrimp to go with my cocktail sauce.

I think I knew how that harpy had felt. Now I was feeling the urge to hit the guy, too.

The man blinked a few times, his eyes trying to focus on me. A shrimp picked that moment to fall out of my hair. Hopefully I didn't look scarier than the harpies.

He fully came to and gasped, his blue eyes wide with fear, horror, confusion; you name it, he had it.

He looked around wildly. "What happened?"

SPI agents were trained to calm any member of the public they might come across who'd just had a close encounter of the supernatural kind. It involved fast thinking and creative explanations. My thinking was plenty fast, but not when it came to lying, especially not when I'd seen three harpies come to life and was wearing shrimp and cocktail sauce on a dress that'd cost me a week's pay.

I decided to go with some truth, not *the* truth, but a little was better than none at all, and maybe it'd be enough for a man with a head injury.

"Your guess is as good as mine, but whatever it was, it's over." I thought for a moment. "At least for now."

That last part was only a partial truth. While it might have been all the way over for him, the shit storm was just cranking up for me and SPI.

I didn't think I should ask him what he'd done to that harpy. He still looked dazed and confused, and I didn't believe it was just due to the near-concussion he'd gotten. I honestly didn't think he was aware he'd done anything. It was rare, but not unheard of, for someone to come into a talent later in life. Usually people were either born with it, or got it in puberty along with pimples. I'd been born with mine.

Before he could ask me anything else, I decided to get some answers of my own.

"What's your name?"

"Ben. Ben Sadler."

"Well, Ben Sadler, I take it you work here?"

He shook his head and winced. "I'm a diamond appraiser at Christie's."

He was here to check out the now-stolen goods. I could see a Christie's employee getting upset enough at the loss of those diamonds to attack a harpy. No diamonds. No auction. No big, honkin' commission.

I gathered my makeshift ice pack, and reapplied it to his head.

He reached up to hold it himself. "Thank you."

Our hands brushed in passing. No zap. He didn't know he'd zapped me. That was both interesting and disconcerting.

"What happened?" I asked Ben. When someone had been turned into a human rag doll, it was best to stick with simple questions.

"Excuse me?"

Okay, maybe that wasn't simple enough. Opting for tact, instead of asking why he'd tried to commit suicide by harpy, I went with: "When you grabbed the, uh . . . thief, there was a flash of light and . . ." My hands moved in vague little circles over my stomach. "Something that felt like I'd swallowed a fistful of electrified Mexican jumping beans. So, what did you do?"

"I only wanted to stop those things from taking the Dragon Eggs. There was bright light and my arm went numb." His pale brow knit in concentration and confusion. "I . . . I don't know anything about jumping beans. Then I woke up here. I remember being hit. I think." He reached up with a shaky hand and gingerly touched his head, the tips of his fingers coming away with blood. His face blanched even paler as he looked around at the destruction and chaos.

By this point, Ben Sadler wasn't the only one with a headache. "Jeez, people," I muttered. "It's over. Stop screaming already."

One of those screams, more of a roar actually, was from one guest in particular, and those roars were in Russian, so I couldn't understand a word except a couple that I'd picked up from a friend and fellow SPI agent who was Russian—and a werewolf—and a believer in expressing himself fully in his mother tongue.

I held my breath. It was Viktor Kain, and he was just around the corner, at the remains of the display case that'd held the pride and joy of his hoard.

A shadow fell over me.

"Where are my diamonds?"

And now he was here.

Each word, in precise, heavily accented English, came from the Russian standing not five feet away. My heart rate shot from eighty to eighty gazillion, and I was dimly aware that I couldn't feel my legs.

What wasn't so dim was the question that was bouncing around in my head: why the hell was he asking me?

He was close enough to inflict more than one kind of violence, but he didn't have to touch to terrify, and he knew it. The reason had everything to do with the dragon aura that reared behind him and loomed over the entire Temple of Dendur. I realized with a flash of panic that somehow the Russian knew I could see him for what he really was. Knew it, and was happy about it.

Viktor Kain reached out, not with his hand or fist, but with his mind. He didn't use words; he didn't need to. In a mere flicker of thought, the Russian dragon showed me what he had done through the centuries to those who had defied him, and what he was fully prepared to do to me with no more thought than squashing a bug.

I knew I should be afraid. I was.

There were supernatural beings that could project their thoughts and words into the mind of another. It took a level of magical skill that was as rare as it was dangerous. I assumed that Vivienne Sagadraco had that skill. I knew her sister, Tiamat, did. A creature so ancient and powerful that the Babylonians had worshiped her as a goddess.

Viktor Kain was probably accustomed to getting the same treatment in the form of bowing, scraping, and cringing from his employees. His three men who'd failed to stop those harpies looked like they were ready to start groveling the instant Kain turned his attention from me to them. The Russian may have caught me kneeling on the floor, but if I was to keep one ounce of my self-respect, I couldn't stay that way. I fought to shove down the whimpers that were trying to escape from my vocal cords. They weren't gonna give up without a fight. Neither was I.

"As you can see, I seldom need to repeat my requests, but for the benefit of your uninformed companion, I will. Once." His dark eyes fell on Ben Sadler and glittered with something ugly. "Where are my diamonds?"

My whimpers turned into a "Huh?" Ben Sadler had tried to stop the robbery. Though if Kain knew I was a seer, knowing appraising diamonds wasn't the only talent in Ben Sadler's skill set would be a no-brainer, and the Russian definitely had a brain.

I put one hand on the table to keep myself from stumbling—or shaking—and got to my feet. It took everything I had and then some to not only stay on the floor, but to go facedown in a full groveling bow. I kept my eyes on his the whole time. Though truth was, I didn't know if I could look away, but I wasn't going to try, and give the Russian the satisfaction if I failed.

He wasn't going to like my answer, but it was the only one I had.

I swallowed on a dry mouth, and hoped my voice didn't shake. "He tried to keep your diamonds from being stolen, Mr. Kain, and nearly got himself killed for it. I would think that deserves thanks, not accusations."

Viktor Kain smiled as he saw through my mustered-up courage.

He could smile all he wanted. It wasn't like I was embarrassed at having to scrape together the guts to stand up to a creature that in his true form and real size had teeth taller than me. There was no shame in being scared of that.

Out of the corner of my eye, I saw Ben Sadler stumble to his feet. He had to brace against the table more than I did, but he'd been whapped by a harpy. Still, he got up. Good for him.

Kain's shadow loomed over us both. "We will see if your answer is the same once—"

"Once you cooperate fully with the authorities in their investigation," Ian said from where he now stood at my side. "I am certain they will do everything in their power to return your property to you."

"And I assure you, agent of SPI," Kain said in a quiet voice used by the crazy-and-proud-of-it brand of criminal the world over, "that I will do everything in *my* power to bring the thieves—and those conspiring against me—to justice. My justice." His tone left no doubt that he considered SPI to be at the front of the conspiracy line.

"There is law in this country, Mr. Kain," Ian responded smoothly. "And you are not it."

"If you had not broken the treaty and come here, this never would have happened." The words were as crisp and cold as only a multi-millennia-old British dragon could make them. That they came from a small woman didn't lessen their impact one bit. She was within lethal violence-dispensing distance of Viktor Kain.

"Agents Byrne and Fraser," Vivienne Sagadraco said, without taking her blazing blue eyes from Viktor Kain, "remove the injured gentleman from this building. Now."

The Russian's full attention was locked on the boss. I didn't know if the glaring contest was some kind of alpha dragon dominance thing, and I didn't care. My boss had just ordered me and Ian to take Ben and get the hell out of Dodge before the gunfight started, and I was going to obey her immediately and without question.

Ben Sadler was understandably unsteady on his feet, either from the knock on the head or from being threatened by what he saw as a Russian mafioso. He made no protest when Ian took one of his arms and pulled it over his shoulder, with the other used to steady him around the waist.

Ian led us out of the Sackler Wing by a door that appeared

to be part of the far wall. It opened into a fluorescent-lit hallway that was wide enough to accommodate people moving exhibits. He closed the door behind us.

My muscles, which had been tensed in quivering readiness for either fight or flight, dissolved into a world-class case of the shakes as I exhaled a word my grandma Fraser would've washed my mouth out with soap if she'd heard.

"Are you all right?" Ian asked.

"Oh yeah." My voice was high and thin, but since I was still alive to speak, I could more than deal with it. "I'm good."

"Why would Mr. Kain . . . think I know where his . . . diamonds are?" It sounded like Ben was running out of steam along with air.

"He's looking for somebody to blame," I told him.

"But why us? I tried to stop the robbery, and you . . ." His still-bleeding forehead creased in confusion. "What *did* you do?"

I opted to downgrade "stop you from being stupid and getting gutted by a harpy" to something less alarming. "I tried to keep you from getting hurt. I didn't quite succeed. Sorry about that."

"I'm certain that you did what you could. Thank you."

Did what I could? I mustered a tight smile. "Don't mention it."

"Let's sit you down here for a minute, sir," Ian said, easing Ben down a wall to sit on the floor. "I need to make a quick call to get us a ride, and we'll be out of here and get you to a hospital."

"I need to contact my supervisor." Ben tried to smile. It didn't make it. "To let him know where I am." The attempt at a smile turned to dread. "And to report an on-the-job accident."

Ian gave him an easy and relaxed smile. "You can use my phone just as soon as I'm finished. Don't worry; we're going to take care of you."

The smile reassured Ben Sadler.

The smile creeped me the hell out.

One, I'd never seen Ian do anything easy and relaxed, especially not smile at a time like this. And two, I'd seen what Ben had done to that harpy, plus gotten myself a free sample, and I knew that in SPI speak, "take care of" could very well mean a cell, an interrogation room back at headquarters, or both. Fortunately, Ben Sadler was still too freaked-out by being attacked by harpies and threatened by the owner of the diamonds his employer was in the running to auction off to take Ian's words at anything other than face value.

"Thank you," the appraiser said. "I believe I could use some assistance."

Ian spoke into his headset. "Mobile Six, we have three for extraction. Request pickup at the west entrance."

Ben's baby blues went even wider than when he'd first laid eyes on those harpies. "Mobile Six? *Extraction?* Who are you people?"

"Take it easy, sir." Ian knelt and quickly placed a steadying hand on Ben's wrist.

The diamond appraiser instantly relaxed.

Way too relaxed, far too fast.

I quickly leaned forward. "What did you—"

Ian flipped his hand open toward me. I saw a flash of a tiny needle.

———— **5**

"A needle? You drugged him?" My voice started rising. Anger does that to me. "You can't just kidnap a man from a thousand-buck-a-head gala."

Ian was patting Ben down for weapons, and found none. "It's not kidnapping." He gripped Ben's arm above the elbow and hauled him halfway to his feet. "It's protective custody." He lowered his shoulder to Ben's midsection and, with no discernible effort, hoisted the Christie's appraiser up into a fireman's carry. "Let's go."

Just because Viktor Kain was on the other side of a re-inforced fire door, didn't mean I couldn't still feel his men-ace clear down to my bones. I scurried on bare feet to catch up with Ian's long strides, realizing that my shoes were still somewhere in the Sackler Wing. High-heeled pumps were death traps; they could stay there.

"Protective custody from Viktor Kain," I conceded. "Okay, I can see that. But did you have to—"

Ian indicated my arm. "He did that?"

I looked where he was looking. My forearm was red and starting to swell. "Yes, but he didn't mean to hurt me. I scared him."

Ian raised an eyebrow.

"I can scare people," I said indignantly.

He glanced at my hair. "Must have been the shrimp." He keyed his mike. "Mobile Six, I need confirmation on that extraction. We have a probable Code Three." He listened for a moment. "Roger that. We'll be there in ten."

I'd been with SPI for nearly a year, but I'd never heard that one before. "Code Three?"

"Rogue talent."

"Rogue?"

"Untrained, untested, unpredictable. Dangerous to himself and everyone else. And after what this guy did, it's not going to take long for a line of people and not-people to form wanting to chat with him. Right now it doesn't matter if he's new to his magic, or if he's just stupid enough to throw it around in public. Viktor Kain isn't the only one wanting to talk to him. This place is about to be overrun with cops and feds, and our boy wonder doesn't need to talk to any of them."

Ian didn't need to explain. Cops meant questions. Questions signaled evasive maneuvers, either verbal, physical, or both.

Most of the witnesses had been too busy watching what their eyes and common sense had told them couldn't be real. But once the cops got hold of the surveillance tape, they'd be able to zoom right in on me and Ben. We needed to make ourselves scarce before the NYPD took that choice way from us. A guy new to his power and who'd literally been smacked upside the head with the reality of the supernatural world did not want to be in a police or FBI interrogation room.

"Until we find out who and what he is," Ian said, "and who he works for, unconscious equals cooperative. That stunt he pulled affected every supernatural being and magic sensitive in the room."

"You mean that electrified-Mexican-jumping-bean-shock-wave thingie?"

"You felt it?"

My belly button and ears were still buzzing from it. "Oh yeah."

"Makes sense. As a seer, you qualify as a sensitive."

"By the way, his name's Ben Sadler," I told Ian. "He's a diamond appraiser at Christie's."

"Did he tell you that?"

"Of course. Who else would—" I stopped and did a mental head smack. How hard was it to give a fake name and job title, Mac? Just because a man has big blue eyes and can act innocent doesn't mean you aren't being played. Now that I didn't have my imminent death hanging over my head and could think straight, it sounded like ninety percent of my dates.

Crap. "Still too trusting, aren't I?"

"Trust isn't bad, but people often are. You just need to make room in your trust to allow for that. We can check his wallet once we get him out of here."

"I still don't think he lied. He'd have to be the best actor on the planet to fake that reaction. I thought he was in shock after seeing those harpies. Too bad he had to snap out of it, get gutsy—"

"Get stupid."

I'd give Ian that one. "Okay, get stupid, and attack that harpy." I paused. "What *did* he do? After that light show, I was blind as a bat." My arm was beginning to seriously throb. "Was that him or the harpy that made those diamonds flash?"

"Harpies don't have magic of their own."

"So Ben did it."

"That's what I saw—me and a lot of other people."

"So what kind of magic is that?"

"It could be any number of things; none of them are anything a beginner should be able to do."

The hallway ended in another door.

Ian hitched Ben up farther on his shoulders. "Time to mingle with the crowd. Stay close."

The door opened on the wide corridor just outside the Sackler Wing. The only civilians remaining inside were the same ones you'd find gawking around any other violent crime scene where there were dismembered and disemboweled bodies. You'd think people had never seen intestines before.

A man up ahead was flagging us down. I tensed until I recognized Eddie Laughlin, our security consultant. Three harpies had been one hell of a security breach. I bet Eddie was grateful that the diamonds' actual security hadn't been his responsibility. And even for a supernatural security consultant, a statue of three harpies coming to life couldn't have been on his "be on guard against" list. That still didn't mean that Vivienne Sagadraco was going to be happy with him.

Eddie fought his way through the crowd. He looked at Ben. "This the guy?" he asked when he got next to us.

"Yep," Ian replied.

"I can have a car here in five minutes," he offered.

"Thanks, but we've got Yasha picking us up."

"Headquarters?" Eddie asked.

"No, safe house on the next block."

"You sure you don't need any help?"

"We've got it."

Eddie listened to someone on his earpiece. "I'll be right there," he said to whoever was on the other end. "Good luck, man," he told Ian. He turned and vanished into the crowd, making his way back to the Sackler Wing.

There was ample chaos and no one gave a second look, or even a first one, at two people carrying a third bloody person away from the scene of the crime and out of the museum. In fact, out was the preferred direction, all we had to do was insert ourselves into the stream of frightened humanity, and let ourselves be swept along. It also helped that all of the men were wearing tuxedos. Unconscious, tuxedo clad, with his head down, no one could identify Ben as the maniac who'd attacked the harpies, and my involvement consisted of a low tackle, out of sight for most people whose eyes were locked on three jewel-thieving harpies.

Running against the tide were at least a dozen of the NYPD's finest.

Ian quickly turned his face away from them, giving me a not-so-subtle clue that he didn't want the boys and girls in blue to see him. Three years ago, Ian had left the NYPD for SPI. He'd been with them for five years, so there was a very real possibility that one or more of that group of cops would have recognized him.

We'd be hearing soon enough what the other witnesses had to say. In SPI training, I'd learned that when people had supernatural experiences, they'd go through all kinds of mental convolutions to find not only a logical explanation, but one that they could personally deal with. The human mind knew how to protect itself, and realized it was in its best interest to keep episodes of catatonic mumbling or hysterics to a lifetime minimum.

The brain could be pretty danged creative when it came to explaining the unexplainable.

Plastic surgeons weren't going to be the only medical professionals with new patients and/or appointments on Monday morning. Manhattan's psychiatric community was about to see an influx of new clients, or old clients with new problems.

I stayed next to Ian. Once clear of the exhibition, the crowd ran across the vast marble-floored Great Hall, out the glass-and-bronze front doors, and down to Fifth Avenue.

"This way." Ian had to shout to be heard over the crowd. "Yasha will be at the end of the block."

With all the mayhem of panicked people running,

gridlocked cabs and police cars, flashing lights and sirens, even Yasha would have trouble getting anywhere near the museum.

Then I saw him. To be more exact, I spotted the tricked-out Suburban he thought of as his baby.

During the day, the sidewalks near the museum played host to food carts and vendors. Tonight the massive black SUV had claimed a big chunk of concrete real estate for its own.

Yasha Kazakov was an accomplished urban off-road driver.

The Russian agent was one of SPI's drivers and trackers. In a city where there were more supernatural baddies than available parking spaces, having a drop-off and pick-up guy you could count on to be there when you needed him was a must-have. The big brush guard mounted on the Suburban's grill had never been used against brush, but saw plenty of action against charging monsters. And Yasha was always willing to take the fight beyond the driver's seat—just not during the full moon.

Yasha Kazakov was a werewolf.

Like most supernatural beings, Yasha used small magics to hide his werewolf form from the public. My seer vision let me see Yasha's large, furry, and red-haired aura. I was grateful this wasn't the full moon. If it had been, Yasha wouldn't have been in any condition to drive.

Older werewolves could change when they wanted to, but all werewolves, regardless of age, changed on the night of the full moon. Werewolves at SPI automatically got three days a month off: the day before, the day of, and the day after a full moon. Though some missions went better and got resolved faster when you had an irate werewolf on your team. Most supernatural bad guys surrendered on the spot to keep from having a full moon–crazed werewolf, who could do zero to sixty in six strides, turned loose on them.

Between Ian and me, we got Ben in the SUV and securely

buckled into the third-row seat. Yasha stayed right where he was, prepared to do his job—get us the hell out of here.

"Go!" Ian shouted, before he even had the door closed.

Yasha proceeded to whip the Suburban into the fastest three-point turn I'd ever had the displeasure to be in a vehicle for. That it was done on the sidewalk of Fifth Avenue half a block from the Metropolitan Museum of Art merely bumped the terror factor up by ten.

I squeezed my eyes shut, winced, cringed, and fully expected a crushing impact any second. We accelerated with only squealing tires, no crashes, thumps, or bumps.

"Still there is no trust in my driving," Yasha said in his thick Russian accent from the driver's seat. Yasha Kazakov was ninety-six years old. Most people would have their driver's license taken away by that age; but as a werewolf, Yasha didn't look any older than thirty-five and was just getting started.

The jury was still out on whether he should have a driver's license.

I opened my eyes all the way. "It's not your driving," I kind of lied. "It's everything else." My hands kept a double death grip on the back of the seat in front of me.

We passed a big network news truck, the kind with its own satellite. I groaned inwardly and thunked my head against the window. I should check YouTube and Twitter, but I just couldn't bring myself to do it. I couldn't do anything about it, so I'd leave it to SPI's damage control people. Their own contributions would be up soon, though they were probably there already.

One of SPI's largest departments was Media and Public Relations. I'd always thought a better name for them would be fire stompers; though in corporate speak, it would be crisis management. Our media and PR department existed with the purpose of dealing with a problem *before* it became a crisis. Proactive "R" Us. They specialized in working behind the scenes to explain the unexplainable, turning actual encounters and sightings into simple hoaxes by those looking for their fifteen minutes of fame, or exposing them as elaborate cover-ups by any number of shadowy government agencies that were ripe for the blaming. No direct accusations, of course, more like the often used "a source close to the investigation speaking on condition of anonymity because they weren't authorized to discuss the investigation publicly."

And not all the people on SPI's media and PR department worked from headquarters. They had people in the highest levels at TV networks, cable news, all across/over/throughout the web, and even in the increasingly archaic print media. Influence had been bought, paid for, and was being well used.

It seemed like everyone had smartphones, and everyplace had security or surveillance cameras. Now not only was Big Brother watching; so was Big Sister and the whole damned family. Yeah, technology gave anyone the ability to photograph a mermaid in New York Harbor, but that same technology gave us endless ways to explain how that photo could have been hoaxed. Privacy was gone; information was there for the spreading—but so was misinformation—and no one could slather it on thicker or to greater effect than our media and PR department.

So as soon as the harpy postings started to go live from the Met, our folks would jump in and throw fistfuls of doubt and disdain at any aspiring photo journalist who thought they had the next *National Geographic* wildlife cover.

It wouldn't surprise me to find out that within ten minutes of the robbery, they had a team in the ceiling above the Sackler Wing installing wires for the investigators to find to explain how those harpies could fly. As for a statue coming to life, Disney World had people dressed and made up completely in white who suddenly moved and scared the bejesus out of kids. And if Cirque du Soleil could make people appear to fly and disappear, so could the thieves. Then there was the ever-popular publicity stunt explanation.

"We've got bigger problems," Ian said, as if reading my mind. It must have been the forehead-to-window thunking that gave me away.

I'd been at SPI long enough to know that if Ian said we had bigger problems, our harpy situation was in reality the size of Godzilla rising out of the Sea of Japan to put the munch-down on Tokyo. I recalled the harpies crashing through that glass wall and into Central Park with a sense of impending doom.

"We both got a good look at that statue before it animated, right?" Ian asked.

I hesitated before responding. I wasn't sure where he was going with this. "Yes."

"And you didn't see anything tipping you off that those harpies were hidden under a veil or held immobile by some sort of spell."

"No."

Ian was leading me to the conclusion he'd already arrived at, but I wasn't doing a good job of following his breadcrumbs.

"Solid rock doesn't come to life. No magic can do that. Meaning those were real harpies that someone was powerful enough to put into suspended animation, harden on the outside to the consistency of stone, keep them that way for at least six days while the exhibition was set up, and release them to steal those diamonds. The beings that have the power to do that can be counted on one hand."

"Have I met any of them?"

"You're alive to ask me that question, so no, you haven't met them."

"How about you?"

"Likewise alive, and I don't plan to get in that reception line anytime soon."

"Now they're in New York with three harpies at their beck and call," I said. "And seven cursed diamonds."

"Do not forget the Russian," Yasha added. "Dragons do not like having part of their hoard stolen."

Nothing like mentioning Viktor Kain to make me want to change the subject. "How long will Ben be out?" I asked Ian.

"One dose lasts an hour."

"And we're not going to headquarters?"

"No. We have several properties in the city where we can take someone of Mr. Sadler's undetermined talents."

That didn't sound good. I got visions of a single chair and a really bright, naked lightbulb.

"There are reasons it's against SPI policy to bring a new talent anywhere near HQ while conscious," Ian said.

"Can't show civilians the Bat Cave, huh?"

"That's one reason. There's also the possibility that Mr. Sadler could have set us up and be working with whatever masterminded tonight's show—or Viktor Kain. Kain saying he wanted him was the perfect way to get back one of his people. If he is Kain's man, *we* want him. We can't risk anyone knowing the location of headquarters."

My mouth dropped open. I didn't even try to stop it. "Holy paranoia, Batman."

"Not paranoia. Past experience. More than once. Agents with more experience than you and me put together have had their instincts proven wrong, and good people have died because of it."

That shut me up. That and Ian's expression at the mention of those "good people." A shadow had passed across his face. He'd known some of them.

"What happens next?"

"They're taken in, given a background check and a psychological evaluation. If their background's clean and they're mentally stable, it's taken on a case-by-case basis as to whether to grant them level one clearance and educate them on their skill."

That was completely different from my experience.

I had attracted SPI's attention working at the only journalism-type job I could get after coming to town—a reporter at a sleazy tabloid that specialized in anything weird or so far out there that just reading a story about it would give you a nosebleed. The vast majority of articles weren't true, but mine were because I could see what the other reporters had to either make up or depend on getting their information from sources who wore tinfoil hats.

I glanced at Ben. "What about the ones packing major mojo?"

"People who come into their talent later in life are particularly dangerous to themselves and others. It has to do with younger minds being more flexible and easily taught."

"Kind of like learning a foreign language. If you're gonna learn one, do it while you're young."

Ian nodded. "They're assigned a mentor of sorts to help them through the adjustment period. The new talent is also required to check in regularly, daily at first, then weekly and monthly as their control—and trustworthiness—progresses."

"Like a parole officer confirming that they haven't been bragging to their friends, or aren't thinking about going into business for themselves knocking over banks."

Ian nodded. "And if the talent is one that would be useful to us, they could be eventually offered a job as an agent."

"Like I was." I thought back for a second. "Wait, I didn't get a psych evaluation."

"Oh, yes, you did. You had tea with the boss, didn't you?"

"Uh-huh."

"Ms. Sagadraco's been around humans long enough to read us at a glance. She cleared you herself—that and your family background didn't hurt."

My family lives in a small town in the far western mountains of North Carolina that through the years has attracted more than its share of people and not-people who wouldn't be described as normal by anyone's definition. My family took it on themselves to protect the prey—supernatural and otherwise—from supernatural predators. Since the town's founding in 1786, there's been a Fraser as marshal, then sheriff, and my aunt was now the police chief.

"Or if the talent is something we don't need often," Ian said, "we contract with them on a job-by-job basis."

"Like Eddie."

"Exactly."

I tilted my head toward the far backseat. "So what do you think is gonna happen with . . .?"

Ian answered by not answering.

I felt kind of responsible for Ben. If tonight had been the first time his talent had stood up and said howdy, I'd been there when it happened. What if I'd come into my talent later in life, and suddenly saw monsters everywhere I looked? I'd be in a funny farm inside of a week.

The thud of something landing on the roof sent a shudder through the massive SUV's steel frame.

As a result, we were all looking up when the harpy fist punched through the bulletproof glass on the rear window. She snapped open her hand to expose claw-tipped fingers that sliced through Ben Sadler's seat belt like a paper party streamer. The harpy then tried to sink those claws into Ben and pluck him out of the SUV like she was one of those steel claws in an arcade machine and Ben was the primo prize.

What the hell?

They stole the diamonds, and now they needed an appraiser?

With two explosive kicks, the talons on her feet punched through the roof of the SUV.

She was anchoring herself on the Suburban's roof while she snatched Ben out the back window.

That was Yasha's final straw.

The Suburban was his baby, his mobile office—hell, she was his partner. And now a bird woman was punching holes all in her.

Yasha spat a continuous stream of Russian profanities. I didn't know any Russian, but there was no denying that Yasha was cussing a blue streak.

Ian had his gun out and was firing through the roof, but all it did was make the harpy work faster to take Ben.

I still wasn't allowed to carry a gun on all missions. Tonight was one of them. Too public. Not to mention no place to hide it in my little black dress.

But I had a knife.

The harpy's claws were grabbing at Ben, who, not being belted in anymore, was flopping and sliding around in the far backseat. Two grabs later, the harpy got lucky and hooked one claw onto his shoulder. If Ben had been conscious, he'd have been screaming his lungs out.

Before she could get a better grip, I turned and threw myself over the back of my seat to return the favor, stabbing her in the forearm.

And broke my blade on her skin.

Son of a bitch.

"Hold on!" Yasha shouted. "I stop."

I grabbed the back of my seat, and Yasha stopped.

Oh boy, did he stop.

The harpy lost her grip on Ben, but not on the roof.

Did your dad ever say, "Don't make me stop this car" or "Don't make me come back there"?

Yasha did both.

Yasha the driver stopped, got out, and went wolf.

Then Yasha the werewolf unleashed a load whole of whoop-ass on a very surprised harpy.

She lost interest real quick in making Ben her personal prize, and opted for retreat over tangling with an enraged werewolf hell-bent on extracting payback out of her stony hide.

The harpy launched herself into the night sky with a shriek that said she wasn't done, not by a long shot.

As pissed as he was, Yasha had had the presence of mind to find a stretch of side street lined with small businesses that were closed for the night. It took a lot of hell being raised to make New Yorkers look out their windows, but apparently a harpy and werewolf going at it in the middle of the street qualified. Lights were coming on in the apartments above the closed businesses. The harpy had messed up the Suburban's body, not the engine, so Yasha got us out of there fast.

The shoulder of Ben Sadler's tux jacket and the shirt beneath were hanging in shreds, and blood was streaming from a puncture just under his collarbone. Ian had his handkerchief out, putting pressure on the wound.

"Get the kit," he told me.

I knew what he was talking about, and better yet, I knew where it was. All SPI vehicles carried military-quality medic kits. Yasha kept his anchored under the middle row of seats. I flipped the clips holding it in place and hauled it up onto the seat with me. I tore into a pack of gauze bandages and passed a handful back to Ian, followed by a roll of heavy-duty gauze wrap.

"Flying stone monsters," Ian said, changing out his soaked-through handkerchief for a stack of gauze bandages. "Sound familiar?"

"If you mean gargoyles ripping apart a borrowed bakery truck to turn us into road paste on my first night on the job, then yeah, it sounds familiar."

He started tightly wrapping Ben's shoulder, bringing the bandage under the appraiser's arm to keep it in place. "I do."

"Then it does."

I didn't need reminding to know how terrifying those

gargoyles had been. Almost as terrifying as those harpies coming to life and raising unholy hell in a crowd of civilians.

Those gargoyles had been after me. That harpy had been after Ben.

The possibility of a connection was the sprinkles on the squashed cupcake of my evening.

───── 6

THE protocol for bringing in a rogue talent was tossed out the nearest window when that harpy punched out the back window of Yasha's Suburban.

Ben Sadler had a deep puncture wound from a harpy claw in his shoulder, and more than a few nasty scratches. He didn't need surgery, but he did require more medical attention than Yasha's first-aid kit could handle.

Increased danger plus serious injury meant we'd be taking Ben home with us.

At SPI, we weren't encouraged to bring friends home to headquarters for sleepovers, but I was sure Mom would be willing to make an exception. One, he was the new kid on the freaky ability block. Two, Viktor Kain thought he was involved with the theft of his diamonds and had looked at him like he was the meat entree on the midnight dragon buffet. Three, whoever had masterminded that robbery was treating the diamonds and Ben Sadler like a matched set they didn't want to break up. They also weren't averse to that harpy poking a few holes in him—and killing us—to get what they wanted.

SPI's resident doctor was presently taking care of Ben, who was still conveniently unconscious from the drug Ian had given him. One of the medics had just finished bandaging the burn from Ben's hand around my lower arm. I'd been burned before, but this didn't feel like any burn I'd ever had. It tingled like a continuous low-voltage electric shock, like when I hit my funny bone, which I'd never found to be funny in the least.

SPI's infirmary looked enough like a hospital that when Ben woke up, it might help alleviate a continuation of the panic attack that had hit him just before Ian stuck him with that needle.

Or not.

When we got to his room, Ben Sadler was still out, or asleep, or playing opossum in his hospital-type bed. The shredded tux was gone, replaced by one of those cotton hospital gowns that were open down the back. *That* was going to be a shocker when he woke up. Spend your evening getting all gussied up for a gala at the Met to get an early look at a priceless clutch of diamonds for your hoity-toity employer. Wake up in a hospital bed, with a hole punched in your shoulder, covered in bumps and bruises you don't remember getting from flopping around unconscious in the backseat of an SUV, and wearing a cotton gown with two ties in the back that left your ass hanging out.

Yep, losing consciousness in one place and waking up in another left you open to all sorts of strangeness.

I knew this from experience.

Ben Sadler woke with a gasp, his eyes darting from one spot in the room to another, desperate for something, anything, to make sense. When those baby blues landed on us, I gave him what I hoped was a reassuring finger wave, since I was pretty sure he wouldn't have happy-fuzzy memories of Ian.

He saw Ian and froze. I think he was afraid to move.

I really couldn't blame him.

"Who are you people?"

He had already asked that question, but before he'd gotten an answer the first time he'd asked it, Ian had stuck him with the nighty-night needle. I think he was hoping for an answer, this time without the needle.

My gut was still telling me that Ben Sadler was a genuinely nice guy who'd ended up in a bad place at the worst time. I'd have been asking the same question, though probably with more than a few colorful vocabulary flourishes. Ben seemed like the polite type. If what had happened to him had happened to me, I'd have kicked everything I'd been taught about being a nice Southern girl to the curb until I'd gotten the answers I wanted.

I wasn't worried about what to tell him. Ian was standing right next to me, and as senior agent, he'd be the one doing the answering. I resisted the urge to look up at my partner, smile sweetly, and ask, "Yeah, who *are* we people?"

"Are you with the government?" Ben asked.

I snorted. "Lord, no."

Ian shot me a look.

I made a zipping motion across my lips.

"We're a private firm responsible for security in such cases," Ian said.

Ben gave him a flat look. "You mean cases such as statues coming to life and stealing diamonds?"

If I hadn't been leaning against the door frame, what my partner said next would've put me on the floor.

"Statues don't come to life, Mr. Sadler. Those were Grecian harpies that had been put in suspended animation by a presently unknown and extremely powerful entity. But yes, they did steal the Dragon Eggs, and their motives are as unknown as their whereabouts."

Ben looked as shocked as I was. Him because he'd just heard the words "harpies," "suspended animation," and "powerful entity" used in a real-life sentence. Me because Ian had actually told him the complete and utter truth.

"I'm sure you have questions," Ian continued without missing a beat, "and I'll answer them, but first I need some honest answers from you."

Ben's glance in my direction wasn't accusing, but it still sent me packing on a brief guilt trip.

"Hey, I didn't need to tell him anything," I told Ben. "He saw what you did—and so did entirely too many other people."

Ben's face paled and he looked a little queasy. He was even worse at hiding his emotions than I was. I gave a little silent cheer. I hoped he got hired. Finally, someone I could beat on agency poker night.

"I don't know what I did," Ben said. "Or how I did it." He eased himself back down on the bed, noticing the bandages for the first time. If he hadn't noticed the pain, the doc must have given him some really good pain killers. "What happened to me?"

That was an essay question if I'd ever heard one. I tossed Ian a "where do we start" look.

I settled at the foot of the bed, close enough to be comforting, yet far enough away not to be threatening. Ben Sadler outweighed me, so I didn't know how I could've pulled off being threatening even if I'd wanted to. I just wanted to regain some of the trust we'd had under that buffet table at the museum.

I glanced at Ian and got a single nod. "You got the crap beaten out of you by a harpy. Twice. You were awake for one, not so much for the other. Though she might have felt justified the first time because you started it."

He tried to sit up, indignant. "Ow. I tried to stop that

thing . . . harpy from stealing the diamonds. I'm the good guy here."

"We're not disputing that, Mr. Sadler," Ian said. "I want to know three things: the real reason why you tried to stop that robbery, what you did to that harpy, and why they would track you down afterward and attack our vehicle with the intent of kidnapping you."

Ben stared down at his bandages with a whole new level of understanding—and fear at where he could have woken up, and what could have been staring down at him. "Kidnapping?"

"Kidnapping," Ian confirmed.

Ben took a shaky breath and let it out. "My client—"

"Who is?"

"The confidentiality agreement we signed—"

"I've got news for you, Mr. Sadler. Those harpies had no problem with going through us to get to you. My team was in danger. That supersedes any agreement you have with your client." He paused meaningfully. "They aren't here. I am."

I spoke up. "Ben, that's as polite as my partner's likely to get, so you might want to stop with the duckin' and weavin'. That harpy wanted you bad. Your commission's not the only thing that nearly became history tonight."

Ben sighed. "Sebastian du Beckett."

"I know Mr. du Beckett," Ian said.

I blinked. "You do?"

"I didn't know what those things were," Ben continued, "but simply *seeing* those seven diamonds—together or separately—was a once-in-a-lifetime opportunity. Four of them haven't been seen publicly for over two hundred years. The Queen of Dreams and the Eye of Destiny had never even been known to exist until Tsar Nicholas bought them for his wife." His expression was stricken. "To have them stolen on the same night they were being shown to the world for the first time . . . I *didn't* think, I had to do something, anything to stop—"

"And you did what?" Ian asked quietly.

Ben fumbled for words, at a loss. "I grabbed the hand with the diamonds."

"Like you grabbed my hand?" I asked.

"Yes . . . No . . . I don't know what I did. You have to believe me. Nothing like that's ever happened before."

"But you're a diamond appraiser," I said. "I'm assuming you've been handling stones for quite a while now."

"Yes."

"And you've never gotten so much as a shiver from one?"

Ben shook his head.

"We don't have to believe you," Ian told him, "but for now, we will. Why would those harpies come after you?"

"I. Don't. Know. I wish I did."

Ian fixed Ben Sadler with a stare. Ben met his eyes, a glimmer of wetness in the corners.

Oh sheesh, don't cry.

My partner's shoulders lowered ever so slightly as he sighed. The threat of waterworks was a wondrous and powerful thing. Even more so when I knew in my gut—and apparently Ian did, too—that Ben Sadler was telling the truth.

"Perhaps we can help you find out," Ian said.

You'd think he'd just thrown Ben a life preserver. "You can?"

"Well, not me, but we have people who specialize in this kind of thing."

I glanced up at Ian and received an imperceptible nod in return. Well, here went everything. "Some people have talents that others don't. Welcome to the club."

"Talent? You call being able to electrocute people a talent?"

"Electrocute is kind of strong, no pun intended. Let's just say you've got a good, defensive zap there."

"It doesn't matter what you call it. I could've killed someone just by touching them. I hurt you."

"Like I said, *defensive zap*. I touched you as you were coming around. The last thing you remembered was getting tossed by that harpy, right?"

Ben thought, then nodded once.

"You were protecting yourself. I don't blame you. If I'd have been in your shoes, I'd have done the same thing myself. Actually, skills like yours aren't as rare as you'd think. People either learn how to hide it . . ." I stopped and caught myself mid-wince. I hadn't meant to go in that direction—that people who couldn't handle any magical woo-woo life handed them often ended up in an institution, on the streets as an addict, or else they self-inflicted themselves into a drawer at the city morgue.

None of those were going to happen to Ben, I told myself. That was why we were here. And nothing forged trust like giving trust.

"I see supernatural people," I told him.

Thank God, I didn't see dead people. Living with that shit would send me screaming right over the edge.

Ben didn't move a muscle. "Supernatural?"

"Those creatures you've read or heard about in fairy tales and urban legends. You've heard the phrase that to every legend there's a grain of truth? Well, there's a lot of grains out there, and they're real. Vampires, werewolves, dragons, elves, goblins, pixies, unicorns, Sasquatch, the Loch Ness, and various other monsters and creatures—they're all real."

During the few times in my life when I'd said a variation of the above to someone, I'd gotten the look Ben was presently giving me, usually combined with the step back, which Ben couldn't do right now, or the person I was drinking with would laugh and order us another round of tequila shots.

"And you never wondered whether you were crazy?" Ben asked.

Ian didn't say a word. He simply went to the door and opened it. The assessment team was waiting outside. Procedure had to be followed.

"Caera, could you step in here for a moment, please?" Ian asked.

Caera Filarion was an attractive human woman in her late twenties—at least she looked like a human woman to human eyes. In reality, she was much older.

She was also an elf.

Ian opted to go with a non-traumatizing example for Ben's introduction to the beings who shared the city and our world with us. Caera was no bigger than a minute, cute as a button, and looked about as threatening as a newborn kitty cat. She was also perfectly capable of kicking Ben Sadler's ass up one side and down the other, but that wasn't part of the example Ian wanted to make.

As a member of the assessment team, one of Caera's tasks was to be a newbie's first walk on the supernatural side.

The elf lowered the magazine she'd been flipping through while she and the other three members of the team waited.

"Need me to flash my ears at him?" she asked Ian.

"If you wouldn't mind."

Caera came in, and Ian closed the door behind her.

The elf crossed the room, hand extended, smiling brightly. It was genuine.

"Mr. Sadler, I'm Caera Filarion."

She didn't give him any choice but to shake her hand, and Ben was too well mannered to refuse, regardless of how surreal all this had to feel.

The handshake was more than an attempt to put a newbie

at ease. It presented them with irrefutable evidence that Caera Filarion was a warm, living, breathing, and charming woman and—as he was about to find out—one who also happened to not be human.

It made the pointy ears she was about to reveal go over a lot easier.

"I'm an elf," she told him simply.

"Pardon me?"

"An elf, Mr. Sadler."

"But there's—"

"No such thing as elves? What was your college degree?"

"Geology."

"And now you're a gemologist and appraiser, which makes you a scientist of sorts, correct?"

"I suppose you could say that, ma'am." Ben had no idea where this was going. I admit Caera was taking me on a walk out in left field, too.

"And as a scientist you're aware that discoveries are made every day."

"Yes," he replied hesitantly.

"Just because one is unaware of the existence of something doesn't alter the fact that it is real—it merely remains undiscovered or hidden. The traits of a good scientist are curiosity and an open mind."

Ben flushed slightly, duly chastised. "But you don't—"

"Look like an elf?" She smiled, and as if on cue, the dimple popped out—and she released the veil covering the tips of her ears and the jeweled glitter of her violet eyes. Dark hair, pale skin, and violet eyes—that combo had worked wonders for Elizabeth Taylor, and it was dazzling the heck out of Ben Sadler.

Ben just sat there, staring, unblinking.

She went to the bed and sat right next to him. I think Ben was the type who would have felt awkward about a woman he'd just met sitting next to him on a bed, but I didn't think

Ben Sadler had a word in his vocabulary for what he thought of the up-close and all-too-real Caera Filarion.

"I, along with most other supernaturals—that's a human term for us, by the way. It lumps us all into one convenient group. Maybe it's easier for them to accept." Caera glanced over at me and Ian, and gave us a wink. "We call ourselves the people. We used the name first. We were here before humans came out of their caves."

Ben swallowed with an audible gulp.

Snuggling up to a newbie wasn't exactly a low-key way to give someone their first gander at the supernatural world, but it sure was effective.

Caera veiled her elven features again. "My disguise for being around unenlightened humans." Then it vanished again. "And the real me."

Ben gazed with growing wonder at the top of Caera's ear closest to him, and raised his right hand ever so slowly. "May I . . ."

"Touch away." She gave him a playful grin. "I never pass up an opportunity to get my tips touched by a handsome man."

Ben sucked in his breath and yanked his hand back, blushing furiously.

"Just messing with you, Mr. Sadler. Another opportunity I never pass up."

Ben slowly reached up and, with one trembling finger, touched the tip of Caera's left ear, holding his breath the entire time.

SPI had other proof of supernaturals' existence lined up for the more thickheaded newbies, but I didn't think they were creatures Ben was ready to meet just yet.

Ben smiled like the sun had just come up. "You're an elf," he marveled.

That was thankfully easy. Though I think getting knocked around by a harpy a few hours ago helped speed things along. There was no denying a puncture, cuts, bruises, and a borderline concussion.

"What can *you* do?" he asked Caera.

Her grin turned wicked. "That depends on what you want to have—"

"Caera," Ian said in a disapproving tone.

"Sorry. Again, I can't resist."

"I mean what talent—" Ben stopped and blushed even more. "That's still not coming out right."

Caera reached over and patted his knee under the covers. "You can stop; I know what you mean. Other than enough magic to conceal my more non-human attributes, no abilities."

"Agent Filarion is too modest," Ian said.

The elf raised a flawlessly arched eyebrow. "Modest, in any sense of the word, is something I have never been called."

"Your talent may not be magic, but we couldn't do without it."

"And it's a heck of a lot more practical than most magic that gets flung around here," I added.

My partner was plain vanilla human, and proud of it. He was hired for his background of five years as an NYPD homicide detective, and for the seven years prior to that doing something in the military that I still hadn't been able to get him to tell me about. He'd probably have to kill me if he did.

Caera shrugged. "You might say I'm good with people."

"And you do a better job of it than any of the certified empaths we have," Ian said.

Ben seemed to shrink back in on himself as it occurred to him that he wasn't in a hospital, at least not a normal one. "Where am I?"

"A secure and safe facility," Ian told him. "It isn't only for your protection, it's for ours."

Ben threw a guilty glance at my arm and started to speak.

I sensed an apology coming on. I held up a hand to ward it off. "Apology heard, received, noted, and accepted. You can stop already."

"Thank you." He hesitated. "Do you think my talen . . . what I can do can really hurt people? Am I dangerous now?"

The poor guy sounded ready to lock *himself* up.

"Honey, you're not dangerous," I told him. "Well, that is unless you want to be."

"What if I can't control it? I couldn't control it at the museum."

I didn't have an answer for that one. He was right. He zapped the hell out of that harpy, and we still had no idea what had set him off. I'd been lucky to end up on the business end of a milder zap. Maybe he'd used up all his mojo on the harpy. Either way, I'd probably dodged a big bullet. I knew it, and from the puppy dog eyes I was getting now, Ben Sadler knew it, too. He'd packed his bags for a guilt trip of his own.

A lot of men would have loved to have that kind of power to throw around. Lucky for us, and for him, Ben wasn't that kind of man. If he had been, Caera wouldn't have been letting him pet her ears, and that wouldn't have been an assessment team waiting outside. When the good Lord had been handing out potentially lethal gifts, he'd picked the right man to have it. Given enough time, we could talk him into believing that it was a gift, but time wasn't something we had a bushel basket of right now.

"What happens now?" he asked.

"Some of my colleagues are going to come in and join us." Caera gave him two comforting pats on the back of his hand that presently had a death grip on the bed railing. "We'll find out exactly what you have and what level of skill you possess."

"But I don't know anything," Ben said. "How are you going to determine . . ." He stopped and I actually heard the railing squeak in protest. My injured arm gave a sympathetic twinge in return.

Caera managed to intertwine her fingers in his. Elves were stronger than we humans, too. "It won't hurt. Our tests won't do any more than I'm doing right now." Her eyes gave a solemn promise. "No one will hurt you, Mr. Sadler; and you are not a prisoner. We're here to help." She paused. "May we have your permission to proceed?"

"I have a choice?"

"You always have a choice."

He didn't look to me or Ian to get a read on whether Caera was telling the truth; he openly assessed the elf's face to judge for himself. Good for him.

Ben took a breath and nodded as he blew it out. "Let's get started."

7

I'D showered and changed clothes.

I kept extra clothes in my locker, and had to use them more often than I liked. If there'd been a company award for the agent most likely to end a mission covered in a food or beverage, I'd win hands down. I didn't seek out greatness; I had it dumped upon me.

Vivienne Sagadraco was back in the office and wanted to see us.

I hadn't done anything wrong—well, other than being photographed by hundreds of people in the most public place possible while tackling the man tangling with harpy jewel thieves—but getting called into the boss's office never marked the beginning of good times.

Dragons as old as the boss and Viktor Kain were rare; but just because they were both dragons who'd seen a lot of water go under the bridge didn't earn the Russian any brownie points with Vivienne Sagadraco. If anything, the opposite was true.

Dragons, especially the ancients, were highly territorial. In the old days it probably had to do with carving out a sufficiently large hunting ground. It took a lot to top off a dragon's tank. Then there was their hoard to consider. Nothing stoked a dragon's fire faster than another dragon getting within stealing distance of their sparklies. Manhattan was Vivienne Sagadraco's territory and Viktor Kain was tracking his big clawed feet all over it.

The boss had started getting antsy the moment the Russian's private jet had touched down at LaGuardia, violating the heck out of whatever treaty or agreement they had to stay out of each other's way.

Dragons were big on etiquette. Being British, the boss took proper manners very seriously. Protocol dictated that the Russian notify her that he'd be spending a few days in the city. Typically this notification took on the tone of a request for an invitation, usually accompanied by a gift of a valued item from their hoard.

Viktor Kain hadn't asked for permission to visit or sent a gift; he simply showed up, like a creepy distant cousin who'd overstayed his welcome five minutes before he'd even arrived. He'd accused Vivienne Sagadraco of orchestrating the theft of his diamonds, and for the cherry on top, he'd threatened me and Ben Sadler. While the boss was protective of her employees, she didn't know Ben from Adam's house cat; but he was a New Yorker, and the boss considered everyone living in the five boroughs to be under her protection. If Viktor Kain racked up any more obnoxiousness points, the boss would personally see to it that he left New York as cargo in his fancy jet.

As Ian and I took the elevator up to the fifth floor executive suites, I could swear the closer we got, the thicker the air became. Dragons were big and so were their emotions. If they were pissed, everyone could sense it. My senses were telling me that Vivienne Sagadraco's mood had passed the point of annoyance and proceeded straight to a low boil.

The carved double doors to her office were open. I hoped we hadn't kept her waiting long.

Ian and I told her what had happened at the museum, about the harpy attack on Yasha's SUV and our conversation with Ben Sadler in the infirmary. We left nothing out, regardless of how insignificant it may have seemed to us at the time.

Ian had learned long ago, and told me, as his partner, that in addition to being one of the oldest living creatures on the planet, the boss was one of the smartest. It made sense that you couldn't exactly survive for thousands of years without being crafty as hell.

We told her everything, and everything we told her ticked her off even more. Ian couldn't see or hear it, but Vivienne Sagadraco filled her office—which had always reminded me of something out of Hogwarts—with a low, rumbling growl. And the aura I detected rearing up behind and around her throne-like desk chair revealed a dragon with peacock blue and green iridescent scales that appeared to be experiencing an overwhelming need to bite the head off of something. Fortunately, I'd been assured that the boss found it counterproductive to kill (and eat) the messenger. She was a firm believer that good help was hard to find.

As Vivienne Sagadraco took a meditative sip from the cup of tea on the desk in front of her, my seer vision saw taloned and scaled fingers holding a dainty teacup and saucer. It was as surreal now as it had been the first time I'd seen it during my final interview before I'd been hired. If there was anything that'd soothe the savage breast of a British dragon, it was a cup of tea. The boss probably owned stock in Twinings. Who was I kidding? She probably had a hand way back when in founding the company. God save the Queen, and God bless tea.

"If Sebastian du Beckett is Mr. Sadler's client through Christie's," she said, "then this young man will meet with our evaluation team's approval." She returned the delicate cup to its saucer. "Bastian is very selective about whom he works with. Though I do think it odd that he would retain the services of a diamond appraiser, especially one so young and presumably less experienced."

"Bastian?" I asked.

Vivienne Sagadraco actually smiled. "The man found and acquired some of the most favored items in my own hoard. There is no one better when it comes to precious gems and diamonds. He shouldn't need an outside appraisal conducted for the Dragon Eggs, with the exception, perhaps, of two of the diamonds. The other five are well-known to him and anyone else in the diamond trade." She shrugged. "That being said, Bastian is reclusive. He regularly retains qualified representatives to do such tasks for him. He has worked with Christie's specialists in the past. They are, quite simply, the best at what they do."

"At least we know one thing for certain, ma'am," Ian said. "Kenji hacked into the Christie's HR department computer, and Ben Sadler does work there as an appraiser. He's the youngest one they have, and he's been there less than a year."

Vivienne Sagadraco stirred her tea, then set the spoon on the saucer. "Then it seems the talent Mr. Sadler exhibited to the public may be part of the reason Bastian chose him. I'll call him and inquire. His accuracy is unfailing when it comes to detecting new talent."

Ian nodded in approval. "Anything he can tell us will help our evaluation team get a better read."

I had a question, one I was reluctant to ask given Viktor Kain accusing the boss of stealing the Dragon Eggs. "Ma'am, why would someone steal diamonds using harpies in front of hundreds of human witnesses? You'd think they would've done their business before or after the exhibition, or at least after hours when all they'd have to deal with were a security system and some guards."

"Because the Dragon Eggs weren't all they desired. Whatever reason they had for stealing the diamonds, perhaps they also wanted to humiliate Viktor Kain, or bring trouble to our doorstep, or expose supernatural beings as real in the most public way possible. Any or all of the above are possible, and more."

Schemes on top of plots, with intricate maneuvering running underneath. That was what Rake Danescu had said about dragons. With his next breath, he'd told me he aspired to be as devious. I was starting to believe that our problem wasn't that we didn't have any suspects; we had too damned many.

"Was Mr. du Beckett having Ben scout out the diamonds because you wanted to buy them?" I asked. "Though if it's none of my business—"

"I prefer diamonds I can wear. None of the Dragon Eggs were cut with the intent of being mounted for jewelry."

"What about the goblin and elven diamonds?" I asked.

Vivienne Sagadraco nodded once. "Neither are of this world, and they have no business being here. They are gems of power, and the presence of such stones from a dimension other than our own seldom occurs without consequences. Often grave consequences."

"What can they do?"

The boss frowned. "Unknown. The fact that our usual sources for such information refuse to divulge what they know only confirms that they are dangerous."

"I'm betting Viktor Kain knows exactly what they're capable of," Ian said. "As well as whoever had those harpies steal them."

Vivienne Sagadraco added another cube of sugar to her tea. "Our sources merely have knowledge of the diamonds' capabilities; unfortunately, Viktor and the thief have knowledge *and* intent. Even the most benign gem of power's capabilities can be twisted to cause harm. As a gem mage, Viktor can access and wield that power."

"Gem mage?" I asked. "I take it you mean more than chakra balancing, crystal healing, New Agey stuff?"

Vivienne Sagadraco raised an inquiring brow. "Not a believer, Agent Fraser?"

"After what I got a gander and taste of tonight? You bet I'm a believer, ma'am. Gullible? Not so much. As for what Viktor Kain can do, I know you're not talking about him waving the right crystal over his forehead to get rid of a hangover."

"No, I am not. A stone of power in the hands of a mage such as Viktor is capable of catastrophic evil, which makes me wonder why he would broadcast his interest in selling such a collection. He has never willingly relinquished power of any kind, especially beautiful objects that conceivably bestow power."

"He's sure not gonna be selling them now," I said.

The boss gave me a ghost of a smile. "Unless that was never his intention."

I'd never thought of that. Rake Danescu was right; dragons were devious thinkers. "Though if those harpies were part of his plan, he put on a fine act."

"Viktor's passions run too close to the surface for his reaction to have been staged. He was as caught off guard as the rest of us were. He did not steal his own diamonds. It would be like him to announce an auction to give his presence in New York extra credibility. The possibility of owning diamonds such as the Dragon Eggs would be irresistible and worth virtually any risk. Whoever is responsible for their theft should pray to whatever gods they may revere that we find them first. If those diamonds are still in this city, I know that Viktor Kain will tear it apart brick by brick until he finds what is his." The boss's eyes glittered. "And he knows that I will protect what is mine."

Vivienne Sagadraco and her evil sister duking it out over Times Square on New Year's Eve was probably nothing compared to the destruction she and Viktor could unleash.

"He had the blame quite ready to lay at my feet," she continued. "He insisted the intelligence I received of a robbery attempt at the Mythos exhibition was merely a cover I fabricated to conceal my own nefarious actions."

"I imagine you've got enough diamonds of your own; why would he think you wanted his?"

"With a dragon, there is no such state as enough of anything we choose to collect. There is always room for more sparklies—as you are so charmingly fond of calling them—in most dragons' hoards. Viktor Kain and I have known each other for two hundred and fifty-seven years, which is precisely two hundred and fifty-seven years too long."

"Uh, not on the best of terms, I take it?"

"Neither on our best nor worst days. Viktor blames me for the death of someone he loved."

"He can love?"

"The presence of evil does not preclude love, Agent Fraser."

"And now he's looking for payback," Ian surmised.

"Oh yes. Viktor insists that our people were inside the museum to enable the robbery, not prevent it. And that if by some slim chance SPI did not steal the diamonds, he believes we know who did and that our actions aided the escape of the harpies."

I nodded in realization. "So that's why he came at Ben."

"Most likely. Regardless of what the diamonds are capable of, Viktor believes that his plans are collapsing around him. Again. He perceives himself as wronged and cornered. It is dangerous for a dragon to feel cornered."

"Why just take the eggs?" I asked. "The dragon in that nest is supposed to be the biggest ruby on the planet, and the nest was woven from twenty-four-karat gold wire. If you're going to go to that much trouble, why not snatch the whole kit and caboodle?"

"Of greater concern to me is what it says about the identity of the thief that they have the ability to put a trio of harpies into a state of stasis resembling stone, and then reanimate them at the exact moment needed to commit the robbery. There are several possible perpetrators, none of which are individuals we want in our city."

"Would the perp have needed to be in the same room to do it?" Ian asked.

Leave it to my former-cop partner to refer to someone that obscenely powerful as a "perp," as if they were no more than a Midtown mugger.

"Visual contact would be necessary," Vivienne Sagadraco confirmed. "Did you see anyone suspicious, Agent Fraser?"

"I didn't sense any magic being worked by anyone near me. And no one else set off any of my other alarms—except for Rake Danescu." He set every alarm I had to clanging, but none of them had to do with diamond theft. "I don't know how good of an actor he is, but I thought his eyes were going to bug out of his head when he saw those harpies waking up, or whatever it was they did."

"Rake Danescu can affect whatever reaction a situation calls for," Vivienne Sagadraco said smoothly. "I was unaware of any talent regarding reanimation; however, he is equally adept at hiding his skills. He will be investigated." The boss's computer beeped, and she turned to check it. "The results from the surveillance tape are starting to come in. Please join me," she told us. "Agent Byrne is familiar with these individuals, but you need to learn to identify them on sight, Agent Fraser. I'll also have their files e-mailed to you."

We got up and went to look over Ms. Sagadraco's shoulder at the images on her monitor. There were seven thumbnail photos. Even though they were small, I could tell that five were men in tuxedos, and two were women. One in a cocktail dress; the other in a full-length gown.

"These are the sorcerers who were in attendance tonight. Of course there were more than are indicated here, but they must possess a high level of skill—and questionable associates and activities—before SPI will put them on our constant surveillance list." She looked at the photos and gave a tired sigh. "And entirely too many of those on that list are in the city for the exhibition and auction. These particular individuals do not bother to hide their power. They know we're watching them, so they simply do not bother with concealment; as a result, we were able to get a clear image of them."

Ms. Sagadraco clicked on the first photo, enlarging it. It was a dark-haired man, medium build, dark eyes. Either he had a really nice tan, or naturally bronzed skin.

"This is Nikolos Portfirio," she said. "He is a human sorcerer based in Cyprus, and is a known business associate of Viktor Kain. His territory is the Eastern Mediterranean and the Middle East."

The boss clicked on the second photo, the woman in the cocktail dress. I couldn't tell how old she was. She wore her blond hair up, her neckline way down. I couldn't really blame her; if I had boobs like that, I'd show 'em off, too. Even more impressive were the diamonds she was wearing. One of the diamonds in her necklace was so large that it was almost wearing her.

"This is Gizela Ingeborg, a gem mage. Last known residence was in Stockholm." The boss's lips twisted with distaste. "We weren't aware that she would be attending, but I cannot say that I am surprised."

"Does she know Viktor Kain?" I asked.

Ms. Sagadraco shook her head. "She does not and does not want to."

"Sounds like a sensible enough lady."

"Gizela's associations are with beings from a much warmer climate."

"I take it you're not talking about the French Riviera."

"Only if it's unfortunately acquired sulfur and brimstone since my last visit. Gizela specializes in the acquisition of cursed objects—for buyers who intend to use them to the fullest extent possible." She clicked on the next thumbnail. "This is Marek Reigory, a goblin dark mage. He is not on the good side of the new goblin king. He recently made a poor choice of allegiance, conspiring with the new king's older brother to assassinate him."

"That wouldn't put him on my good side, either," I murmured.

"Lord Reigory has been banished; not only from the goblin court, but his entire home dimension."

"So what's he doing here?"

"This is where he was banished to," Ian said.

I blinked. "New York's a punishment?"

"He can go anywhere in the world, but he can't leave."

"Forgive me if I don't cry the boy a river. There's nothing like finding out the goblins consider Earth a penal colony." I thought of something and grinned. "Though that might explain what Rake Danescu's doing here."

"Danescu is here by choice," Ian said. "His. Definitely not anyone else's."

"You don't have much use for him, do you?"

My partner snorted. "Even less, if that's possible."

"Don't let Lord Danescu get to you, Agent Byrne," Ms. Sagadraco said. "It serves no purpose other than amusing Rake. The last thing he needs is more amusement. I will admit that his skill level puts him firmly in the dangerous category; however, he has yet to use his power against us, or given us any reason to take action against him."

"No, ma'am, he hasn't," Ian agreed politely. "That we know of. But give him time."

I detected the faintest upward twitch of one side of Vivienne Sagadraco's lips. "And until then, we will give him the same benefit of the doubt that we would any mage living in our city."

Ian drew breath to speak. Vivienne Sagadraco held up her hand.

"As always, while keeping him under surveillance from a respectful distance," she said.

That seemed to satisfy my partner.

"Next is Gerald Blackburn from Scotland," the boss continued smoothly. "Sadira Kansibar from Turkey, Stephan Javier of France, and Dietrich Wolf from Germany. All have places of dishonor on our most watched list."

"Not most wanted?" I asked.

"Always suspected," Ian said. "Never convicted. Unfortunately, they're that good. We can pin crimes on them; we just can't make them stick."

"I won't go into their past criminal offenses now," Ms. Sagadraco told me. "They will be in the files I'll have sent to you. Study them well."

"Yes, ma'am."

I didn't need to ask why she wanted me to study up on six humans and one goblin who didn't use any kind of glamour to hide anything about them. Normally people and creatures that didn't use glamours to hide didn't need a seer to point them out. When I started at SPI, I already had a bull's-eye on my back. My three predecessors had met with messy deaths. Someone with a lot of magical power and influence in the supernatural world was determined to keep SPI without a seer. I'd been here nearly a year and had managed to keep myself among the living, mostly thanks to Ian.

I knew exactly what the boss was telling me. One of these people could want me dead.

"Of more concern to me are those who had tamped down

the auras generated by their magical power," Ms. Sagadraco was saying. "Until tonight, these individuals have been completely unknown to us. We have images from the surveillance cameras, but so great were the forces restraining their auras that the images are distorted. We have agents who are specially attuned to those with excessive magical strength. They are working with our artists to get accurate renderings. We gather as much intelligence as we can on people with this level of power. If anything good can be said to have come out of this evening, it is learning of their existence. Better the devil you know than the devil you don't."

There were two artist renderings: one of a man, the other a woman. Next to each was a still image captured from the museum's cameras. For the most part, you could see their bodies okay, but their faces looked like TV static. That wasn't helpful.

"Not the greatest resolution," I noted. "But the drawings are incredible." Heck, it was even better than some of the art at the exhibition tonight.

The man looked mid-sixties, the woman mid-thirties. While the drawings were beautiful, the subjects themselves looked completely ordinary, meaning about as dangerous as serial jaywalkers.

"Do we have any estimate as to how strong they are?" Ian asked.

"The agent who spotted and documented these two is one of our best and most accurate. She would not exaggerate what she saw. The darkness of their auras and the psychic vibrations from how tightly they were being contained indicates that these two individuals could be more powerful than all but one of the known suspects in attendance."

I was incredulous. "And no one here's even seen or heard of them before?"

"Correct."

"Dang, that's scary."

"Yes, Agent Fraser, it is. And these are merely the first two to be recorded. There were five others, all with nearly the same strength estimate." She paused. "One, in particular, possessed power beyond any of the sorcerers present. I'm having our best artist working on that rendering now."

"And no one had ever seen him before?"

"Her," the boss corrected me.

Oh crap.

I resisted the urge to look over my shoulder. "Your sister isn't in town, is she?"

"No, she is not. I would almost prefer if this woman had been her. As I said, the devil you know . . ."

And I'd met that devil before, up close and personal—and in my head. Before she'd tangled with her sister in the sky over Times Square, Tiamat had herself a little fun taunting me with how her grendels and their dozens of hatchlings were going to eat their way through the New Year's Eve crowds beginning at midnight. Having a crazy, megalomaniacal dragon traipsing through my gray matter was a sensation I did not want repeated.

But it had happened again tonight with Viktor Kain. He hadn't used words in my head, just images, like showing me his personal scrapbook of evil.

"That level of power does not simply appear overnight," the boss was saying. "There have been those like Mr. Sadler, but they are the exception rather than the rule. We'll start the files on the new ones, and share what information we may be able to uncover. Every attempt will be made through our international offices and contacts to keep them under surveillance, but considering that tonight was the first known record of their existence, they obviously know how to maintain a low profile." She blew out a weary breath. "Agent Byrne, I believe you have a contact or two in the supernatural fine art black market?"

"Yes, ma'am."

"Please reach out to them regarding any sudden actions such as gatherings or transfers of large sums of money or gold—either in this world or the supernatural realms."

"I'll get right on it."

"Monsieur Moreau is having a list compiled of suspects capable of putting harpies into suspended animation, and who would benefit either from owning or selling the Dragon Eggs. Our Research department is investigating what, if any, magical capabilities the Dragon Eggs possess—either individually or combined. It would go a long way towards explaining Viktor's anger at having the diamonds stolen. If he had wanted to sell them, he could have done so perfectly well from St. Petersburg or any other location where he has homes. There was no need for him to travel here. He would never risk coming here for a mere auction. There is one thing I can always count on my Russian nemesis to have—a plan that goes ten steps beyond what he wants me to think he is doing." She scowled. "I dislike having an opponent with an advantage."

I shifted uneasily. I didn't know if Ms. Sagadraco realized what had happened tonight between me and Viktor Kain, but if she didn't, she needed to—and I needed to know why it was happening to *me*, and if there was anything I could do to stop it from happening again. I didn't want anyone in my head, least of all psychotic dragons.

I wouldn't be the first person in my family to pick up a strange, new ability. My cousin Charlie could communicate with birds. The other men in the family thought the only time that was useful was during duck season. My aunt Blanche swore up and down that she knew exactly what each one of her fifteen cats was thinking. The rest of the family pretty much took that claim with a grain of salt, and told Aunt Blanche she needed to get out of the house more.

To the best of my knowledge, I was the only Fraser whom dragons could talk to telepathically. Though considering how rare dragons were, I might have been the only member of my family who'd ever been close enough to a dragon to have a chat.

"Uh . . . Ms. Sagadraco?"

"Yes, Agent Fraser?"

"Viktor Kain and I had a little . . . run-in this evening."

"That is another thing he has to answer for. I will not have my agents threatened—"

"It wasn't the threats, ma'am. It was the movie that went along with it."

"I beg your pardon?"

"It only lasted a few seconds. I mean, it felt a lot longer, but I'm sure it only took up a couple of seconds."

The boss's expression darkened, and her dragon aura loomed behind her, flowing up the wall like a shadow. I knew it wasn't directed at me, and she couldn't help that she did it, but that didn't keep me from wishing I'd just kept my mouth shut.

Her eyes glittered dangerously. "What happened, Agent Fraser?"

"He was trying to scare the hell out of—I mean, he was trying to intimidate me by showing me what he'd done to other people who didn't tell him what he wanted to know. It was . . . impressive. FYI, ma'am, the file we have on him really doesn't do his past activities justice."

The spooky shadow flowed back down the wall as Ms. Sagadraco made an effort to calm herself. Her expression softened along with it. "Words, regardless of the language, have difficulty capturing the horror of a situation. Visuals, such as photographs or videos, do a much more effective job."

"It was effective, all right."

She gave me a small smile. "And you did not back down."

"I didn't see it as an option, ma'am. I don't give in to bullies. And that's what Viktor Kain is, a bully. Albeit one

with a wider mean streak, who's had a lot longer to practice."
I hesitated. "The problem is, your sister talked to me in my
head on New Year's Eve, and tonight Viktor Kain bragged
on how many ways he's killed people who sassed him."

Vivienne Sagadraco raised a single eyebrow.

"Who defied him," I clarified.

"Oh."

"That's not anything I've been able to hear or see before
I came to New York. Then again, so far it's only happened
with dragons, and until I'd moved here, I'd never met a
dragon."

"Have you heard my thoughts?"

"No, ma'am, but I just figured it was because you were
too much of a lady to barge in to my head without knocking."

A tiny grin curled the boss's lips. "So my sister isn't a lady?"

"I'll acknowledge that she's female. No offense, ma'am,
but that's about as far as I'd be willing to go."

Vivienne Sagadraco gave a short laugh. "I couldn't agree
more, Agent Fraser. I had thought the incident with my sister might have been a fluke. Having become accustomed to
being worshiped as a goddess, Tiamat became quite adept
at forcing her thoughts into the minds of her human priest-
esses."

"I'm a dragon priestess?" My voice rose and my alarm
along with it.

"There is no such thing, Agent Fraser; merely those who
are sensitive to the thoughts of our kind. My sister must have
sensed this in you and taken advantage of it." Her expression
grew solemn. "May I have your permission to try something?"

I tensed even more than I already was. "To talk to me in
my head?"

"Yes. If it is an ability you have, then it is a rare gift
indeed—and one that could prove most advantageous to the
entire agency." She paused. "You have not experienced any

uncomfortable aftereffects as a result of the contact, have you?"

"Just a galloping case of the creeps after having a pair of psychos pull a Hannibal Lecter and Clarice Starling in my head." I stopped. "Sorry, ma'am, but I—"

"I know, Agent Fraser. You call them as you see them. It is a quality I've always admired in you, and in this case I agree. Both my sister and Viktor Kain are undeniably psychotic, among many other distasteful things."

"May I sit down?"

She searched my face, concerned. "Do you feel that you need to?"

"I wasn't sitting down either time before." I gave her a tired little smile. "But it's been a long night, ma'am."

"That it has, Agent Fraser. Please, do be seated."

Ian spoke for the first time in about five minutes. "May I stay, ma'am?"

"Of course." She glanced at me. "If you do not mind?"

"Mind?" I turned to Ian. "Why wouldn't I want you here?"

My partner looked uncharacteristically uncomfortable. It was kinda cute. "It isn't . . . personal?"

I coughed back a chortle. Ian was serious, and I didn't want to laugh at him. "No more personal than the two of *us* having a chat. Me and Ms. Sagadraco will just be looking at each other. You won't hear a thing. We will. That is, if it works." I looked back at our boss. "Are you ready, ma'am?"

I felt a push behind my eyes.

"Always."

I froze and my eyes went wide.

"I take it that means you can hear me?" my dragon boss asked.

I managed a series of tiny nods.

"Is it working?" Ian whispered.

"Oh yeah," I whispered right back, not taking my eyes off of Ms. Sagadraco. *"So, how am I able to do this?"*

"I've never heard of it manifesting in a seer. However, there are not many dragons left, and it is a rare gift, so perhaps you are merely the first."

"Oh wonderful. I'm a trailblazer."

"Actually, it is wonderful. Especially if we can also communicate over distance. Do I have your permission to try later?"

"Could you give me a call on my phone first? It might not be quite so . . . startling that way."

"Of course."

She glanced over my shoulder at Ian. "That went exceptionally well," she told him out loud.

He looked from me to the boss and back again. "It worked?"

"Perfectly," she said.

I went with more nods and what I hoped wasn't a freaked-out rictus of a smile.

There was a soft tap on the door. It opened a crack and Caera Filarion stuck her head in.

"I'm sorry to interrupt, ma'am. Mr. Moreau wasn't at his desk, and I knew you'd want to hear this."

I went still. "Ben?"

"Oh yeah. But don't worry, he's fine. He simply has more horsepower under his hood than we thought possible."

Vivienne Sagadraco beckoned with a bejeweled hand. "Come in, Agent Filarion."

Caera did and closed the door behind her.

"It's rather too soon for your team to have a full report," the boss noted.

"We're still testing Mr. Sadler, but I knew you'd want to know that our preliminary results indicate that Ben Sadler is at least a level ten gem mage."

That was confusing. "I thought the scale only goes to ten."

"It does. Tall, blond, and beautiful you brought home with you is testing off the charts—all of them."

"So he's not a newbie?"

"Oh, we're pretty sure he's just coming into his power." Caera bit back a snicker. "He has absolutely zero control. We had a test gem that's been especially responsive to mage stimuli in the past. He blew out every light and electrical outlet in the infirmary, and that was from simply looking at the thing. Bob from Research was observing the test. Unfortunately he was standing in front of an outlet; now he's sporting a bad perm."

Ian chortled. "So Ben Sadler was telling the truth."

"In my opinion, yes. He was open to our questioning and forthright in his responses. Mac, you saving him from that harpy made our job infinitely easier," she told me. "He trusts you. Ian? Uh, not so much. Ben sees his talent as more of an incurable medical condition, and we're the only available specialists. Unfortunate that he perceives it that way, but it's a normal human reaction."

Ian turned to the boss. "Ma'am, you said that Viktor Kain is a gem mage. Do you think he could sense a like talent?"

"Definitely."

"If he really thinks we're behind the robbery, you ordering us to get Ben Sadler out of the museum would play right up his paranoid alley."

"Because he would believe that I would be using Mr. Sadler to activate the diamonds to do whatever it is they can do."

Ian nodded.

"So what's next?" I asked. "We can't keep him locked up."

"We could," Caera said. "But we won't, at least not if he continues to be cooperative. He's been honest with us; we'll be honest with him. It's not safe for him anywhere in the city right now. Aside from Viktor Kain, those harpies are a concern, but so are the police and the media."

"I'd almost rather face a harpy than a swarm of folks sticking cameras and mikes in my face," I said.

"It's also not in our best interests for Ben to be picked up by the police," Caera said. "Open and honest to our questions is good; it wouldn't be good at all if the FBI got hold of him."

Ian nodded. "There were plenty of high-profile internationals at the Met tonight. The diamonds belonged to the head of a known Russian criminal organization. Every alphabet agency out there will want a piece of the action."

Vivienne reached for her slender phone. "Perhaps I should call Bastian now."

8

IT was after midnight. There was too much happening too fast to even think about getting any sleep.

What had happened at the Met and to us on the way back to headquarters had activated SPI's version of DEFCON 2. Supernatural creatures had been seen by hundreds of people. Enemy combatants were on the ground in the city—that would be Viktor Kain, and whoever had masterminded the robbery and was pulling those harpies' strings. And last, but certainly not least, possible weapons of mass destruction had been stolen and were in the hands of a powerful, but as yet unknown, adversary. The only thing needed to bump it to a DEFCON 1 would be one of the enemy combatants taking open action in the city.

SPI's media and PR team, on the other hand, had gone into DEFCON 1 mode the instant photos and videos of those harpies had started popping up online, and then in network news coverage of the incident, and pop up they had. The Media department was on the second floor of our headquarters' complex, which was located right under Washington Square Park, and was nearly as big as the park itself. The complex was centered around what we called the bull pen, which was where most of the field agents had their offices. Above were five stories of steel catwalks connecting labs, more offices, and conference rooms.

Our media team was in full crisis management mode. They were used to having to deal with the occasional urban legend, but this was exactly what they trained for. This situation may have been SPI's worst nightmare, but these people were living the dream. I'd never seen them happier.

Overseeing the gleeful, perfectly orchestrated chaos that the second floor had become was a petite powerhouse of a woman who was the greatest irony of all.

Kylie O'Hara—SPI Media department director, world-renowned debunker of the supernatural, and the ultimate mistress of misinformation—wasn't even human herself.

She was a dryad.

Her real name was something unpronounceable with way too many apostrophes. You know the ones; the kind of names you see in fantasy novels, but have no idea how to say. You'd be surprised at the amount of stuff those authors got right. Unfortunately, rampant use of apostrophes was one of them. The extremely shortened form of her first name was similar enough to Kylie, and she used O'Hara because it was the name of the state forest near the shore of Lake Ontario in upstate New York where she was born.

And people thought her green eyes and last name meant she was Irish.

At five foot and a handful of change tall, Kylie O'Hara didn't do her hoax busting from the shadows. Far from it. She put herself front and center on TV and radio talk shows, and was accepted by respected journalists as an expert on the exposé. I'd heard last week that Syfy had offered Kylie her own series where she would reveal and demonstrate how hoaxes were perpetrated, and how paranormal frauds pulled the wool over the eyes of the masses. Heck, even if I didn't know and like her, I'd watch that. Whenever we'd gone out to lunch together, we never had to wait for a table. It didn't matter how crowded the restaurant was; we always got a table—a good one.

Kylie and I had more than a few things in common. One was our jobs. I exposed supernatural criminals by seeing through their glamours. Kylie exposed paranormal hoaxes, either by revealing a fake, or by debunking the real thing to cover it up. We both had journalism degrees, though Kylie had gone to Columbia, and I, well, hadn't. Last, but not least, we were both country girls. I was from a small town in the North Carolina mountains; Kylie was from a large tree in a New York state forest.

Her website, hoaxbusters.com, had become a daily entertainment stop for millions; she'd recently passed two million followers on Twitter; and just because she hadn't yet displaced cat videos from its YouTube throne didn't mean she wasn't working on it. In her downtime—what there was of it—she loved World of Warcraft, which was the one place other than SPI where she could be herself.

The door to the Media department's version of their bull pen opened and Kylie stepped out onto the catwalk leading to the elevators. Her dark hair was swept up into a twist, and she was wearing what'd become her standard TV interview look. I called it "business funky." Her bright blue suit was classic cut, but Kylie knew how to have fun with accessories. It told viewers, "I take my job seriously, not myself." Her most famous accessory was her collection of eyeglasses. She changed them to suit her outfit and her mood. Like most supernaturals, Kylie's vision was perfect, better than human perfect; but she thought glasses were fun. Combine all of the above with a voracious love of the latest technology, and Kylie O'Hara had earned a place among geek royalty.

Right now, she was geek royalty with a job to do. I'd seen the video that'd been released in the last hour from a witness at the Met, someone who'd been close enough and had the skill to get some damned good—and damning—footage. Footage that'd been liberally smeared all over the Internet and networks. The chance of making this go away quietly was gone for good. Kylie had an impossible task ahead of her.

From the impish grin on her face, gleam in her eyes, and determined stride, you'd think that video and those that were sure to follow were a lifetime of birthday presents given to her on one night. I had no clue how she was going to pull it off, but Kylie apparently felt armed for battle and was confident of victory.

"Go get 'em, tiger!" yelled one of the field agents in our bull pen.

Kylie rewarded him with a megawatt smile and a thumbs-up.

The bull pens on both floors erupted in applause, whistles, and cheers. I joined in.

Then I saw a sight I'd never beheld—my partner standing next to the stairs with a big, goofy grin on his face. The instant he sensed me watching him, the grin vanished.

"Hey, don't stop on my account," I teased. "Kylie isn't the only one putting on an enjoyable show."

Kylie had started at SPI a few months before I had. Ian dated, but it was no one serious, and it definitely wasn't anyone from the office. I'd surmised that my partner was one of those "no workplace romance" kind of guys. Which, when you thought about it, was pretty smart. If a relationship went sour, you'd be biting that lemon every day at work.

But from what I'd just witnessed and sensed before that,

that didn't mean he didn't want to. I'd told him more than once to just ask the girl out already.

Kylie O'Hara was beautiful, brilliant, fun, and could turn the most adamant witness of a supernatural event into a doubting Thomas in under five minutes flat. She'd have made one hell of a lawyer. I was glad she'd picked us instead.

As far as I was concerned, there came a time when some rules were meant to be broken—or at least bent to be more accommodating. If anyone had learned the lesson the hard way that life was too uncertain not to bend a few rules, it would be Ian.

Before joining SPI, he'd been a homicide detective with the NYPD. All that came to an end the night he and his partner were ambushed by a gang of ghouls. Three of them had used their claws on Ian like switchblades—while their leader had eaten his partner.

As a result of that attack, Ian had spent a month in the hospital. One night, Vivienne Sagadraco had paid him a visit and made him an offer he didn't want to refuse. He'd sworn to get the thing that'd butchered his partner. The boss offered him a job that would take "to protect and serve" to a whole new level. When he'd been released from the hospital, he turned in his resignation with the NYPD and came to work for SPI.

I was glad Ian had picked SPI, too. I was alive because Ian had been there for me, determined that he would *not* lose another partner. He'd taken good care of me, and I'd done all that I was able to do the same for him.

I'd decided several months ago that it was best if Ian and I kept to being partners of the professional kind. Ian was teaching me how to stay alive until I could fend for myself better. I'd decided that my real life was more important than my love life. I could get a love life elsewhere. Eventually.

Maybe. Starting a romantic relationship with Ian and having it go bad would make our time at work awkward. In our line of work, awkward would be a distraction, and distractions could and would get you killed.

As far as I was concerned, Ian's rule about no workplace romance should be more of a guideline than a rule. Rules could bend, but could he? For his sake, I hope he learned.

I glanced over to the stairs. Ian was gone. I turned back to my computer.

I didn't worry about missing whatever news program or show Kylie was scheduled for. Every monitor in the bull pen would be playing it as soon as her segment started. Until Kylie went live for the opening move in her game of smoke and mirrors, I thought about trying to grab a power nap, but almost immediately nixed that idea.

SPI had dorm-style accommodations here for when we went "all hands" so that folks could get some shut-eye in shifts. I could have grabbed a couple of hours. Call me overly sensitive, but two harpy attacks and a chewing-out by a Russian dragon in one hour was doing a better job keeping me awake than a whole six-pack of Mountain Dew.

I didn't think I was ever gonna sleep again.

Bob and Rob in Research—or "the Roberts," as the boss called them—would be giving her a full report on the Dragon Eggs, but had I decided to do a little digging on my own.

If I couldn't afford to own world-class diamonds, at least I could look at them. Google gave me almost more information than I knew what to do with. Though the more I read, the less enthused I was about having any one of the Dragon Eggs hanging around my neck, let alone having the entire clutch in my possession. Whoever had stolen the things just moved up in my estimation from jewel thief to certifiable psycho.

I already knew that two of the diamonds weren't of this

world. The pink Queen of Dreams had been stolen from the goblin crown jewels, and the pale blue Eye of Destiny had been taken from the elven royal treasury. SPI employed elves and a few goblins who were the living equivalent of the Internet when it came to the races: culture, politics, and history. All of which we needed on a daily and occasionally hourly basis, since trouble could be brewing at any time in any place in the world. When our people had to step in and mediate a situation between the two races that on a friendly day merely despised each other, it was critical to know not only who you were dealing with, but also how to deal with them, and this meant having access to knowledge-able people.

Unlike elf and goblin nobles, our elven and goblin agents got along just fine. Some of them even socialized together after work. It must have something to do with the atmo-sphere of New York. It was a worldwide melting pot; so it wasn't that big of a step to make it an inter-dimensional melting pot. Maybe all elven and goblin nobles should have to live in New York for a month. Maybe if they didn't kill one another, they'd learn to get along.

The Queen of Dreams and Eye of Destiny were impor-tant to goblin and elven royalty; therefore the pink and pale blue diamonds—and their whereabouts—were important to us.

Both stones had been stolen from their respective royal treasuries around the time that they joined the five diamonds from our world and came into the possession of the supremely unlucky Alexandra, matriarch of the soon-to-be-murdered-and-buried-in-a-pit Russian imperial family.

It said a lot about elven and goblin life spans that a hun-dred years wasn't all that long for the diamonds to be stolen and still missing. The same elven royal was still on the throne, and just recently the youngest son of the goblin queen who'd had the diamond stolen from her had become king of the goblins.

The five diamonds from our world had left quite a bloody trail to follow. The Star of Asia was the red one in the cursed clutch. Legend had it that there had originally been a pair of red diamonds that were the eyes of a god in a temple—now in ruins—in a Thai jungle. The first documented owner, an Englishman, died with his entire family in a carriage crash. Subsequent owners had experienced overwhelming desires to take long walks on short skyscraper ledges.

The Green Ghost, which had also been known as Le Fantomê Vert by one of its French owners, had also been stolen from the eye of a statue. You had to wonder if any of these guys robbing temples ever seriously asked themselves: "Is this a good idea?" Apparently not. Though you also had to wonder what'd happened to the greedy, stupid schmucks. The oracle that was Google did not reveal their fates. The Green Ghost was one of the eyes belonging to a statue of Buddha. His peace-loving followers notwithstanding, this particular representation of the serene one appeared to take grave offense at having one of his eyeballs popped out with some temple raider's knife, and proceeded to take it out on every human who crossed its glittery path for the next four hundred years.

The Sun King's moniker was given to it by its first official owner, Louis XIV. No excessive ego involved there. The canary yellow diamond must have been happy with its name; it kept its bad mojo to itself. Not so much with the next two guys named Louis to sit on the French throne. In the beginning of his reign, Louis XV was called "Louis le Bien-Aimé" (Louis the Well-Beloved). By the end of his time wearing the crown, he'd made so many monumentally crappy decisions that when he died in 1774, he was the most hated man in France, and had the distinction of being identified by many as the excuse for the French Revolution. But it was the next Louis and his wife, Marie Antoinette, who bore the brunt of the Sun King's bad karma, and it certainly didn't delay their wagon ride to the guillotine that they also owned the Hope Diamond, another famously cursed gem.

The last two diamonds weren't slouches in the death, destruction, and despair department, either.

The London Blue had been used by Henry VIII to woo Anne Boleyn.

We all know how well *that* turned out.

After sending the *first* Anne he'd married to the chopping block, ol' Henry dangled the diamond in front of wives numbers three through six.

Enough said.

And before coming into Viktor Kain's hands/claws, the Heart of Darkness had surfaced briefly—after taking care of business in Russia with the Romanov family—to find its way into the hands of the SS, who had a nasty habit of liberating paintings and jewels from their owners to enrich themselves and the coffers of the Third Reich. The black diamond came into the possession of Adolf Hitler, who gave it to Eva Braun as a wedding gift the day of their marriage—and one day before their joint suicide.

"Damn, that little rock didn't mess around," I muttered.

But there'd been no mention of the diamonds ever having been used for anything other than deadly adornment. At least not individually.

The one and only time (before now) that all seven diamonds had been together had been with the Romanovs. I clicked through several photos of the royal family, which naturally included some with Rasputin. I clicked on one to make it bigger. "Mad Monk" was right. Those were some seriously crazy eyes.

So when a hand touched my shoulder, I damned near jumped out of my skin.

It was Ian with two coffees in one of those carry-out holders.

I pressed my hand into my chest and tried to remember how to breathe.

Ian held up the hand he'd touched me with. "Before you say it, I did not sneak up on you. You weren't paying attention."

"Another training opportunity."

He handed me a coffee and a cheese danish. "You made this one; not me."

I took both gratefully. "Thank you. Cream?"

"Yes."

"A lot?"

"Enough to refill a cow."

I took a sip. "Perfect."

His own coffee would be black, and the longer it'd sat in the pot, the better. Between his time in the military and the NYPD, the need for any froufrou coffee fixins had been programmed right out of him. Like he'd told me once, "Soldiers and cops are grateful to get coffee any way they can."

SPI now had a functioning cafeteria. Entirely too many of our cases involved twenty-four hours or more of being awake and working. We'd lured a hotshot incubus barista from an East Village Starbucks. Most of us were a little more discerning than Ian when it came to our coffee. If we needed caffeine to stay awake, it'd better be good.

The coffee served here was also hot. As SPI agents, we were expected to know how to use virtually anything as a weapon. Coffee in our cafeteria qualified as a weapon, only our take-out cups didn't have some fancy version of "It's hot, stupid" printed on them. As SPI agents, we were expected to have enough sense to know it.

Since my coffee had enough cream to qualify as a latte, I could've guzzled mine without risking third-degree burns.

I couldn't resist it; I had to ask. "I noticed you popped out of here pretty quick when Kylie left. Did you get a chance to talk to her?"

I had waited until Ian had just started to take that first cautious sip of coffee before asking my question. Not that I wanted him to burn himself, but it was a lot harder to hide a reaction while your tongue was being scorched.

Ian must have gotten some seriously intensive anti-interrogation/torture training in the military. He didn't even wince at what had to have been nuclear-hot black coffee.

My partner was a rock of resistance.

Ian glanced at my screen. "Looks like you're reading up on our AWOL diamonds."

I sighed and nodded. "And they're as nasty as those harpies." I gave him the *Reader's Digest* condensed version of their history. "What about your black market art dealer? You get up with him?"

"Nothing yet. Considering what went down tonight, I imagine he's busy right about now, and hopefully it has everything to do with the Dragon Eggs. I left a message. He always calls back."

"Know where he might be?"

"He doesn't trust anyone that much. I've met him in a different place every time."

"Speaking of contacts, this du Beckett guy—I've heard that name before, but I can't remember where and from who."

"Eddie does work for him."

"Security?"

Ian shook his head. "Acquisitions."

"Fancy way of saying that Eddie's his picker?"

"You got it. Mr. du Beckett hears about a piece through that grapevine of his, and he sends Eddie out to go get it and bring it back. While he's out there, if he and his team see anything else they think du Beckett will like, they bag it and bring it home with them. World travel, exotic locations, danger around every corner, and at the end of the day, the big bucks."

"Crappy sounding job, but I guess somebody's gotta do it." I glanced over to where Kenji Hayashi and his people were going over the Met surveillance tape. There wasn't any code the elf tech couldn't crack, any encryption he couldn't decipher, or computer system he couldn't hack. Kylie considered Kenji her brother from another mother. From the looks of the scowl on Kenji's face, the identity of our heist mastermind was eluding him and endangering his perfect record, and Kenji was not amused.

"Doesn't look like they've hit pay dirt yet," I noted.

"Nope," Ian said. "I took a look and saw a lot of familiar faces. I was surprised some of them could scrape off enough blood and brimstone to mix with polite company."

I froze. "Demons? I didn't see any demons there."

"The figurative kind. The things that like to walk on the dark side—like Rake Danescu. Word has it he's put together enough gold to turn Viktor Kain's head when the bidding starts, but tonight he might have been too clever for his own good."

"Meaning?" I asked.

"You weren't all Rake was admiring."

I remembered. "The harpy statue."

Ian flicked his finger across the tip of his nose. "And he's strong enough to do what happened tonight. Whether he has the talent or not is another question, but whenever a crime goes down in this city with a supernatural perp, if Danescu doesn't have a hand in it, he at least has information."

"When Ben was about to go after those harpies," I said, "Rake was gone."

"Maybe his work there was done. Not accusing him, I'm just saying what I saw."

"He did advise that I step away from the harpies right before they broke loose."

"That was nice of him."

I snorted. "First time for everything."

Ian started toward his desk, stopped, and looked at me over his shoulder. His lips twitched at the corners. "Nice try with the hot coffee."

9

BY the time the sun came up, we'd discovered another thing Ben Sadler was good at—healing fast. He didn't have any special healing skills, just the stubbornness that came with being in the middle of a crappy situation that involved him, and refusing to stay in an infirmary bed while others did the legwork of solving the problem. Part of me did a face-palm when I'd heard he wanted to go with us, but the other part was proud of him. When your problem involved a Russian mafia boss who also happened to be a dragon large enough to eat you and use one of your ribs to pick his teeth afterward, that problem needed solving quick.

It said a lot about Ben Sadler that he wanted in. On second thought, maybe it just said he was nuts.

There were two other things Ben was adamant about: going to his apartment to get clothes, and going to see Sebastian du Beckett with us. Vivienne Sagadraco's acquirer of unacquirables had been less than forthcoming about Ben, Viktor Kain, and what his interest was in the Dragon

THE DRAGON CONSPIRACY 101

Eggs, but he'd said he "owed it to the boy" to tell him in person.

Ben told us he had wondered why a client of Sebastian du Beckett's wealth and influence had requested an inexperienced junior appraiser to evaluate the Dragon Eggs for him. Now that he knew about his "condition," as he had taken to calling it, he knew that du Beckett had ulterior motives, not necessarily nefarious, but Ben wanted to hear what they were straight from the horse's mouth. So we took the necessary security precautions and Ben got to go along on our morning field trip to the Upper West Side.

The first errand didn't need to be done by Ben. SPI dispatched a couple of our guys posing as air-conditioning repairmen to Ben's West Village apartment. Tool cases and duffels were empty going in, full coming out.

Clothes obtained. Objective achieved.

The second errand was trickier.

It involved getting back into a moving vehicle with Ben Sadler. I wasn't superstitious or anything, but I had to admit to being nervous. As usual, Yasha was our driver, and I wouldn't call him nervous, more like growly.

The SUV was a Tahoe, not Yasha's beloved Suburban.

Ben reached for the door handle and tensed. "Is he growling at me?" he whispered.

I remembered that Ben had been unconscious last night and hadn't been properly introduced to Yasha. Some things Ben wasn't ready for yet. Like the fact that our driver *was* growling at him, was a werewolf, and that it was futile to whisper because Yasha could hear a tick burp at fifty yards.

"Yasha, this is Ben Sadler," I said. "Ben, this is Yasha Kazakov. He was our driver last night."

Ian got in the passenger seat, and shot the Russian a look. "He's not growling; he's clearing his throat."

I patted Yasha on the shoulder as I slid across the backseat. "How is she?"

"Looks worse than is, but looks bad."

"She's got the best looking after her. I'm sure she'll be fine."

That was the truth. The mechanics in SPI's motor pool could repair any automotive damage. Bullets, claws, steel-dissolving alien secretions, you name it, those guys and gals could make the vehicular victim look and run like new.

They'd had a lot of practice.

Ben looked confused at my and Yasha's exchange, but didn't ask any questions. Wise man.

Regardless of how secure the line was, Sebastian du Beckett had refused to talk about Ben over the phone last night with Vivienne Sagadraco. Her growl when she'd hung up the phone had probably rumbled the Old Masters paintings plum off her office walls.

She was sending Alain Moreau, her chief legal counsel who also happened to be my manager, to "inquire as to his reticence to discuss the matter."

I think she was sending Moreau rather than going herself because she would've been too pissed to be polite. As a Brit, there wasn't anything more important than politeness, unless it was not alienating the man who kept her hoard topped off. It was known throughout the supernatural world that Alain Moreau spoke for Vivienne Sagadraco, so du Beckett shouldn't be offended. Heck, if he had a lick of sense, he'd be relieved to have a vampire knocking on his door rather than a dragon whose real form was as tall as his brownstone.

On second thought, du Beckett might be in more danger from Alain Moreau. He was hundreds of years old and had impeccable Old World manners to go with each and every year. However, any attempt to harm or even show the slightest disrespect to Vivienne Sagadraco, and he would make the offending party regret they'd ever been born. He looked proper and like he didn't like getting his hands dirty with violence, but I had no doubt he could unleash copious amounts of chastisement if he had to.

Alain Moreau had somewhere else to go first, so he took another car, but he was there waiting for us as we pulled up to the front of the Upper West Side brownstone. With his fangs retracted, my vampire manager looked like Anderson Cooper in need of a week of sun in the Hamptons. He was his usual flawlessly dressed and dapper self. He was old enough to be able to be out during the day. Most vamps his age still avoided daylight; for Moreau, it gave him a chance to add yet another stylish accessory to his ensemble. His sunglasses probably cost more than I made in a month.

The street was quiet. It was an affluent, residential neighborhood and it was before nine in the morning, but that didn't do a thing to stop my heebie-jeebies.

If anyone was watching, I glanced around just as a person who'd never been here before would have, mildly curious, taking in the surroundings. Perfectly normal. In reality, I was as jumpy as a long-tailed cat in a room full of rocking chairs. Not that I expected to see a harpy walking down the street, but when you worked for SPI, you saw stranger things, several times a day, often before lunch.

"Tell me you've got heavily armed folks posted around here," I said to my partner, trying not to move my lips.

"Hidden and in plain view," Ian assured me.

"The two yuppie moms with strollers down the block?"

"You don't recognize Elana?"

I looked closer without trying to be obvious. I'd been working off and on with Elana since my first night with SPI. If there was a dark alley that needed investigating, Elana was the go-getter who wanted to go in first. She was *that* person, the one who didn't necessarily start the bar fight, but come hell or high water, she was gonna be the one to finish it.

"Wig and glasses," Ian said helpfully. "The woman with

her is one of our new recruits. Early retirement from the Navy. She got tired of waiting for the SEALs to accept women."

"Uh . . . lucky us?"

"Yes, lucky us."

"And I'm betting the NYPD wouldn't approve of what they have in those strollers."

"Probably not. I also have three lookouts on surrounding rooftops alert to incoming anything, especially harpies." With the barest nod, he indicated a manhole cover about five feet away. "And you'd be amazed at how quickly that manhole cover can come off with a motivated ogre under it, right, Carl?"

A disconcerting mix of grunt and evil chuckle came up from beneath the street.

Jeez. Our backup was scarier than what was after us.

We went up the brownstone steps beside Ben and behind Alain Moreau. My manager rang the doorbell, and we all waited.

And waited.

"He's got a camera mounted out here somewhere," Ben told us. "And all around the outside of the house. I've seen the monitor in his office. He's always answered right away before."

"I imagine you didn't bring this much company with you then," I murmured, in case the old guy was watching *and* listening.

Ian smoothly pushed back his jacket, clearing the way for his hand to his gun. A gun that was always loaded with silver bullets, casings cooled in holy water when they'd been made. "Moreau?"

"I agree. Something's wrong." The vampire reached for the knob and turned it. Locked. Then the fingers of his hand tightened and gave the knob a sharp jerk. There was the distinct and unnerving sound of door hardware breaking and clattering to the floor on the other side.

The door opened.

Moreau led the way. No gun, no need.

Sebastian du Beckett's house looked like a live-in museum in need of a good cleaning. The walls were wood paneled, the furniture was leather, and stuff that looked really old and expensive was everywhere. I wondered if he knew my friend Ollie Barrington-Smythe. A rich guy with a house full of spooky shit definitely needed an introduction to a snooty little Englishman who ran a shop full of the same.

Moreau and Ben had been here before and took off down a side hall.

Moreau's sharp command came from the end of the hall. "Monsieur Sadler, don't move."

Ian had his gun in his hand, and swept me behind him as we followed. When I got a good look at what was in the room, I had to nix the idea of an introduction to Ollie.

There was a man sitting upright behind a desk in an office chair.

He couldn't be any more dead.

Getting turned to stone would do that to you.

"Sebastian du Beckett?" I asked.

Ian lowered his gun, but didn't put it away. "Yeah."

There was no sign of a struggle. The two guest chairs were angled in front of the desk, a small table between them. No other visible way in except the door we'd used. A nice, big window behind the desk looked out over a small backyard, or maybe folks who lived in brownstones called it a garden.

Alain Moreau had his phone out. "Madame, Monsieur du Beckett is dead." Without hesitation he went right up to the presumed corpse and poked at him with one long finger. "Stone, Madame. It appears to be gorgon inflicted."

"Gorgon?" Ben gaped. "As in Medusa?"

I nodded and tried to look everywhere at once. Ian was on his own headset, hopefully calling for backup in case du Beckett's earlier visitor was still here.

"Just another member of our not-so-little community," I told Ben, wishing I had a gun to hold on to, or best of all, considering there was a gorgon on the loose, a pair of mirrored sunglasses. After last night, I wasn't exactly batting a thousand with my little knife.

Sebastian du Beckett's expression didn't appear to be terrified. Actually, if I had to pick an emotion, I'd say that the art and diamond broker looked surprised. Getting turned to a slab of rock would certainly surprise me. Maybe the killer moved so fast du Beckett didn't have time to change expression. Or maybe he knew his attacker. Either was a possibility; neither would be a surprise.

His entire body had been turned to stone. His clothes had not. Neither had his unbelievably thick glasses, though the left lens was cracked. That just looked freaky. My favorite *Clash of the Titans* was the cheesy but cool Harry Hamlin version. In that movie, Medusa's victims were turned to stone—along with their clothing, which when you thought about it was ridiculous. A gorgon's stare or touch turned skin to stone, not clothes. Leave it to a human-made movie to go for cool over accuracy.

I remembered back to the last office I'd been in with a dead person. There'd been no chance of being mistaken then, either. He'd been gutted, torn limb from limb (some of them missing), and his intestines had been hanging from the overhead light fixture like a squishy party streamer. The murderer in that case had made so much noise that the cops had shown up within minutes. They'd arrested me and Ian, and the NYPD had scraped together what was left of the victim into a body bag.

This situation presented a very different problem. There'd been no noise, no cops, and there was no way in hell to get a petrified person sitting behind a desk into a body bag.

Ben was staring at his concreted client in unblinking horror. "Do you think he's alive in there?" he whispered.

Alain Moreau answered him. "I assure you that Monsieur du Beckett is no longer with us."

"Are you sure it was a gorgon?" Ian asked. "Not a basilisk?"

"I have no doubt."

Screw ineffective. I got my little knife in my hand. It wasn't much, but it was something.

"Think it's still here?" I asked.

"Unlikely," Moreau said. "Monsieur du Beckett was not a small man. It would have taken at least an hour for petrification to progress this far."

I felt sick. "Progress? He was still alive for that long?"

"Unless the murderer was directly from Medusa's line or very old, he was alive until petrification reached his heart and brain. The stone would continue to harden for at least the next half hour."

"Who would want to kill Mr. du Beckett?" Ben asked. "I wouldn't think he'd have an enemy in the world."

"It's often not a matter of enemies, but of possessing an object that the killer wanted. Monsieur du Beckett owned much that would appeal to the criminally inclined." He was studying the top of the dead man's desk. There wasn't a computer, but there was a notebook just to the right of the body; Moreau scanned the page it was open to. "According to Monsieur du Beckett's calendar, we weren't his first visitors this morning. Rake Danescu had an appointment here two hours ago."

Ian and I exchanged glances.

"Rake was at the museum last night," I said. "Aside from me, he was the closest to the harpy statue."

"Interesting."

Rake could turn women to putty, but as far as I knew, he couldn't turn a man to stone.

Ian keyed his mike. "Yeah, what is it?" His eyes snapped toward the window. "Run!" he shouted at us.

The word was still leaving his lips as a harpy crashed through the big office window—and this time, she'd brought backup. She hadn't been able to get the job done last night, so she'd brought her two sisters this morning.

The talons that had punched holes in the roof of Yasha's Suburban last night sent splinters flying from Sebastian du Beckett's desk this morning—and chunks of stone from du Beckett's arm that'd been resting on the desktop.

Obviously hell hath no fury like thwarted kidnappers.

The things screeched loud enough to burst our eardrums after having destroyed the window frame and most of the surrounding wall shouldering their wings into the office. All I could think was that they looked much bigger in full daylight.

Moreau's fangs were out and he launched himself onto the back of the nearest harpy, and the screeching, hissing, and clawing that ensued could only be described as the world's biggest catfight. As much as I wanted to watch my manager hand that harpy her tail feathers on a platter, I had a harpy trying to do the same to me.

I was closest to Ben, and I was determined to stay there.

Ian had found out last night that bullets, even the silver-infused kind, didn't do squat against a harpy. He'd found a spear among the late Mr. du Beckett's office clutter, and was putting it to good use—until one swat from the harpy snapped the shaft in half.

If Yasha, Carl, and the girls didn't join us soon, all they would find was what would be left of us.

A vampire, werewolf, and an ogre walk into an office . . . It sounded like the beginning of a really bad joke with an even worse ending.

The third harpy had me and Ben all to herself, and was standing squarely between us and the office door, our only means of escape. Ben desperately looked around for somewhere to hide, even though we both knew it was useless unless either of us could suddenly shrink to the size of an action figure.

Nice thing about clutter was that it gave me plenty of stuff to throw. If I couldn't take down a harpy, at least I could hopefully keep her from killing us long enough for Carl the ogre to get here.

My hand fumbled around on a crowded shelf and came away with some kind of stone monkey god. It was uglier than homemade sin, but it fit in my hand.

I brought a rock down hard on the harpy's bird-clawed foot. The harpy didn't so much as blink.

It did get her attention away from Ben.

And on to me.

"Oh shit," Ben said for both of us.

That was good because my brain was too busy watching my life flash before it—and a talon-tipped hand, close to being around what was soon to be left of my throat. The claws whistled past my neck, but didn't take any of me with them. I sucked in my breath, as if that'd help me plaster myself any closer to the wall, and saw the tips of one wing sticking through the crack where the office door hinge met the wall. I didn't know how much damage it'd do, but I figured it wouldn't feel good.

I grabbed the back edge of the door and slammed it back against the wall.

And heard a gratifying snap.

Note to self: slamming a harpy's wing in a door hurts like hell.

Alain Moreau flung the harpy attacking him against the wall over our heads. Chunks of wall, pieces of ceiling, and the dust of who knew how many decades filled the air and my lungs as breathing became the next fight for survival.

I desperately raked through the debris for a weapon, and came out with a shiny rock. It was blue, sparkly, and about the size of my fist. Was it what the boss had called a gem of power? I didn't know. Ben would know once he touched it. At the very least, he could chuck it at the harpy.

"Ben, catch!"

I tossed the rock and Ben caught it.

The instant the gem touched his hand, it flashed.

I squeezed my eyes shut—for all the good it did me. I saw the blast of blue light through my closed eyelids.

Blinded by the light, I didn't see Ben zap the harpy, but I sure smelled it. I didn't know if it was the same harpy Ben had tangled with last night, but the pain hadn't stopped her from taking those diamonds last night, and it didn't keep her from taking Ben this morning.

Ben had his back to the wall. He wasn't going anywhere and the harpy knew it. A pleased and entirely too hungry growl rumbled the floor under our feet as she knocked me aside. In one lightning-quick move, the harpy grabbed Ben's forearm, slamming it and the hand holding the blue stone against the wall, shattering the stone—and breaking Ben's arm. There was no mistaking that sound.

The only supernatural Ben had ever seen had been Caera Filarion. Cute, sweet, funny Caera the elf. The harpy was none of those things. She grabbed and wrapped her indestructible arms around the struggling Ben as if the six footer was no bigger than a toddler.

Ben hadn't screamed last night. Between his broken arm, and the harpy reopening last night's wound when she grabbed him, he screamed now.

I damned near joined him.

One harpy had come after us last night. Between me and Ian, but mostly Yasha, we'd persuaded her to retreat. She'd brought her sisters this morning, and even though we'd substituted a vampire for the werewolf, we were outnumbered. And they had talons that might as well have been made out of surgical steel.

The girls had worked fast.

Our backup never had time to reach us.

The first beat of her wings launched her into the air; the second beat took her up and through the shattered window.

The instant she was clear, her sisters broke off their fight with Ian and Moreau, and were out the window, flanking the harpy carrying Ben like a pair of fighter jet escorts, though thanks to Moreau's efforts, one was missing half a wing.

They were headed north. We'd be able to keep visual contact for only so long—unless they weren't going far. Though as soon as they dropped below the tops of any buildings, we'd lose sight of them. I couldn't imagine them staying airborne for any length of time; half of Manhattan would see them. Then again, the girls hadn't been shy about being seen last night. It looked like Kylie would be getting another couple hundred sightings to explain, but at least it'd give us a way to track the harpies and rescue Ben.

Ian appeared next to me at the window. "Where'd they go?"

That was a puzzler. I pointed. "They're right there, headed north."

"I can't see them."

Oh hell.

Last New Year's Eve, Vivienne Sagadraco's sister Tiamat had orchestrated a grendel infestation that was to reach its bloodbath of a conclusion in Times Square at midnight. Part of her evil master plan had involved equipping the two adult grendels with a small device that rendered them invisible to everyone and everything except me. I'd found out that being a seer also allowed me to see through mechanical as well as magical veils. In the cleanup of the grendel nest afterward, several more of the devices had been found. What I now saw flying away from us—and Ian didn't—told me that SPI apparently wasn't the only possessor of that technology. I hadn't seen the harpies wearing the devices, but then I had better things to do than admire any jewelry the harpies might have been wearing.

I told Ian my theory.

We heard sirens in the distance.

Ian swore and keyed his mike. "Yasha, get to the alley round back. Now. Du Beckett's dead; we need to get him out of here." He ran over to the desk and started shoving debris away from the body. Moreau quickly searched the room for anything else the NYPD didn't need to find.

Damn, Ian was right. We did have to take du Beckett with us. A regular dead body could be left for mortal authorities to find. One that had been turned to stone? No way in hell.

I willed the cheese danish I'd eaten an hour ago to stay put and dropped down to the floor, doing what a SPI agent had to do—find the rest of Sebastian du Beckett's left arm.

The hand and wrist was still in one piece. It was next to a small trash can. I grabbed a crumpled piece of paper out, turned the can on its side, and, with the paper over my hand, scooped up what looked like Thing from *The Addams Family* prop department. Smaller bits of the shattered forearm were mostly in one area. I got those, too.

I popped up from beside the desk. "Got the hand and as much of the arm as I could find."

"Good." Ian was pushing the rest of du Beckett, still in his office chair, toward the door. He'd wrapped the braided cord from the ruined drapes around the corpse's chest and the back of the office chair, tying him in place.

The clock on the mantle had chimed nine o'clock an instant before the first harpy had blasted through that window.

It was only two minutes after nine.

10

RAKE Danescu had an appointment when he'd visited Sebastian du Beckett this morning.

We didn't have an appointment when we showed up at Rake Danescu's front door.

Though technically it was the front door of his very exclusive apartment building on Central Park West.

Yasha had taken Sebastian du Beckett's remains back to the lab at headquarters. We took Alain Moreau's car to see Rake Danescu.

If it had just been me and Ian, we wouldn't have gotten past the doorman, at least not without a lot of lying.

That was when having a centuries-old vampire for whom mind control was just another form of communication came in handy. Alain Moreau did a smooth Jedi-mind-trick thing on the doorman, the security at the front desk and the elevators, and we were on our way up to the penthouse.

Naturally the goblin who owned and operated the most exclusive sex club in the city would live in a penthouse.

Rake Danescu answered his own door, and didn't appear to be surprised in the least to see us. Though he did seem mildly taken aback, or at least amused, to see me standing in his building's opulent hallway coated in what I kept repeating to myself was only plaster dust, and not some of the pulverized remains of Sebastian du Beckett. Ian looked like he usually did—on the winning side of an ass kicking. Moreau had ripped half a wing off a harpy but didn't have a hair out of place or a wrinkle in his still-immaculate suit.

Moreau spoke. "Lord Danescu."

Lord?

The goblin made no move, either to step aside or invite us in. Where I came from, a lack of hospitality equaled bad manners.

"To what do I owe the pleasure of this visit?"

Moreau didn't bat an eye. "I don't think you want me to say in front of your building's security cameras."

"Speaking of my security . . ."

"They were most accommodating—unlike one of their residents."

"Ah, I should have known." He smiled, showing fangs.

Moreau's were on full display, too.

I wondered if fang size was as important to male goblins and vamps as another body part was to human guys. Probably. I would have asked them, but didn't want to step on my manager's toes—or whatever—when he seemed to be winning what was going on here.

Rake Danescu stepped aside and waved his arm with a flourish. "By all means, do come in."

We did.

I looked around and was surprised. I half expected there to be mirrors on the ceiling and fur rugs on the floor.

Rake Danescu's décor was downright tasteful, even though he was the owner of a supernatural sex club. What I assumed was the living room could have been the centerfold of *Architectural Digest*. I wondered if the goblin had done the decorating himself or hired someone—or both. He'd probably hired someone, a human female someone, with the stipulation that they work very closely together—

"Agent Fraser?"

Crap.

Alain Moreau had asked me a question. Rake was smirking. Ian was inscrutable.

Honesty, at least partial, was best. "I'm sorry, sir. I was admiring the décor. It's lovely, Mr. Danescu." I didn't care what he was; there was no way I was calling him "lord."

The goblin graciously inclined his head, his eyes gleaming. "I can hardly take all the credit. My interior designer is incomparably talented. She selected most of the furniture. I was telling Monsieur Moreau that while I was ill prepared for company, I would be a poor host indeed if I did not at least offer tea."

"None for me; thank you."

"Three declines. Then we can proceed to what has brought you uninvited, though not unwelcome, to my door. Please be seated."

I perched on the edge of a small pale gray sofa that more or less matched the dust I'd brought in with me. Ian seated himself next to me—and between me and Rake.

Ian had been with SPI a heck of a lot longer than I had, and from what I'd been able to gather, he'd known Rake Danescu for most of that time. I hadn't managed to pry any of the finer details out of my partner, but I knew for a fact that he didn't trust and didn't like the goblin mage, as in *really* didn't like him. I didn't know if the feeling was mutual; Rake—and goblins in general—kept people guessing as to where they fell on the whole like/dislike/burning hatred scale. I guess it made killing your enemies easier if they didn't actually know that they were your enemy. Yeah, like goblins weren't confusing enough.

The first time I'd run into Rake Danescu was my first night on the job at SPI. I'd kind of gotten myself enthralled by him—at least that was what my more magically-in-the-know coworkers had called it. As a dark mage, Rake was gifted in many of the magical arts that most sane people would run away from. Some of that magic was of the personal kind, the kind that allowed a mage to get inside the mind of a person of their choosing. Rake had chosen me and he'd gotten into my mind that night. I had to admit I'd liked the way he'd knocked. As a result, the goblin could now read me like an open book, though it wasn't like I was exactly inscrutable before. There was a reason nearly every one of my coworkers wanted me to join their table on company poker nights—I was a fluffy sheep ready for the fleecing. Though as far down the corporate ladder as I was, it wasn't like I had much fluff for them to fleece.

Rake Danescu saw me as a sheep, too. A sheep to his big, bad, wicked wolf.

I didn't know if it was that thought or something else, but the center of my chest, right below the first button of my shirt, was starting to itch like crazy. There was no way I was going to stick a finger down there and scratch myself. Something shifted and I quickly glanced down.

And bit back a squeak.

I had Sebastian du Beckett crumbs down the front of my bra.

It wasn't plaster dust. I could tell myself that it was until the cows came home, but that wouldn't make it true. This was grit, coarse grit, like pulverized stone.

Pulverized, petrified Sebastian du Beckett.

I tried slow, calming breaths. I couldn't lose it, especially not here. Excusing myself to Rake Danescu's bathroom and ripping my clothes off wasn't going to happen. It wouldn't surprise me if Rake had cameras in his home bathroom just like he did in the ladies' room (and probably the men's room) in his club. I hadn't gone in the men's room. The leprechauns I was after had opted to do their illegal smoking in the ladies' room in a stall that could have easily held ten people doing Lord knows what.

"You had an appointment at seven this morning with Sebastian du Beckett." Moreau wasn't beating around the bush. Good for him. Better for me. The quicker I could get out of here and into yet another change of clothes, the better.

Ian nudged me.

At least no one had just asked me a question.

"I met with Mr. du Beckett this morning from seven to seven twenty," Rake freely admitted.

"May I ask why?"

"You just did, but I don't have to tell you."

"Do you have something to hide?"

"I am a goblin; there are many aspects of my personal and business lives that I prefer to keep private."

"Monsieur du Beckett was murdered this morning."

Rake Danescu's only reaction was the raising of one eyebrow. "How unfortunate for him, and how inconvenient for me. But you didn't magic your way up to my home merely to inform me of Bastian's untimely demise. To save you from having to be so gauche as to ask me directly if I killed him, my answer is no. And again, keeping you from the social discomfort of questioning my integrity, yes, that is an honest and true response. I did not murder, harm, or in any way threaten Sebastian du Beckett—at least not this month. Does this answer the questions that brought you here?"

"Yes."

"I am glad to hear it—"

"And no."

"My, aren't we the curious one this morning." His words were playful, his expression anything but. "You're not the only one with questions. How was Bastian killed?"

"Gorgon."

Rake Dansecu's expression told me that one had come at him out of left field.

"That's unexpected," was all he said.

"I'm certain Monsieur du Beckett felt the same way."

"I seriously doubt that Bastian was too terribly surprised. He was not, as humans say, a Boy Scout. Pay him enough and don't ask too many questions, and there was nothing that man couldn't acquire. Vivienne knows this only too well. There are any number of individuals who have taken enough issue with Bastian's practices to put him 'out of business' permanently."

"Do you know of one who would have employed a gorgon to do so—or a gorgon who would have felt wronged?"

"First you accuse me of murder, then you want my help. Will you be making up your mind anytime soon?"

"I merely need explanation of a coincidence. You had an appointment with Monsieur du Beckett, and he was killed soon after you left."

"From the dusty appearance of the usually fair Makenna, your own visit to Bastian's was more eventful than you anticipated."

"Harpies," I said. "From last night."

"Those girls have been busy for the past twelve hours," Ian told Rake. "They stole the Dragon Eggs, then attacked a SPI vehicle last night in an attempt to kidnap the young man who tried to stop the robbery. He's a diamond appraiser at Christie's. Sebastian du Beckett was his client. Apparently one of du Beckett's clients—or even du Beckett himself— wanted in on Viktor Kain's auction. Mr. Sadler went with us to du Beckett's home this morning, and somehow the harpies knew he'd be there. He's been kidnapped." Ian paused meaningfully. "We are not happy."

"You'd already flown the coop when all hell broke loose at the museum," I told Rake. "Thanks for that, by the way."

"I saw everything, my dear Makenna, and had deemed

you perfectly capable of handling the incident. I merely removed myself from what was sure to become, at least for me, an incriminating situation."

"Now, why would anyone think you had anything to do with a priceless diamond heist?" Ian drawled.

"Yet another benefit of being me, Agent Byrne. If an exotic or daring supernatural crime is perpetrated, my name lands near the top of each list every time."

"Naturally, you're innocent."

"Sometimes, yes; other times, no. Regardless, I've always found it prudent to remove myself from situations in which I do not wish to become entangled. Last night was one such example. No doubt, Viktor Kain is upset, as are the Dragon Eggs' potential buyers."

"Yourself included—along with Marek Reigory."

Rake Danescu leaned back in his chair, smiling. "Ah, I'd wondered when my countryman was going to be brought into this."

"You knew he was at the exhibition?"

"Naturally. Aside from a nod in passing, I had nothing to say to Marek, nor will I. Let's say we don't see eye to eye politically. I'm rather fond of our new king, who is a vast improvement over the rule of his insane—and now thankfully dead—older brother." Rake's dark eyes softened as if at a pleasant memory. "That assassin's crossbow bolt through his chest was the best accessory I'd ever seen him wear." Then pleasant memories went bye-bye. "I enjoy unpredictability and games as much as the next goblin, but His late-and-not-lamented Majesty's favorite guessing games included which noble would he accuse of treason that day, followed by the ever unpopular what would he choose as this poor unfortunate's punishment for an imaginary crime: torture, prison, or immediate beheading? Marek—for some inane reason known only to him—prefers his kings insane. He made his choice, was rightfully banished for it, and I do not wish to sully my reputation by association. As to my interest in the Dragon Eggs, I did not keep it a secret. However, rumor had it that Viktor had no intention of actually selling the diamonds, or he had a buyer already lined up and merely announced the possibility of an auction to drive up the price. The Queen of Dreams belongs to the goblin crown. My government will not pay for something that was stolen from us." The goblin's expression darkened. "If anyone should fund its reacquisition, it should be the elves, seeing that it was an elf who stole it from us in the first place."

Now, that last, snippy tidbit was interesting; I hadn't heard that part of the story.

"I want to find the thief just as badly as you, if not more so," Rake continued. "My government has authorized me to obtain the Queen of Dreams by any means necessary before it can be illegally purchased as stolen property and vanish for another hundred years. The rapidly shifting situation dictates that I remain flexible in my acquisition methods. I'm a direct sort. I never would have thought of harpies. I must admit it was ingenious, though the way the robbery was executed suffered from an excess of convolution."

Ian snorted. "Direct? Since when?"

Rake's dark eyes flicked ever so briefly at me. "When there is something I want quite badly, I have been known to dispense with games."

"Why the sudden need to do your civic duty?" Moreau asked.

"For the most part, my government leaves me to my own devices in this dimension. I would very much like for their disinterest to continue."

"You graduated from the magical gifted and talented program," Ian said. "If you saw what happened at the Met, then you know those harpies weren't ordered to get Ben Sadler to appraise the Dragon Eggs."

"What level gem mage is he?" Rake looked at each of us

in turn. "Oh, come now, the boy didn't even have to touch those diamonds last night. He grabbed the harpy that held them and the stones lit like tiny suns."

"Our assessment team has evaluated him as a level ten," Moreau said.

"Merci, Monsieur. Direct talk will serve you well over the coming hours. You may not have time for much else."

"Then, like yourself, I will be very direct," Moreau continued. "We have information on the Queen of Dreams, but anything else you can tell us concerning what it's capable of would be greatly appreciated. It is documented that it was stolen from your people. We will do everything within our power to see it returned to you."

Rake Danescu's expression went from surprise, to suspicion, to cautious acceptance, finally settling on reserved gratitude. "If you accomplish this, you will have my thanks as well as the gratitude of His Majesty, King Chigaru Mal'Salin. Aside from being part of the goblin crown jewels, the Queen of Dreams cures disorders of the mind and diseases of the body, an ironic ability I've always thought considering its color."

I was confused. "But isn't the Queen of Dreams the pink diamond?"

"It is."

"But pink's a nice color."

"Not for goblins. Pink is the color of pure evil."

I had a flashback to shopping for one of my nieces in the all-pink Barbie aisle at Toys "R" Us. I had to admit, it had creeped me out. I nodded. "I can see that."

"If you're familiar with our royal family," Rake continued, "you know that insanity is a problem every few generations. We've been fortunate for at least half of this generation, but fate is one lady I do not wish to tempt."

"A diamond that heals," Ian noted. "That's certainly motive enough for a theft. Perhaps our thief needs someone's disease cured—or needs healing themselves. Does it only work with goblins?"

"It has been found to work on any supernatural, from any dimension."

"Making it even more valuable," I said.

"Indeed."

"As to why the thief took all of the diamonds, maybe they didn't want to risk Viktor Kain splitting up the Dragon Eggs and auctioning them off separately."

"What about the elf diamond?" Ian asked Rake.

"The Eye of Destiny is said to enable the seeing of the truth in all things and expose that which is hidden."

Oh, wonderful. A rock that did my job. I was glad the boss had already assured me that she wasn't interested in owning any of the Dragon Eggs. "How does it do that?"

"By negating magic," Rake said.

Those three words hit our collective pause button.

Depending on who was throwing the magic around, and what kind they were tossing, that could be a very good—or an exceptionally bad—thing.

"How wide of an area would be affected and for how long?" Moreau asked.

Rake shrugged. "That would depend entirely on the strength and control of the gem mage using it."

And the thief had just kidnapped a level ten—a level ten with no control whatsoever. I wondered if the thief would let Ben Sadler go once he found out he'd snatched himself a loose cannon. As soon as I thought the question, I knew the answer. They may have gone to a lot of trouble to kidnap Ben, but getting rid of him would be easy. There were endless ways to kill someone.

"The other five diamonds came from this world," Rake was saying. "Any gem that appears to possess any kind of supernatural power, humans usually refer to it as cursed. Stones typically don't bring bad luck by themselves. That's simply what happens when a stone's power is activated, but not controlled."

"Like a car that gets put in gear on a hill and turned loose," I said.

"A more accurate analogy would be the parts to a particularly large bomb," Moreau said. "Each isn't necessarily dangerous by itself, but once combined and activated . . ."

"When would it be set to go off?" Ian asked.

"The veils between the dimensions are at their thinnest twice a year," Rake said. "The summer solstice and what mortals call All Hallows' Eve. The goblin and elven diamonds will be at their strongest, equal in strength to the others. At any other time of the year, the Queen of Dreams and Eye of Destiny would be weaker than the diamonds from this dimension. But tonight at midnight, the power of all will be able to unite equally as one."

"But to do what?" I asked.

"Unknown, my dear Makenna. But regardless of the seemingly benign capabilities of the elf and goblin stone, no one steals, murders, and kidnaps, then turns around and begins bestowing gifts."

"The first time all seven diamonds were together was when they were owned by Nicholas and Alexandra of Russia," Moreau said. "The stones were split up again and lost during the Russian Revolution until Viktor Kain found them and brought them together again."

We all pondered that for a moment.

"To release those harpies from stasis required proximity," Moreau continued. "Other than Agent Fraser and Ben Sadler, you were closest to that statue when the spell holding them immobile was dropped."

A faint shadow of a smile creased Rake's lips. "You of all people know what I'm capable of, Alain. Have you ever seen me petrify a living creature, much less keep them in stasis for how long?"

"Six days," Ian said. "That's the length of time the 'statue' was in the Sackler Wing before last night."

"Six days. Not an inconsequential length of time, and then release them, immediately bringing them back to full awareness, so they can carry out my evil and brazen master plan?"

"I am not accusing you personally, Rake," Moreau said.

"But you believe I am involved in some way."

"I believe you know more than you are telling us."

The goblin smiled. "Always, *mon ami*. But were I to attempt such a feat of criminal daring, I would be much more circumspect. Less truly is more. The successful theft of what are at this time the seven most famous diamonds in the world would be enough of a coup even for the most inflated of egos. It would be wise to carry out the theft when there are the fewest people around. The more people, the more unknown elements. Even though he—or she—was successful, they should consider themselves the luckiest person in this world, or any other, because they now not only possess the diamonds, but a master gem mage to wield them. The persistence in the abduction of Mr. Sadler tells me that the thief knows what the Dragon Eggs are capable of," Rake was saying, "but didn't have a gem mage, or not one who would be willing to risk his life activating those diamonds. You must admit that Mr. Sadler gave a dazzling audition. He activated the stones without even directly touching them, and if that harpy hadn't hit him, he would have been none the worse for wear for the experience. In less than twelve hours, not only was this individual success- ful in acquiring the Dragon Eggs, but their persistence with their harpies paid off handsomely with the capture of quite possibly the most powerful human gem mage in this world. Since five of the diamonds are of this world, the thief would need a human to do the heavy lifting, so to speak."

"Which brings up the question of why Sebastian du

Beckett wanted Ben in the first place," I said. "He's a junior-level diamond appraiser, and Ms. Sagadraco said that du Beckett had a good eye for magical talent. He had to have known what Ben could do. Heck, he even had a gem of power in his office. Ben used it on one of the harpies."

Moreau sighed in frustration. "Unfortunately, Monsieur du Beckett is in no condition to answer that or any other question we have."

"I can't imagine you not knowing who your competition was in Kain's auction," Ian said to Rake. "Especially the powerful ones who preferred to fly under the radar."

"They, or their representatives, were all in attendance at last night's rudely interrupted gathering. These individuals are like myself in that they value their privacy. They form an intricate network, a web, if you will. The slightest touch at any point sends a tremor down every strand. Were I to give you names, Bastian's fate could very well be mine."

"Afraid of a little gravel in your hair?"

"Merely the annoyance of having to add another individual to the list of those already queuing up to kill me. Eventually someone's luck will triumph over my skill. Though being immortalized in stone does have its appeal." He eyed me. "Unless a clumsy harpy obliterates the masterpiece. I do not wish to be reduced to dust."

The corner of my left eyelid began to twitch.

"Would you like to avail yourself of my shower, dearest Makenna? I'm certain these two gentlemen could think of more rudely invasive questions. I can assure you my bath has everything you could possibly desire in your hour of need."

The slightest emphasis he put on "desire" and "need" elevated the twitch to a spasm. I had to put my finger on my eyelid to make it stop.

Everyone noticed.

Rake smiled.

I resisted the urge to flip Rake the bird.

"Thank you," I told him. "I'll be fine."

Alain Moreau stood. "And we need to be going. I have asked the questions that needed to be asked."

"I trust my answers were to your satisfaction?"

"They were what I expected."

"I'm always glad to be what SPI expects." The charming banter vanished along with Rake Danescu's smile. "Though if you want to get all the answers, you'll need to ask the one creature who has them. Viktor Kain."

11

IT was noon on Halloween. Twelve hours until midnight on Halloween, and we were no closer to finding where the harpies had taken Ben and the diamonds.

Until last night, Ben Sadler had been blissfully ignorant that the three largest populations in New York weren't humans, pigeons, and rats. Within a few hours of finding out that monsters were real, he'd been kidnapped by three of them.

Last night was supposed to have been fun for him. Get dressed up, go to a museum gala, size up some diamonds for a client, have a few drinks, maybe meet a nice girl—a normal, human one, like a lawyer, stockbroker, actress, advertising exec—anything but three reanimated harpies.

Why the hell couldn't he have run away like every other human in the room with a lick of good sense?

I hadn't run, but crap like that was my job, as was protecting people like him who should've escaped outside, jumped in a cab with the cute lawyer he'd just met, hit the nearest bar, and tried to convince each other that their eyes and the lighting had been playing tricks on them, or the museum sure did pull out all the stops with the special effects. Then maybe end up back at her place—not unconscious in the back of a Suburban with a werewolf outside kicking a harpy's ass who ten seconds before was trying to drag you out a back window she'd bashed in with one punch.

Ben had wanted to hear for himself what Sebastian du Beckett knew about him. He'd insisted on going with us. We were armed, we had backup, and it still hadn't been enough.

I ran what had happened over and over in my head, searching for a missed opportunity, or an action I could have done better to change the outcome.

Nada.

I was still relatively new and untrained. I had an excuse, even if I didn't want to take it.

Ian and Alain Moreau were seasoned veterans of monster combat, and this morning, a man under their protection had been taken. Pissed didn't even begin to describe what I'd seen burning in their eyes. They wanted a rematch, they were going to have one, and the outcome would be different.

Ian's desk was next to mine in the bull pen. He'd been on the phone since we'd gotten back. One of his calls sounded like he'd finally gotten in touch with his black market art guy.

Moreau had gone to check on progress with Sebastian du Beckett's remains in the lab, and then it was to the boss's office to tell her about Ben and fill her in on our visit with Rake Danescu.

"They will not hurt him." Yasha put his big hand on my shoulder. It was warm and reassuring. "They need him."

The Russian was six five in his bare feet, and well over seven feet tall in his bare paw pads, but that didn't keep him from moving like ninja.

"Thank you, Yasha."

He was right. The thief or thieves wouldn't hurt Ben as long as he was useful to them. Whatever the Dragon Eggs were capable of, they needed Ben to wake them up and put them to work. But it didn't mean they'd say "please" while asking him to do whatever it was they needed him to do.

That's why they're called bad guys, Mac. They're not nice.

With Ben's left arm being broken, half of their job would be done for them. I'd had a broken arm before, and until it'd been set, I'd scream if the wind blew the wrong way. "Hurt like hell" didn't even *begin* to describe how it'd felt when those broken bits of bone had shifted.

Ben was new to his gift. What if he couldn't do what the thieves wanted?

Then they wouldn't need him.

Ian got off the phone and rolled his chair over to us.

"So where do harpies roost?" I asked them. "Obviously they don't have a problem with sunlight. Do they leave a trail a werewolf can follow? What do they eat? Are pigeon brains a delicacy? Maybe Midtown's having a rash of mangled pigeon corpses with the heads bitten off—I don't know. There's got to be *something* we can do."

"We've put out an APB."

I damned near jumped out of my skin. Again.

Alain Moreau. Right behind me. At least Yasha had the consideration to displace air when he moved.

"Sir, don't take this the wrong way," I said, "but could you walk louder? At least when you're coming up behind me?"

My vampire manager almost smiled. "I will make every effort, Agent Fraser. The APB is for Monsieur Sadler, the harpies, and any trace of gorgon activity. Normally we would not want to frighten the city's supernatural population unnecessarily, but Madame Sagadraco has just learned that the disturbance that was felt by the supernaturals in the museum when Monsieur Sadler made contact with the harpy and the Dragon Eggs was felt by every supernatural and magic sensitive on the island of Manhattan and two of the other boroughs."

Holy crap.

Ian and Yasha's stunned expressions told me they were thinking pretty much the same thing.

"Madame agrees with Rake Danescu's theory that the thief is on a schedule," Moreau continued. "Whatever the Dragon Eggs are capable of doing, the best time to use them will be midnight tonight. That leaves us only twelve hours to find the diamonds and Monsieur Sandler." He paused. "He will be unharmed until at least after midnight—and perhaps longer, depending on what use the thief has for the diamonds. A gem mage of his ability is rare, and the thief went to a great deal of trouble to abduct him."

"How far can harpies fly?" I asked him.

One corner of his lips quirked in amusement. "And how am I supposed to know that, Agent Fraser?"

"You're . . . you know . . ."

His pale blue eyes glittered. "Old?"

"I wouldn't have used that word. I was going to go with 'experienced'."

"Of course," he said smoothly. "I do not know what a comfortable flight distance for a harpy would be. But if I had to make a guess based on their performance in Monsieur du Beckett's office, I would say that a harpy, even with an injured wing or laden with the weight of a human, could fly as far as she needed to go. I would guess their destination would be within the five boroughs, which leaves us with entirely too many possibilities. Madame Sagadraco is having Agent Hayashi and his team monitor both human and supernatural news sources for reports of any winged creatures. Perhaps one good thing that came from the harpies appearing before the human public is that the people of this city are now alert to the unusual."

"And who is searching?" I asked.

"Every agent we can spare."

Ian leaned back in his chair. "Viktor Kain wouldn't have brought the Dragon Eggs to Ms. Sagadraco's doorstep unless he intended to not only use them against her, but against the city as well. He has to know how protective she is of this place. If he wanted to hurt her, hurt her city."

Moreau nodded. "She is aware of this. Until we know the threat, we do not know what precautions to take."

"If we knew what the diamonds could do," I said, "and what the thief plans to do with them, we could at least narrow down possible hideouts, lair—"

"Nests," Moreau said. "Harpies have nests. But your other word choices would be the correct ones for their master. Harpies do not act of their own initiative. They are but tools for whoever is behind this."

Ian scowled. "For someone who threw a public tantrum, Viktor Kain must be a happy man right now. Still think his hands are clean?"

Moreau gave a haughty sniff of derision. "They never have been. I do not think that has now changed. However, Madame believes that he is not directly responsible; indirect involvement is another thing altogether."

"Ms. Sagadraco said that Viktor Kain's real motive for coming to New York wasn't to sell those diamonds," I said. "That he could have done that a lot easier from home. Does this mean that whatever Kain planned to do with the diamonds is what the thief will try to do, now that they have Ben? I don't know how this kind of thing works. Can two gem mages do something completely different with the same set of stones? Or is it dependent on the stones what kind of magic is worked, and the mage is just the switch to get them started?"

"The latter, Agent Fraser," Moreau replied.

"If Kain hasn't left town yet, then whatever the thief plans to have Ben do with those diamonds must not be too bad." I stopped. "Kain hasn't left town, has he?"

"No," Moreau replied. "He hasn't. He and his entourage are staying on the top two floors of the Mandarin Oriental. Kain himself is in the Presidential Suite."

"Central Park," Ian noted. "High enough so he can survey Vivienne Sagadraco's domain, and only a diamond's throw from her penthouse—and Rake Danescu's."

"Do we have anybody other than Ms. Sagadraco who could stand a chance of getting Kain to talk?" I asked.

"No." Moreau's response was blunt and not what I wanted to hear, and from the tightness of his voice, it wasn't the response he wanted to give. "If he came here with lethal intent, nothing will get it out of him, unless he's certain that she or we won't be able to stop him. Then he'd probably be only too happy to tell us everything."

"Whatever it is the Dragon Eggs can do, it must be something that Kain wanted done in or to New York," I said. "Hopefully the thief isn't planning the same thing, but I'm not gonna hold my breath. Kain's pissed at the boss; that's his motive. Revenge. What are the chances the thief wants the same thing? Or same thing but with a different motive?"

"When you have lived for as long as Madame Sagadraco, you accumulate enemies along with those years. Powerful enemies. That is the first possibility Madame considered. She's cross-referencing them with any known association with harpies."

I couldn't imagine living so long as to have accumulated enough enemies to cross-reference. Made me glad I was human.

As the head of an international crime cartel, Viktor Kain and his organization thrived on chaos and fear. Through SPI, Vivienne Sagadraco had given those in the supernatural world a place to turn to for help against supernatural criminals. It wasn't like they could go to the human authorities. If humans ever got confirmation that supernaturals lived among them, there would be monster hunters and vigilantes everywhere. Supernaturals would either be constantly on the run, or decide to stand and fight. Many of the vampire covens and more than a few of the goblins and elves were fed up with hiding, and thought it was high time they made themselves known to humans, whom the vamps considered food, and the goblins and elves thought were beneath them.

Vivienne Sagadraco didn't think that way. Compared to her, humans had the life expectancy of fruit flies. That she didn't think of earth as a giant petri dish said a lot about her, all of it good.

"I know people in Russia," Yasha said. "Well, people part of time, werewolves rest of time. One of them is a friend. Mercenary, but with honor. Will only work for those who also have honor."

"I take it this means he has not worked for Viktor Kain," Moreau said.

"No, he has not. He has worked for men who were destroyed by Kain."

"Sounds like a survivor," Ian noted.

Yasha gave us a sad smile. "Werewolves are good survivors. Men pay my friend for work, not to die. Russians are practical people." He looked at Moreau. "When you learned that Viktor Kain would be coming here and bringing the Dragon Eggs with him, I called my friend in St. Petersburg for information. He calls friends he trusts—friends inside Kain's organization. Not high in organization; he only accepts werewolves as outer circle guards." Yasha grinned. "But we have big ears, very good for hearing. Some consider guards like furniture. They are there, but not there. Last year, Viktor Kain tries to buy red diamond from businessman in Berlin. Price is too low, businessman did not want to sell. Viktor makes another offer. Not much higher than first. Man still refuses. Kain orders man's family taken. Ransom is red diamond plus ten million dollars for refusing to sell when first asked. Businessman is to deliver it himself.

He brings diamond and money, and Kain has the man's family shot through their heads one by one. Then after this poor man sees his wife and children murdered, Viktor Kain burns him to a crisp. When he locates the owner of the black diamond and makes offer, owner takes first offer made." Yasha paused, and I could hear the clock ticking on the wall. "Word gets around."

"So it would seem," Moreau said quietly.

"Sir, would be a great favor to entire world if Viktor Kain could be . . . what is fitting word . . . exterminated."

"That is the perfect word, Agent Kazakov. Attempts have been made and those attempts have failed. There are many beings who agree with you, myself and Madame included, and those efforts will not cease until there is success."

"So within a month of getting his hands on all seven diamonds," Ian said, "the first thing he does is bring them here, in Ms. Sagadraco's territory, for show-and-tell and sets loose a rumor about an inter-dimensional auction to sell the lot."

"It seems odd to say it," I began, "but those harpies busting out those museum windows and taking those diamonds with them is sounding more and more like a good thing. I mean, what are the odds that someone worse than Viktor Kain is in town?"

As soon as I said it, I realized I really should've kept my mouth shut.

12

"KENJI, we need you to check the database—"

"For gorgons," the elf finished for him. "Just sent the report to your phones."

We looked down. Sure enough.

The elf knew it was us without even looking away from his screen. His fingers never slowed from flying across the keyboard. Kenji Hayashi was a wizard with anything computerized or electronic, but that was it. To the best of my knowledge, he didn't have eyes in the back of his head—some of SPI's employees actually did.

"Gorgons," he continued. "Gaze turns you to stone, poisonous touch, snake hair. Though that last one's not politically correct nowadays."

"And physiologically incorrect," Ian said.

"That, too. Though that's too bad, because the snakes were the coolest feature."

"Not sure the guy upstairs would agree," I told him.

That made Kenji's fingers stop clicking keys. "God?"

"Sebastian du Beckett. On a slab up in the lab."

He winced. "Oh, right. The dragon lady herself asked for the report, and wanted it quick."

"How did you know it was us?" I asked. "You don't have any of those little rearview mirrors on your monitor."

Kenji spun his chair to face us, smiling, quite obviously pleased with himself. "I have something infinitely more effective. I got tired of having *The Shining* twins over there sneaking up on me."

Agents Calri and Gormi Dorgan looked up from their desks and grinned evilly. Oh jeez. Dwarves and elves had never gotten along. It was a cruel twist of fate—or bone-headed mistake of HSR (Human and Supernatural Resources)—that put twin dwarves directly across the aisle and just out of an elf's peripheral vision. The twins kind of reminded me of Shrek's pint-sized, ugly cousins after a weekend bender. Most agents didn't bother to use any spells to hide what they were while they were in the office. Calri and Gormi, in particular, had always enjoyed strolling up beside people and then just standing there, staring at them. It didn't matter what species you were; glancing up to find a pair of identical and identically dressed twins staring at you was creepy as hell. We all have Stephen King to thank for that.

That being said, they were the best at what they did. The Dorgan family—in their human disguises—were involved in just about every city excavation project, going back to when the first sewer and subway lines were carved out under Manhattan. The twins knew the eight hundred miles of sub-way tracks and the thousands of miles of sewer tunnels running under the city like the backs of their hands. More than a few of the supernatural baddies SPI ended up going after took to the darkness under the city in an attempt to elude capture. The twin Dorgan agents were our blood-hounds, bloodhounds that had a tendency to become annoy-ing when they were bored. And when dwarves were bored, any elf in their immediate vicinity was going to get a double dose of obnoxious.

I had news for the boys; they were messing with the wrong elf.

"I wrote a little program," Kenji was saying, "installed some sensors under the floor tiles, and rigged a few of the security cameras to scroll across the bottom of my monitor the name of anyone who comes inside my perimeter."

"Perimeter?" Ian asked. "That sounds paranoid."

Kenji raised a finger in dispute. "Sounds smart. Keeps Agents Fun 'n' Games over there from shaving five years off my life twice a day. I'm running out of years, and I've long been out of patience." He shot the twins a dirty look. "And if that doesn't work, I'll put collars on the little bastards and install one of those invisible fences—right after I tweak the system to quadruple the voltage."

I opened the e-mail on my phone. "So we've got a list of gorgons in the tristate area? That was fast."

"It's a short list. Though it only covers the registered or suspected gorgons."

"Registered?"

"Any supernatural that is on a list of those considered dangerous to humans are requested to register with us," Ian said.

"It's not a requirement?"

"It's a strongly worded request. We can't make them."

"But if they don't," Kenji added, "and we find out about them, they get a star by their name, and it's not for good behavior."

"Meaning they can find themselves at the top of a suspect list when a violent crime is committed by one of their species," Ian said.

I opened the e-mail and keyed in my password to unencrypt the file with the list.

Three names and brief bios.

That was all.

"You weren't kidding when you said it was a short list," I told Kenji.

"Like I said, those are the registered and suspected gorgons. One registered and two suspected."

"If they're not planning to go on a crime spree, why not just register? Yeah, it's an invasion of privacy, but—"

"Gorgons have to kill to survive," Ian said point-blank. "Otherwise their disease will kill them in a similar way."

"On the other hand, vampires don't need to kill their victims." Kenji paused uncomfortably. "Well, at least not after the first time they feed. Gorgons don't have a choice. They survive by taking their victim's life essence—all of it. The victim's remains turn to the consistency of stone."

"So gorgons have to do unto others before their disease can do unto them. I take it there's no cure?"

"Not that's been discovered yet."

"That would be a good enough reason," I readily admitted. "So the doctor tells them to turn someone to stone twice a day and call him in the morning?"

"More like once a month."

"That's better, but not to the poor schlubs who get stoned."

"Gorgons often go into careers that require them to travel," Ian explained. "They murder while away from home, then pound the corpse to gravel, which no human law enforcement agency can determine was ever a human being, resulting in a nearly perfect murder. No body that can even be identified as a body, let alone a specific individual, so the victims become just another missing person. There are things still unknown about gorgonism, and since those with the disease have to kill until they are caught and killed themselves, it's not like the sufferers are willing to sit down with researchers and chat openly about the details of the disease, and what all they are capable of and how. The only info on this in SPI's database is what was gathered as a result of investigating crime scenes where a gorgon was the murderer, or what was observed and experienced by agents while hunting gorgons. Of course, this information was only available from agents who survived their encounter."

"Most gorgons use a combination of eye contact and physical touch," Kenji said. "There are a few who use only their eyes, though you can count the number of those left on one hand."

"I'd rather not count them at all. How is the disease passed?"

"The nest of snakes for hair is a myth," Ian said. "It's a type of vampirism—at least, the method of transmitting the disease is. There's a pair of flexible, needle-thin fangs under the tongue—"

I blinked. "Tongue?"

"That is to transmit the disease. Gorgons can paralyze the outer muscles with a gaze. Physical contact resulting in broken skin transfers a small amount of venom which turns the victim to stone. But the disease itself is only transferred through a bite in a major vein. Gorgons older than five centuries only need their gaze to turn a victim instantly to stone."

"Could a gorgon have turned those harpies into something resembling stone?"

Ian shook his head. "I wish that mystery could be solved that easily. When a gorgon paralyzes their prey, I've heard that it's possible to release them from that state, but only if done within a very short length of time; after that the paralysis becomes permanent. I don't know the exact time frame, but I do know that six days is way outside what's possible. I think we're talking hours here."

"Crap. That shoots down that theory." I thought a moment, horror dawning along with realization. "When you say 'permanent paralysis,' you mean the person is still alive in there, they just can't move or talk?"

"Yes."

"Oh God."

"However, if they aren't released, the victim begins to petrify from the outside in. As to how long the final petrification takes . . . the facts we have are sketchy at best. Gorgons aren't volunteering to tell us the details, though the victim would die once the petrification reached the major organs."

"But during all that, they would be aware of what was happening to them."

Ian didn't speak; he simply nodded.

"I can see why gorgons aren't exactly lining up to give us their names." So how does that work for the registered one?" I looked again at my phone and did a double take at her age.

Ian noted my reaction. "Yeah, gorgons older than a thousand years no longer need to kill to survive. They can take what they need without turning their prey to stone. As with vampires, if the source of a gorgon's nourishment is a willing participant, it's not illegal."

"That would explain why she'd registered." My brow furrowed. "But she lives here in Manhattan. Convenient."

"The two suspected gorgons are under surveillance," Kenji told us. "The reports from this morning have one in Cleveland on business, the other is in Richmond, Virginia, attending a family reunion." He gave a short snort. "Makes you hope they get along better than most families. If not, that'd be a seriously fertile hunting ground."

"Do you think our registered gorgon fell off the wagon?" I asked Ian.

"Possible, but unlikely."

"*Im*possible," said a cool, crisp voice.

Vivienne Sagadraco didn't come down to the bull pen often, but when she did, you knew things were on the verge of going to hades in a handbasket. I turned to see the rare sight of SPI's director in chief in the bull pen, walking down the aisle between the field agents' desks.

Looking right at me.

I wondered if the boss might have a wee bit of gorgon in her, too. Her eyes locked me to the spot where I was standing.

"I wasn't implying suspicion, ma'am," Ian said. "I'm merely keeping all avenues of inquiry open."

"You can eliminate Helena Thanos as a suspect, Agent Byrne."

Ian opened his mouth to respond, presumably to apologize. The boss held up a hand.

"It's early in the investigation, and you are following protocol, as you should. I will be having tea with Helena within the hour. I will ask the question to officially eliminate her from the list of suspects. The other two gorgons are out of town and are likewise eliminated. Correct, Agent Hayashi?"

"Yes, ma'am."

"Which leaves us with no viable suspects. Meaning we have an unregistered and unknown gorgon at large in Manhattan. While Helena seldom leaves her apartment, she does have an extensive and trustworthy network of contacts, and has been of immeasurable help to us in the past. She is also one of the world's foremost experts on Greek history and mythology—she was there. I have questions for her, and since this is your case, Agent Fraser, you should come with me."

"It's Ian's—I mean, Agent Byrne's case, too. And as senior agent, shouldn't—"

"No, Agent Fraser. He should not. Helena was infected with gorgonism by a man and, through the centuries, has been hunted by men. As a result, she's not overly fond of them, and I would not offend her sensibilities by bringing a man into her home. This will be an excellent learning opportunity for you."

Why is it that opportunities, either training or learning, end up being extremely unpleasant experiences?

"If there is a rogue gorgon killing humans in our city, she would want them dealt with."

"How do we do that?" I asked. "Deal with them."

"Helena Thanos is one of only five known gorgons who are old enough not to need to kill to keep their disease from consuming them. It is exceedingly difficult to capture a gorgon. However, when one is caught and their actions connected to specific deaths, there are only two solutions: solitary confinement until they reach a thousand years old, or execution. Were I afflicted with gorgonism, I would choose the latter."

13

THE Dakota.

I'd heard of it. I mean, who hadn't?

Exclusive and expensive home to celebrities and the absurdly rich. Where John Lennon had lived and was killed a couple of years before I was born. But I'd never seen it in person. The apartment building looming over a chunk of Central Park was part French chateau, part fortress.

In my opinion, it couldn't have been a more perfect home to New York's only registered gorgon.

Vivienne Sagadraco's limo stopped in front of the arched carriageway that extended through the thick walls of the sand-colored building. I half expected to see an iron portcullis over the entrance, ready to drop on any who had the audacity to pass through without an invitation from one of the residents. There was a guard in an actual sentry box like something you'd find outside Buckingham Palace, minus the big, furry hat. God help you if your name wasn't on the guard's list.

Naturally, the boss was on the list, and surprisingly, my name was on there as well. It didn't merely say "and guest." The guard directed the two of us through the carriageway and into an amazingly quiet inner courtyard. The sound of the water in the bronze fountains was actually louder than the traffic on the street outside.

We crossed the courtyard and entered a small lobby. I turned toward the elevator, and felt Vivienne Sagadraco's light touch on my arm.

"This way, Agent Fraser."

"But—"

"Helena has a private elevator to her apartment. She prefers to avoid contact with the other residents."

I could certainly understand that. Turning people into life-sized action figures would be a surefire way to alienate your neighbors.

The boss led me to the far end of the narrow lobby where there was a small keypad set into a blank wall. Her delicate fingers flew over the keypad, hitting I had no idea how many numbers. There was a click and an elevator door–sized section of wall silently slid back, revealing a dark wood-paneled elevator illuminated by a pair of alabaster sconces set into either side of the back wall.

The elevator went up as quietly as the door had opened, so I couldn't tell how many floors we passed going up. How we were getting there was less of a concern to me right now than what the heck I was going to say when I got there. Best to ask now than to embarrass myself soon.

"Ma'am, I don't want to offend Ms. Thanos or embarrass you, but I have no idea how to act around . . . someone with her affliction. I was raised to believe that it's rude not to look people in the eye when you talk to them, but with a—"

"I've told Helena that I will be bringing a guest. She will wear special glasses over her eyes out of consideration for you. It will be perfectly safe for you to look at her."

I didn't want to ask, but I had to. "Are you sure it's safe, ma'am?" I spoke quietly. I didn't doubt her word, but after seeing what'd happened to Sebastian du Beckett . . .

She gave me a reassuring smile. "Quite certain, Agent Fraser. No human has ever been turned to stone by looking at Helena's glasses. And skin contact can only transfer the disease if Helena wills it—and she has not done so for hundreds of years."

"What about you, ma'am?"

"The glasses are not necessary when I am her only visitor. I am immune to the unfortunate side effect of eye or skin contact with a gorgon."

"That must be a comfort to Ms. Thanos to have a friend with similar interests and life experiences who she can talk to and be herself around."

Vivienne Sagadraco was facing the closed door, her profile to me. I glimpsed a shadow of a smile. "Very diplomatic, Agent Fraser."

"Pardon?"

"Since Helena and I were both around when Plato was teaching in Athens, we're two old ladies who can gossip."

Lucky for me, the elevator picked that moment to stop. The door opened into a small room with another door on the opposite wall. It had a bronze knocker in the center in the shape of a Medusa head complete with hair of all-too-lifelike snakes. After what had happened with a certain statue of three harpies, there was no way I was touching it. Good thing the boss didn't share my squeamishness or we'd have been standing out there all day.

A petite woman wearing dark Jackie O–style sunglasses opened the door. She had to be Helena Thanos; that was, unless her staff had to wear incredibly stylish protective sunglasses, too.

Between knowing that the gorgon was conservatively two thousand years old, and Vivienne Sagadraco telling us that she rarely left her apartment, I expected someone who was a combination of a reclusive silent movie star and Miss Havisham from *Great Expectations*.

Helena Thanos was neither.

After entirely too many surprises since last night, it was nice to have a pleasant one.

She couldn't have been much more than two inches over five feet tall. Though it was only in recent human history that people have been growing taller. In ancient Greece, she was probably quite tall. I knew how old she was, but she looked to be in her early forties, a very attractive early forties.

I could only see the lower half of her face; the top half was covered by the sunglasses. Vivienne Sagadraco was right; I didn't turn into stone by looking at the glasses. That was good because I hadn't been able to resist looking at her.

Her hair was cut in a dark bob that perfectly complemented her glasses. She was dressed in casual, but elegant, cream-colored slacks and ivory silk blouse that were tastefully accented with gold jewelry.

But it was her aura that had clued me in immediately that Helena Thanos was more than a snappy dresser with a flair for accessorizing. The auras of humans and supernaturals had one thing in common—they encompassed the entire body. Helena Thanos's aura was centered around her head. It was green, and damned if it didn't look like she had snakes for hair. I wondered if that was where the myth had started— a seer in ancient Greece had gotten a good look at a gorgon and lived to tell about it. And speaking of living to tell about it, my instincts were telling me rather forcefully to forget the elevator that'd brought me here; find the stairs, find them now, and run until I got to the street, and when I got to the street, keep running.

Helena Thanos gave us a warm smile. "Vivienne, how good to see you!" Watching a dragon and a gorgon hug and do the double-cheek-kissing thing was surreal.

The gorgon turned her attention to me, and I tried my best not to close my eyes or cringe, and especially not to run.

"And you must be Makenna Fraser."

"Yes, ma'am."

She must have been all too aware of how humans who knew what she was reacted the first time they met her. The warm and welcoming smile stayed in place, but she made no move to touch me.

God, I really felt bad for her.

Do it, Mac.

I took a step forward and extended my hand.

Helena Thanos's smile brightened as she took my hand in a warm handshake.

Judging from the upward slope of the ceiling, Helena Thanos's apartment was on the Dakota's top floor, and included one of the pair of two-story gables that dominated the front of the building. I couldn't even begin to imagine how much this apartment must have cost.

There were flowers, real trees, and even a small, shallow stream winding through the room and continuing into the next through a low arch cut into the wall.

The walls were continuous, photo-realistic murals of a meadow at the edge of the woods. The illusion continued from the walls to the vaults of the gables that were painted like a blue sky, and it all glowed with sun that streamed in through a progression of windows set into the gables, the last set so high as to qualify as skylights rather than windows. There were artificial sources of light, but they were recessed into the ceiling to supplement and mimic natural light. The sun coming in through the windows dimmed with the passing of a cloud, and the room's lighting adjusted to match.

"Wow," was all I could think to say.

Way to be the articulate representative of mortals, Mac.

"Thank you, Agent Fraser." Helena Thanos sounded genuinely pleased. "The lighting in this room is a great source of enjoyment. It can also duplicate a sunset, through twilight, and on into a starry night sky with moonlight." She gestured through a pair of white marble columns twined with climbing roses. "Please, come in. Doria has prepared tea for us."

The boss and Helena Thanos traded brief pleasantries, and then it was down to business.

Harpies.

But most of all, gorgons.

"As much as I wish we could linger and chat," Vivienne Sagadraco said, "we have a rapidly deteriorating situation that won't allow it." She hesitated. "Unfortunately, circumstances also dictate that I officially ask you a question, which, considering that you almost never leave your apartment, is in extremely bad taste. Where were you this morning between six and nine?"

Helena Thanos waved a dismissive hand. "I understand completely. I was here. Until seven o'clock, I was still in bed. From then until approximately eight thirty, I was out on the terrace enjoying a real sunrise and my morning coffee and paper. I then went inside to prepare for a nine o'clock meeting with my assistant to go over my tasks for her for the next few days. And the only person who can vouch for me is my housekeeper, Doria. And so you don't have to suffer the discomfort of asking, our building does have security cameras that show the area of my terrace where I was sitting." She reached for the smartphone on the table beside her. "I will call down and ask that they release—"

Vivienne Sagadrago shook her head. "Helena, that's not necessary."

"For you, my dear friend, I know it is not. However, the circumstances that bring you here must be dire for you to ask. I will gladly put your organization's mind at ease. Will the hour and a half that I was on my terrace be sufficient? Only Doria saw where I was from—"

"It will be more than sufficient, Helena. I'm mortified to even—"

"Think nothing of it."

Helena Thanos made the call and the request for the security footage from her terrace from seven to eight thirty this morning. That would definitely be sufficient. Unless Ms. Thanos could sprout wings, it'd be impossible for her to have gone to Sebastian du Beckett's brownstone, turned the old guy to stone, and returned to her penthouse. Ian hadn't mentioned anything about gorgons being able to fly, and if they could have, I was certain he'd have mentioned it.

"If I may inquire," Helena Thanos asked once she'd completed the call, "what happened that prompted you to ask?"

"Sebastian du Beckett was found dead in his office this morning," Ms. Sagadraco said. "Turned to stone."

"That would certainly be a good reason to know the whereabouts of every gorgon in the city. Do you believe it is connected to the theft of the Dragon Eggs last night?"

"We do."

"I read it in the paper and saw it on the news, Agent Fraser," Helena Thanos explained in response to what must have been my surprised expression. "My reluctance to venture out does not extend to completely cutting myself off from civilization. I enjoy all of the technology this exciting age has to offer." She indicated the phone she'd just used. "I upgraded my iPhone last week." With an impish grin, she flipped it over to reveal a phone case featuring a brightly colored Medusa head. "We all are what we are, Agent Fraser. Life goes down a lot easier when we accept it and move on."

I smiled at the cover. "I love it."

"I do, too. Another benefit of the twenty-first century—online shopping. Who needs to leave home?"

Ms. Sagadraco proceeded to tell her friend the details of what had happened this morning: Sebastian du Beckett's death, Ben Sadler's kidnapping, and the now less-than-twelve-hour window we had to stop the diamonds from being activated.

"If you have any knowledge that would assist us in locating this individual, as always, I value your wisdom."

Helena Thanos gave a mirthless laugh. "You know as well as I that wisdom has nothing to do with it. Living for thousands of years doesn't make us wise, it simply makes us old. Who donated the harpy statue?"

Vivienne set her teacup on its saucer. "A Madame Pointe-Cozeur from Nice."

"I take it her statue never made it to New York?"

Vivienne nodded. "It was found in a warehouse outside of Heathrow. The jewel thief—and now kidnapper—arranged his tableau to match, placed it in the real statue's crate along with the corresponding paperwork. It was put on the flight to JFK as originally scheduled."

"So you have a team of thieves as opposed to an individual."

"An individual powerful enough to immobilize three harpies in a crate long enough for a transatlantic flight, time in customs, and then sitting in a museum exhibit for six days before it was opened."

"Harpies aren't known for their patience," Helena noted wryly. "Which probably accounted for their crankiness when they were released from stasis. The mortal authorities are fortunate only the two guards were killed. If the harpies' orders hadn't been so precise, there would have been many more deaths. So they can put harpies in stasis, but they need a human gem mage to use what they stole?"

"Correct. Does that sound like anyone you know?"

"I wish I could say it did. Not that I would want to know this person but at least if I did, I could be more helpful. How good is the gem mage who was abducted?"

"Our preliminary testing puts him at the top of the scale for a gem mage—at the very least."

"Our folks think he's a total newbie," I added.

Helena Thanos's lips curled in a smile. "Total newbie?"

"Sorry, ma'am. He's just now come into his power and while he's got a lot of it, he has absolutely zero control."

"I believe Bastian knew more about Mr. Sadler but he refused to discuss it over the phone," Vivienne Sagadraco said.

"And now he can't. What about this Madame Pointe-Cozeur?"

"I sent a pair of investigators from our Paris office to interview her. The statue has been in her family since her great-grandfather brought it back from Cyprus in the 1840s."

I got the impression of an eye roll from behind the glamorous sunglasses. "Yet another acquisition from a Grand Tour. Why couldn't nineteenth-century French and English bring back tacky souvenirs like everyone else? Must they carry off our culture?"

"The request from the Metropolitan Museum was legitimate," the boss said. "Madame Pointe-Cozeur has loaned the statue to museums in the past, most recently the Louvre."

"One thing I can tell you for certain is that locating and securing the cooperation of three harpies was not done on the spur of the moment. Your jewel thief is much more than a diamond aficionado. They would have a network of contacts in the art world, and possess the intellect and patience to manipulate events behind the scenes. And since your mastermind has retained the specialized services of others, it stands to reason that he or she may not have been the one to release those harpies." Helena paused. "Have you heard from your sister lately?"

"She was my very first suspect," Vivienne said. "I have confirmation from a trusted source that Tiamat is nursing her wounded pride in a cave in Tibet, no doubt planning revenge, but the trouble that landed at our front door last night isn't her doing."

Helena gave a little half smile. "Maybe next week. You're certain that Viktor Kain is not responsible?"

"He did not release those harpies. I was close enough to him that I would have felt that much power go out."

"And he's blaming you."

"Naturally."

Helena raised her teacup. "Just like old times." She turned her sunglass-covered eyes toward me.

It took some effort, but I didn't look down, around, or away.

"Vivienne tells me that you were close to the harpies when they were awakened."

"Yes, ma'am."

"Tell me what you saw and heard."

"I heard moaning coming from the statues just before the harpies reanimated," I told her.

"How long until they regained full movement?"

"Less than thirty seconds. More like ten to fifteen."

"That was not the work of a gorgon, Vivienne. Harpies have thicker skin than humans, and are stronger and more resilient, so there is less chance that they would go into shock from lack of blood flow to their outer layers once that circulation was restored. That being said, it is impossible that a gorgon could have paralyzed a harpy for six days. The maximum length of time before the process is irreversible is twelve hours. Any longer than that and petrification sets in. They would only survive for another few hours at most, long enough for the process to overtake the major organs. The only other option I can think of would be a spell of some kind. Physically, blood flow to the skin and extremity muscles would not be affected. And harpies can put themselves into a state resembling hibernation. In short, they are an ideal choice if one needed to create a living statue capable of reanimating immediately into action."

Vivienne Sagadraco shook her head. "I've heard of sleep spells that can last for years, but those induce a state resembling a coma. So we're talking about something else."

Helena nodded.

"If the harpies had been put into suspended animation for six days, how could the spellcaster, for lack of a better description, have made them immediately do a smash-and-grab robbery?" I asked.

"They would have to be under a compulsion that was implanted in their minds prior to them being put into stasis," Helena Thanos said.

"So harpies aren't big on independent thinking?"

"It's fortunate that they are not. Equally fortunate that the number of beings who have the power to influence or control a harpy is very small. Harpies are appallingly efficient, single-minded weapons. They do best with simple and clear instructions."

"Smash, grab, and kidnap."

"Correct."

"What about the gorgon from this morning?" Vivienne Sagadraco asked quietly.

Helena Thanos's entire demeanor changed. Her posture became rigid, and I didn't need to see her eyes to know they were cold.

"You said the door was locked?" she asked me.

"Yes, ma'am."

"Sebastian du Beckett's death was a murder," she said. "It was personal, and he knew his killer."

"Because he let them in?" I asked.

Helena Thanos nodded. "That, and he was seated behind his desk when they struck. That says familiarity. I knew Mr. du Beckett only by professional reputation, but he did not seem to be the careless type. And as he regularly had to deal with people who, shall we say, were on the fringes of legality, he had every reason to exercise caution. When a gorgon kills, the choice of victim is either completely random or highly personal. The majority of our victims are selected by opportunity and ease of disposal, not choice. Sebastian du Beckett was chosen. To my knowledge—and it was certainly true with me—no one has ever been willingly infected with gorgonism. Being forced to kill to survive, condemned to a solitary existence; that is, unless one is fortunate enough to have a friend who is a dragon or other supernatural being who is immune. And during your first century—assuming you can keep your sanity for that long—you cannot even touch another living creature without turning them to stone. I can't imagine being infected with gorgonism and having no knowledge of the supernatural world and those who would be immune to you who you could reach out to. Without this knowledge, the infected individual would be truly alone. Forget Hell, Agent Fraser. *That* is eternal damnation."

The silence grew. I didn't know what to say, but I knew what I wanted to ask.

"Ma'am, I'd really like to ask a question."

"From your hesitation, I'm guessing this question is of a personal and presumably indelicate nature."

I responded with a single nod.

"I'm old enough to be past offending, Agent Fraser."

"You can call me Makenna, if you'd like, ma'am."

"Vivienne tells me your fellow agents call you Mac."

"They do. My grandmother calls me Makenna." I paused. "As does a lady back home. She's been through a lot in her life, and she's been kind enough over the years to give me some of the best advice I've ever gotten. I think the world of her. She calls me Makenna."

"Very well . . . Makenna. Ask your question." She smiled slowly. "But only if you will call me Helena."

I returned the smile. "Miss Helena."

"Helena will be fine."

I shook my head. "Where I come from, when you address an older lady who you admire, you put 'Miss' in front of her name as a courtesy and a sign of respect."

Her smile broadened. "Miss Helena it is, then."

"How did you do it?"

"Do what, Makenna?"

"Get past the anger, the resentment?"

She gave a bitter little laugh. "Who says I'm past it? I've just gotten better at controlling it. When I was first infected, I preyed on the shadows of society, the criminals. At first I had no control. I killed when I had no need, telling myself that since I preyed only on the criminal, I was doing society a service. Trying to buy back my humanity with lives, to kill so many, so often, so as to leave me no time to think on, to admit, what I truly was. A monster."

I started to speak, but she held up her hand.

"If I couldn't be a part of society, I convinced myself that I could help it. I became a one-woman judge, jury, and executioner. Society would be better off without these creatures who call themselves people, who feed upon humanity's weakest and most vulnerable. Society would also be better off without me, but I discovered that it's very difficult to decapitate one's self, which is one of only two ways to kill a gorgon. If I remained for too long in any one place, or made an effort to be careless in disposing of my victims' remains, I'm sure the mortal authorities could have eventually caught and executed me; but by then, I'd convinced myself that I was better at their jobs than they were."

"You probably were."

"Being a vigilante gave me a sense of purpose. To make it through your first century, let alone your first millennium, you must find a purpose for your continued existence. I found mine. I became a self-appointed goddess of vengeance. In the back of my mind was the doubt, the guilt. Who was I to make that decision, to end the lives of others? I was as much of a monster as the men and women I killed."

"But you continued to do it."

"I did. Until one day I no longer felt the ache in my joints, the pain of the hardness beginning to grow inside of me that had always signaled the need to find a life to take, to make the pain recede for a while until it came again. But it never came again. While I no longer have to kill, the curse remains."

I didn't know how to respond, so I went with how I felt. "I'm so sorry, Miss Helena."

"As am I, Makenna. But thanks to friends like Vivienne, I am beginning to learn to venture out. After so long a solitary existence, it is not easy. She has provided me with modern technology to enable me to see the world without having to step outside the security of my home."

"You're making excellent progress," Ms. Sagadraco assured her.

"Small steps. In the meantime, my interior gardens bring me great comfort. Vivienne found artists and a landscaper who have transformed this space into a lovely home."

"You are most welcome, dear Helena."

I raised my hand a little. "Miss Helena, I have another possibly insensitive question. I'm only asking because it'd be a good thing to know if we run into Mr. du Beckett's killer."

"I'm sure it's not insensitive coming from you, Makenna. What is it?"

"What's the second way to kill a gorgon?"

"It's a way that you should be eternally grateful you cannot use. An older gorgon can turn a younger gorgon to stone. I am not proud to say that I have used this more than a few times. Gorgons are territorial by necessity. Newly infected gorgons tend not to be very selective in their choice of victims, and where they feed can draw unwanted attention to an older gorgon's territory. Once I decided that I wanted to live, I wasn't about to have youngsters with poor table manners attract people with axes."

"Understood."

"What will be even less pleasant to hear is that since a gorgon was not responsible for the harpies at the museum, there's a good possibility that Bastian's murder may be unrelated to either the robbery or the kidnapping. The gorgon could very well have been connected to one of his other clients—a very dissatisfied client."

"I know. We're concentrating our efforts on the Dragon Eggs, since we have it on better than good authority that whatever the thief intends to use the stones to do, they'll be doing it at midnight tonight." Vivienne gave Helena a brief summary of what we knew about the diamonds.

The boss's phone rang from her purse.

"Forgive me, Helena. It's Alain. He would not call unless it was urgent."

Helena and I sat quietly while Vivienne Sagadraco was on the phone. She mostly listened while Alain Moreau spoke, her lips a thin, tense line. She asked a few questions, none of which gave me any clear indication of what had hit the fan at headquarters.

"Tell Dr. Riley to keep me posted," the boss said. She pressed the hang-up button on her phone and put it back in her purse. "Dr. Riley was able to estimate the time of Bastian's death at eight o'clock this morning."

A time when Helena Thanos had an airtight alibi, soon to be confirmed by the Dakota's security footage.

However, it was forty minutes after Rake Danescu *said* he'd left—with no confirmation, either by a witness or security footage.

"Dr. Riley said that Bastian's remains were softer on the inside than at the surface of his skin," Vivienne Sagadraco said. "The interior of his torso, where his major organs were located, was more of the consistency of ash. Does this tell you any—"

"That Sebastian du Beckett's killer is a very young gorgon," Helena said. "One that was turned less than a year ago, probably less than six months. A gorgon gains strength with each victim, and after the first year of the disease, they will cause the internal organs of their victims to petrify as solidly as the rest of the body. This gorgon will need to feed again soon, within the next few hours. A powdery consistency to the internal organs indicates less than optimal . . . I'm sorry, but 'digestion' is the only word that's truly accurate. A gorgon this young is still learning to feed properly. The more solid the remains, the more satisfying the feeding and the longer the gorgon can last until they have to kill again. Some youngsters are careless when they're this hungry."

"So our killer will make a mistake?" I asked.

"*Some* youngsters, Makenna. This one gained entrance to Sebastian du Beckett's home and struck him down where he sat, leaving behind nothing but a locked door. This gorgon was an accomplished murderer already. He or she won't make mistakes; they'll make more victims—and soon."

—— **14**

TO crack a case, you connect the facts.

We didn't have enough facts to fill a shot glass.

We were really hoping Ian's black market art dealer contact could help change that.

Denton Sykes was waiting for us in a coffeehouse on Fifty-ninth Street across from Central Park. It was closing in on five o'clock on Halloween. The place was almost empty. People would be getting off work and going home to get ready for the night ahead. For the not-clued-in humans, that meant makeup and costumes, many going to parties as supernatural creatures. Supernaturals could simply drop their glamours and do the "come as you are" thing, though they might have to do some quick thinking to explain to their friends and coworkers why their makeup looked so realistic.

The coffeehouse was almost empty. After the morning rush and the early afternoon caffeine fix, there was a lull until the night crowd started coming in. Considering that tonight was Halloween, that bunch was gonna look a heck of a lot different from the T-shirt-and-jeans-clad guy slouched over his laptop in a faded, overstuffed chair in the far corner.

If Denton Sykes wanted to be in a public place and still have privacy, he'd done a fine job picking our meeting location.

He was waiting for us at the opposite side of the coffee-house from web-surfer dude. He had his back to the wall and his eyes on the door. He also had a large coffee with barista shorthand for three shots written in Sharpie on the side. There were at least five empty, colorful packets of not-sugar next to the cup.

According to Ian, Sykes would have been nervous when he came in, and was about to toss enough caffeine and sweetened cancer powder on top of those nerves to be able to climb the wall behind him like a fly.

I flipped on my seer vision to take a quick look.

Denton Sykes wasn't a fly, just a highly caffeinated human. Jeff Goldblum still had the neat, yet disgusting, human-turning-into-a-fly trick all to himself.

"That stuff will kill you, you know," Ian told Sykes.

"It'll have to get in a long line." Sykes winked, though it might have been a nervous tic. "Sit down and let's get this over with."

"In a rush because you've got big plans this evening?"

"If by big plans, you mean leaving town? Then yeah, big plans."

"Denny, this is my partner, Makenna Fraser. Mac, this is Denny Sykes. Denny's usually a regular silver-tongued charmer. He seems a little out of sorts. Tell me, Denny, what's got you out of sorts?"

"A line of potential customers from here to the East River docks, and nothing I've got to sell is anything they want to buy."

"So who's the lucky salesman who does have the business?"

"Nobody—at least not anybody I know. Those rotten eggs haven't surfaced. It's looking like the thief decided to hang on to his haul."

"Or cut out middlemen like you," Ian said.

"Possible, but even then I'd have heard something."

"Quiet?"

"As a tomb—the kind with an actually dead occupant."

"Letting the diamonds cool off?"

"Rocks like the Dragon Eggs don't cool, not even a little. Even if they cut them up, the colors would be a dead giveaway."

"We recognized a few of the interested parties on the security video from the Met, but some were from out of town. Your reputation runs far and wide. Any of the foreigners contact you?"

"If they did, it was through a local third party. Anyone who called me I already know. The Dragon Eggs aren't a once-in-a-lifetime score; they're a once-in-a-*millennium* score. When they were stolen, every wannabe buyer in that room knew that their competition now included Viktor Kain—and the Russian is deadly competition. Nobody's taking any chances. If those diamonds were to come up for sale, and one of them had the winning bid, they'd know Kain would be hot on their trail. That was enough to make some turn tail and run." Sykes grinned. "Most of them weren't bothered by that at all and are sticking around to see what happens, though they're taking precautions and operating through representatives. Hell, their aliases have aliases." He took a goodly chug of his coffee. "The value of the stones has quadrupled overnight. I don't think there's a limit to what I could ask—if I knew where they hell they were, I'd never have to work another day in ten lives." Denny spread his hands. "But it's a moot point because I can't sell what I ain't got."

"Never stopped you before," Ian said.

"True. But there's a difference between almost in my

possession, and no way in hell I'm going to get them. Whoever stole those seven diamonds means to keep them."

"Did any of your potential customers hire themselves some jewel thieves when they got to town?"

Sykes laughed loud enough to make the surfer dude look up and glare at us. "Every hotshot thief in town is on a retainer. Most of the foreigners brought their own. If there had been an auction, there were going to be a lot of losers. These people aren't used to losing, and each and every one of them was prepared to do something about it."

"Got any names?"

"A few, but I want to live to see the sun come up tomorrow. You don't go around saying certain names out loud, especially those belonging to people who could pop my heart out with a spoon all the way from Jersey. Discretion is the better part of survival. My regulars have been calling. But like I said, whoever has them is keeping them. They're also keeping quiet. There should at least be a rumor or two, but nothing. And the more cautious types scrambled back under the slime-covered rocks they live under once word got around that Sebastian du Beckett went and got himself stoned this morning."

Ian gave him a flat look.

"Really? Nothing? That's priceless."

"Glad it tickles your funny bone. We found him, so we were less than amused."

"Men like me and du Beckett gotta watch our backs and our fronts. When you have monsters and freaks for customers, chances are one day one of them will be the one to take you out."

Ian leaned back in his chair. "And when it's your turn, it won't have happened to a more deserving guy."

"Du Beckett's customers dress nicer and talk better, but they're all monsters and freaks."

Oh yeah, somewhere a charmer was missing his snake.

"Your buddy Eddie Laughlin must have heard what happened to du Beckett this morning," Sykes said. "He's gone to ground. In our business, if your boss gets plugged, you start seeing bull's-eyes on yourself, you know?" Sykes pushed back his chair and picked up his coffee. "If you'll excuse me, those eggs aren't the only action in town. I got people to see and customers to make happy before I make myself scarce for the night."

Sykes left the coffeehouse, stepped out to the curb, looked both ways, and ran across Fifty-ninth Street and into Central Park.

"I thought you said that guy was a friend of yours," I said.

"I never said 'friend'; I said 'contact.' You assumed."

"And I've never been more glad to be wrong. I didn't get any more food dumped on me, but after sitting across from that guy, I'm feeling the need for another shower."

"Denny has that effect on people. He also makes people want to kick his ass."

"That'd involve touching him. Then you'd *really* need a shower."

"Yeah, but the ass kicking would be worth it."

Movement out of the corner of my eye caught our attention. A flock of birds that should've been roosting for the night by now flew out the top of the park's trees. They scattered and didn't come back.

It took a lot to scare birds once they'd settled in for the night.

Ian stood. "I'm taking a short walk in the park. Stay here."

I stood. "Like hell."

"Then stay behind me."

"Could you at least say 'cover my six'? Give me a little dignity here."

"Okay. Cover my six—just don't shoot me in the ass."

"How about I kick it?" Sykes wasn't the only one asking for it.

I heard the grin in his voice. "You're always welcome to try."

Ian and I crossed Fifty-ninth and entered the park.

It was quiet. Sykes's analogy came back to me. Like a tomb.

It turned out to be accurate.

Central Park had a new statue complete with a pigeon perched on its head.

Denny Sykes was stoned. I'd bet he wouldn't find that phrase nearly as funny now. The pigeon saw me and Ian and flew away, but not before leaving a gift on Sykes's shoulder.

In the immortal words of the now late Denny Sykes—that was priceless.

Ian had his anti-gorgon-glare glasses hooked in the front of his shirt. He put them on with one hand, while getting his gun in his other—simultaneous and slick.

I was still fumbling in my purse.

After meeting with Helena Thanos this afternoon, and hearing that we had a young and hungry gorgon aspiring to use the city as its personal buffet, the boss had deemed it prudent for field agents who'd be out in the city tonight to be carrying protective eyewear.

Ian scanned the surrounding area for threats. "Got your glasses?" he asked without looking at me.

"Trying."

"Try faster, and don't look up until you do."

Oh crap. "Gorgon's here?"

"Not yet."

I fumbled, found, and put on SPI's version of safety glasses. Guaranteed protection against gorgon stares, Mongolian Death Worm spit (normally found in the Gobi Desert, seen last month in the desert outside Vegas), and Amazonian chimera loogies (recently spotted in a Louisiana swamp).

We went back to back and scanned the area.

Plenty of trees.

Lots of almost dark.

No birds, no people, no gorgon.

And no way in hell this was a coincidence. Denny Sykes had been right to be paranoid.

He—and we—were being watched.

___ **15**

IAN called Yasha for pickup, and we hightailed it to Eddie Laughlin's place, hoping we weren't too late.

Why the sudden concern for Sebastian du Beckett's picker?

One, Denny had said that Eddie Laughlin had gone to ground. Two, we hadn't heard a peep out of Eddie since he'd offered us a ride at the Met last night. In light of points one and two—and what'd just happened to Denny—Ian thought it'd be a good idea to check in on Eddie.

The gorgon seemed to be starting a series of sculptures entitled "Still Life with Art Dealers." Technically Eddie was a picker, not a dealer, but when you're a hungry young gorgon on a killing spree/feeding frenzy, you probably didn't bother with a little detail like that.

Eddie Laughlin's apartment building wasn't in the worst part of town, but with a gorgon running amuck, having a heavily armed werewolf friend two days shy of a full moon made me feel a lot less jumpy about being there.

Unlike last night at the museum, I had a gun and it was a comforting weight under my jacket. It'd taken me a while to get used to carrying, but now I felt downright naked when I wasn't. My official security blanket was two pounds of steel with silver bullets. It wasn't warm or fuzzy, but it was a heck of a lot better at keeping nightmares away.

Ian didn't buzz Eddie to be let in. He put the face of his watch against the door's locking mechanism. Like nearly every building in Manhattan and the outer boroughs, you could only get in if a resident buzzed you in—or if your employer's R&D department developed gadgets that Q would have been proud to give to 007.

The door obediently opened with a click, and we were in.

Until we knew what, if anything, was presently visiting Eddie, my partner preferred to keep our visit a surprise. At the same time, we didn't want any surprises of our own. It was dark, and we were wearing what looked like sunglasses.

That extended to taking the stairs rather than the small elevator. Ian had taught me from the get-go that unless you needed to get to the top of the Empire State Building and had to have enough wind to talk King Kong off the ledge when you got there, you always took the stairs. Elevators were just coffins with bad Muzak. When you dealt with shapeshifters that could go from two legs to eight, and could scuttle down an elevator cable like a web, stairs were the safest way to get where you needed to be.

It was also the best way to get the drop on a gorgon possibly getting the drop on a colleague.

There was no window on the fire door opening onto the fourth floor. I knew the drill. I stood with my back against the wall next to Ian as he opened the door just enough to know if anything was on the other side waiting to bite our faces off or stare us into statuary. If my partner deemed our faces and the rest of us safe, we went in.

In an ideal world, the door opened on silent hinges; on a less than optimal day, they had a creak that'd wake the dead. Believe me, if you're tracking something dead, you don't want it awake when you find it. Luck was smiling on us; the fire door was quiet.

Ian took a set of lock picks out of his jacket pocket, and worked his magic on Eddie's five locks. Even in this part of town, five seemed a mite excessive unless you had stuff you didn't want stolen or stuff you'd stolen yourself.

Less than a minute later, we were inside.

No Eddie.

No gorgon.

There were avid collectors and there were hoarders.

Looking around Eddie's place, I decided that avid collectors were basically hoarders, only with better focus. And, fortunately for us in Eddie's case, taste.

Sebastian du Beckett's Upper West Side brownstone looked like a museum in need of a curator.

Eddie Laughlin's Lower East Side apartment looked like a museum reject bin in need of dusting—and with entirely too many items that needed explanation. Eddie hadn't been turned to stone, but from the looks of his wall art, he might have taken a left turn toward the dark side. He wasn't at home, but he'd left us plenty of presents that were a veritable treasure trove of incriminating evidence.

Floor plans of the Sackler Wing. Photos detailing security camera placement. But most damning of all—up-close photos of the sloped wall of windows the harpies had broken through to escape.

Ian's jaw was doing that clench/unclench thing that said loud and clear that Eddie better be glad he wasn't here.

We'd had to leave Denny's body in Central Park, but Ian had called Vivienne Sagadraco and told her what we'd learned from Denny—and the surprise Denny had gotten from the gorgon while strolling in the park. The boss would arrange to have Denny retrieved and taken to the lab where I guessed he'd be keeping Sebastian du Beckett company.

When what we'd found was evidence linking Eddie to the robbery rather than a gorgon turning Eddie into the human version of a garden gnome, Ian decided we should turn what'd been a search-and-rescue mission into a search-and-seizure operation.

The apartment wasn't large, but there was a lot to go through. Ian and I didn't trash the place, but we didn't worry about being tidy or leaving fingerprints. The boss had given us the green light to do a little breaking and entering. Once we'd gotten to the apartment and seen what there was to see, Ian phoned home again, and the boss had added evidence collection to our list of permitted activities.

If Eddie came back while we were there, Ian had several very pointed questions to ask him; and if Eddie didn't like that we'd let ourselves in and made ourselves at home, he could take it up with Vivienne Sagadraco, who'd authorized it. With Sebastian du Beckett dead, Eddie had already lost one employer today. If he wasn't guilty of anything, I couldn't see him pissing off the only other source of gainful employment he had left.

Our presence here was bound to surprise Eddie, but if he was taking a walk on the dark side, it'd be a bad idea to let Eddie surprise us.

Yasha's job was to search the front of the apartment and keep his wonderwolf ears perked for any sign of incoming company. Like I'd said before, Yasha could hear a tick burp at fifty yards. Hearing a breathing human coming down the hall would be easy peasy. I was almost hoping that Eddie would come home so Ian could ask nicely for him to tell us what the hell he was up to. And if nicely didn't work, Yasha could hoist him upside down by one ankle. That'd always had an encouraging tendency to work.

Ian had found Eddie's laptop and I was going through papers on his organizational disaster of a desk, while occasionally peeking over Ian's shoulder. I'm a multitasking snoop.

Presently on the screen was what looked like some kind of schematic.

"What's that?" I asked.

"Just the specs for the glass in the window wall of the Sackler Wing."

So much for innocent. Eddie's computer was doing a fine job of proving him guilty. "That little son of a bitch."

"Yeah."

"So you're saying that *Eddie* is our criminal mastermind?"

"Hardly. More like a man on the inside of SPI."

Yasha's growl was rippling, drawn out, and perfectly conveyed his feelings.

Ian grunted. "Couldn't agree more, buddy. You got anything?" he asked me.

The contents of the top of Eddie's desk had yielded if not pay dirt, at least something worth sharing. "Looks like Eddie's developed a sudden interest in Russia's last royal family."

"Sounds promising."

"Maybe I just haven't reached the promised layer yet. Yasha, some of these books are in Russian." I picked up four old-looking books with cracked leather bindings, and handed them over. "Would you see if you can find any juicy parts? One has a lot of photos of handwritten pages."

"Eddie can read Russian?" Ian asked.

"There's a ton of yellow Post-its attached to the pages," I said. "Comments are written in English. Unless Eddie has someone else making notes for him, it appears there's quite a few things we didn't know about him."

I started speed-reading both the Post-its and the loose printouts of whatever I found that was in English. I ran across a couple of pages that'd been copied from handwritten Russian originals, and passed those off to Yasha.

We worked quickly and in silence for several minutes.

"I may have something," Yasha said.

I went over to have a look.

"These are copies of letters from Rasputin to Alexandra. He tells her that he bought what she wanted, though it took all of the gold she gave him." Yasha ran his finger down the page to the end. "Then here he promises to be back at court in three weeks and he will bring the two eggs with him—for young Alexei."

"I don't think he's talking about either the fresh-laid variety or Fabergé," I said.

"Agreed," Ian said.

I scanned the page Yasha held, trying to will the Cyrillic letters to turn to something I could read myself. "I don't suppose it says what color those eggs are?"

"*Nyet.*"

"So the Romanovs didn't get the Dragon Eggs in one convenient carton," I said. "They had to collect them, just like Viktor Kain. Think Rasputin might have gotten a line on a way to heal Alexei? He was the heir, he had hemophilia, and his parents were willing to move heaven and earth to find a cure, and they had more than enough money to do it."

"Rasputin was rumored to be a wizard of black magic," Yasha told us. "It was said to be how he had gained power over Nicholas and Alexandra. He claimed to be a healer."

And being an evil wizard would explain those freaky crazy eyes I'd seen in that photo online.

"Maybe he had 'gem mage' on his resume, too," I said. "Or considering that he couldn't cure Alexei, maybe he just fancied himself one. Either way, he couldn't deliver on his promise. What's the date on that letter?"

"October 7, 1916."

"About three weeks from Halloween," I noted. "The timing's right for him to try to use the diamonds to heal Alexei. Though Russians wouldn't have known it as Halloween, but if Rasputin was a wizard with contacts in the elven or goblin realms, he'd have known when the barriers would be the thinnest and the diamonds would be the strongest." I remembered something else. "And it was about two months before his bullet-riddled body was found tied up and weighted down in a frozen river. Russian aristocrats trying to save the monarchy supposedly did the deed, though it danged near took them all night to finally kill the guy. I wonder if that could've been fueled by a smidgen of royal disappointment at Rasputin failing to cure Alexei. It's one of those things that make you go hmm."

Ian was only half hearing me; he was staring out the room's one window. Now, just because I was a history buff, I didn't expect everyone else would be enthralled. My little factoids didn't have any bearing on our problem. But still.

Then I realized Ian wasn't staring out the window; he was looking at something on the windowsill.

What on earth?

Ian went to the window and I followed.

A pigeon statue?

On a side table by the window was another one. Eddie had been using it as a paperweight.

Ian opened the window.

On the fire escape was a birdcage. Not the kind for keeping pet birds; this one was for trapping birds.

There was a live pigeon inside next to some scraps of bread and a few peanuts.

"One trapped pigeon plus two stone pigeons." I did the math and got a completely unexpected conclusion. "*Eddie?* It couldn't be."

"A monkey demon spit in his eye, my ass," Ian snarled.

"Someone's been practicing," I said. "Or else, snacking on pigeons between meals."

Eddie Laughlin was our gorgon.

16

"EDDIE the Gorgon," I said, trying it out. "Okay, I'm sorry, but that just sounds ridiculous."

We'd freed the pigeon, and Ian had called Ms. Sagadraco yet again, this time to drop the bomb that one of her security consultants was a gorgon, and an indiscriminate killer of people and pigeons. When Ian finished his call, he'd run into the tiny kitchen and come out with a handful of those big, black trash bags. "Yasha, watch the front door."

The big Russian gave a grim nod and an affirmative grunt as he pulled on gloves.

Gloves? Huh?

"What are you doing?" I asked my partner.

Ian cleared Eddie's desk of papers with a single rake of his arm, dumping everything in a garbage bag. "Getting the evidence and getting out." He tossed me a bag. "Get to it."

I did. "We're scared of Eddie? But we're wearing glasses."

"And one touch from Eddie on bare skin will get you just

as stoned as a stare. I'd rather not go hand to hand with him right now."

Oh yeah.

Oh shit. That was why Yasha had gloved up.

Then I remembered what Helena Thanos had said about the only way to kill a gorgon. "When you were ransacking the kitchen," I asked Ian, "you didn't happen to have seen a big-ass knife, did you?"

My partner answered my question with another question. "Yasha?"

The Russian reached behind his head and under the collar of his leather coat—and pulled out a freakin' machete.

So much for whether Ian and Yasha knew how to dispatch a gorgon. I felt safer already.

I started shoveling. And while I shoveled, I thought out loud. "So Eddie killed Denny?"

"That's what I'm going with."

"So that was Eddie out there watching us."

"Stands to reason." Ian scooped up the laptop and dug around under the desk until he found a messenger bag Eddie must have used as a case.

I didn't need Ian to tell me that the only reason Eddie probably hadn't gone for three outs in Central Park was that we were ready for a gorgon. We had glasses and guns—and a werewolf with a machete who was about two days shy of going furry. Silver bullets wouldn't kill a gorgon, but it'd put a hurtin' on him long enough for Yasha to do his thing.

Right now I almost wished Eddie would come home. A good, old-fashioned ass kicking could be delivered via boot, no hands needed. Because in addition to Denny—whom I didn't think many, if any, people would miss—Eddie had killed Sebastian du Beckett, an old man who'd taken Ben Sadler under his wing and kept the boss happy with high-quality sparklies.

"Sebastian du Beckett would have just let Eddie in the house this morning," I said. "The old guy trusted him. No wonder he was killed sitting behind his desk; he didn't suspect a thing. Why would Eddie kill Sebastian du Beckett? He worked for the guy, liked him even."

"Ms. Sagadraco said Bastian had a keen eye for new talent," Ian replied. "What if Eddie checked in this morning and du Beckett knew on first sight that Eddie's eye problems weren't from monkey demon spit? He probably recognized gorgonism when he saw it. Eddie had to kill him to keep his secret."

I stopped shoveling and stuffing. "Wait a minute. I'd never seen a gorgon before this morning." I waved my fingers around my head. "Kenji said the whole snake-hair thing is a myth, but that's what I saw going on with Helena Thanos's aura. At the museum, I just saw a thick film over Eddie's usual aura caused by the magic monkey spit. Eddie had to know there were people who'd realize he was a gorgon. Maybe he actually did goad a monkey demon to spit in his eye, just for the aura disguise, and to give him a real excuse to wear dark glasses. Eddie being our gorgon also means that Helena Thanos was right. Mr. du Beckett knew his killer, and it was a young gorgon. Eddie must have been turned recently."

"He came back last Thursday from three weeks in Thailand on a buying trip for du Beckett."

"And while he was there, he made a new friend."

"More like really pissed them off. If he did get infected in Thailand, that Thai gorgon could have turned him to stone, but gave him gorgonism instead."

I thought of Miss Helena and what she'd said about the curse being an eternal damnation and worse than Hell. "Whatever comes after 'pissed off' must have been what Eddie did." Then I realized what he was doing now. "Eddie's a new gorgon looking for a cure."

"Uh-huh," Ian said. "Once I get this laptop to Kenji, I imagine he's going to find a lot of searches on cures for gorgonism."

"Rasputin used the Dragon Eggs to try to heal Alexei," I said. "It didn't work. Eddie's a gorgon looking for a cure. From all these papers and books lying around here, he must know the Dragon Eggs didn't cure the tsar's son. Why would Eddie think the diamonds would work for him?"

A proverbial ton of bricks fell on my head.

Holy crap.

"Alexei was human; Eddie's a gorgon, but even before he got infected he wasn't human. He's an elf/goblin hybrid, a supernatural. Like the goblins who have been using the Queen of Dreams to heal for thousands of years. Since there's no known cure for gorgonism, that diamond would be his only hope."

"Eddie's a smart guy," Ian said, "and he's got some connections, but a harpy-wrangling, criminal mastermind he's not." My partner thought of something, swore, and kicked one of the three full garbage bags over to the door where Yasha was tossing them into the hall. "And last night I told him where we were taking Ben Sadler."

"*He* sent that harpy after us?"

Ian shook his head. "Not his job. His job was to be the inside man in SPI. He and his *real* boss had to have seen us leaving with Ben."

"Eddie offered his car."

"And when he couldn't get Ben into his car, he asked where we were taking him, and like an idiot, I told him."

"Hey, we all trusted Eddie."

"But I was the one to do everything but stick a bow on the kid's head. Ben attacking those harpies must have been a lifetime of Christmas presents rolled into one. They'd found their gem mage; now all they had to do was snatch him."

"And Eddie told someone on his earpiece that he'd be

right there," I said. "What you wanna bet he wasn't talking to any of our people?"

"Or no one at all. Just an excuse to leave fast once we wouldn't put Ben in his car."

"To run back into the Sackler Wing to report to the guy who's been pulling *all* of our strings." This still wasn't making any sense. "The goblin diamond cures goblins, elves, all supernaturals. The elf diamond negates magic. I could see a lack of magic as being a bad thing, but curing?"

Ian stopped. "Curing who?"

"Uh . . . supernaturals."

"And curing them from what?" He asked it like he already knew the answer.

The lightbulb in my head came on, and I looked at my partner in dawning horror.

"From the diseases that made us what we are." It was Yasha. He was standing by the door, a full garbage bag held by suddenly loose fingers. He dropped it to the floor. "To be cured would make me what I used to be many years ago, a human man." He looked at us—disbelief and fear in his eyes. "A ninety-six-year-old human man."

Oh. Oh no. No, no.

Yasha didn't need to say anything else. We knew.

He'd be cured of being a werewolf, but the shock of it would probably kill a ninety-six-year-old human.

"Moreau," Yasha said, his voice a quiet rumble. "And all others."

As with werewolves, vampirism was a disease, spread through blood. Alain Moreau would be cured of being a vampire; but as a human, he was centuries old. He'd be instantly reduced to bones.

I plopped down on Eddie's couch. My legs didn't really want to hold me up right now.

Miss Helena? She'd be dust.

"Ms. Sagadraco," I whispered. "A disease didn't make

her a dragon, but she uses magic to hide what she is. The elf diamond negates magic. If that happened, she wouldn't be able to hide. Everyone would know she's a dragon."

Ian nodded. "If Ben is forced to activate those diamonds at midnight, every supernatural within their range will lose their ability to use magical glamours to hide what they are." He put the final piece in place, and we could see it all. "Viktor Kain brought the Dragon Eggs to New York. Vivienne Sagadraco's territory, SPI headquarters, home to the world's largest concentration of supernaturals and undead. Viktor Kain wants to destroy everything the boss ever built, and force her into hiding—or to be hunted down."

It wouldn't take the military long to find a dragon as large as Vivienne Sagadraco. As soon as a blue dragon the length of three city buses was seen flying over New York or anywhere else, I guarantee the military would get involved. I remembered back to the night I'd first seen the boss go dragon. It'd happened inside headquarters; she had to fight a male grendel and dozens of his hatchlings. Vivienne Sagadraco's head had nearly reached the top of the fourth story. Later that night, she and her sister Tiamat had battled in the skies over Times Square. They'd each had a device to make them invisible to humans. If all magic was negated, even that wouldn't save her. My *King Kong* analogy came back to me. Biplanes with machines guns buzzing around him like hornets. Substitute Ms. Sagadraco for King Kong . . .

The modern U.S. military used fighter jets with not only guns, but rockets, missiles, and bombs. With technology that could find terrorists in caves, they'd have no problem locating a dragon anywhere in the world.

"When Ben touched those diamonds, every supernatural in Manhattan and two other boroughs felt it," I said. "It could 'heal' all those undead and expose every supernatural in that area."

"Or further. Ben only touched the harpy that held the diamonds."

"And whoever Eddie's working for promised to cure him, meaning they plan to use the Dragon Eggs for the exact same thing. So why hasn't Viktor Kain flown home with his scaly tail between his legs?"

"He still has time to leave."

"How are we going to find those diamonds?"

Yasha had all three bags clenched in his huge hands, his eyes glittering gold with determination. "First we must warn our people, then we find the diamonds, and the *real* monster who would murder us all."

17

BAD news travels fast.

News of imminent supernatural Armageddon breaks the sound barrier.

It was eight o'clock Halloween night. While humans dressed up as vampires and werewolves would be coming into the city for parties, the real deal was getting the hell out of town. Part of me wished I could have been leaving with them; the other half knew that while fake monsters would be out partying until the wee hours, many vamps and weres—considered real monsters by humans—would be dying permanently at midnight.

Four hours from now.

Four hours and we still didn't know where Ben Sadler and the Dragon Eggs were.

Since it was Halloween, the chaos wouldn't start immediately at midnight, but when morning came and the humans took their makeup off, the supernaturals wouldn't be able to put their glamours back on. Those who didn't turn to dust would be exposed to every human who saw them. Manhattan and the other boroughs would be turned into the urban version of villagers with torches and pitchforks.

It was going to get nasty.

The three of us had gotten out of Eddie's apartment with three trash bags full of evidence and hopefully a computer with the location of the bitch and/or bastard behind this, Ben Sadler, and the Dragon Eggs. If we couldn't find the diamonds and stop their activation, that location would become ground zero for the largest mass murder in the history of the supernatural world.

Fortunately for the fate of the world, Eddie's apartment wasn't far from SPI headquarters, and Yasha had never been more determined to get us all there with all of our pieces and parts intact.

We did a conference call from the speeding SUV. The three of us summarized what we'd found and what we feared it meant to the boss, Alain Moreau, and Bob and Rob, aka the Roberts.

Bob, Rob, and their team would be waiting to take in the trash.

SPI's Research team had the best analytical minds Vivienne Sagadraco could lure away from the human private and government sectors, and from the courts of the supernatural realms. They'd absorb the evidence, and hopefully shoot our theory down in flames. I'd love to see that. God, we hoped we were wrong, but my gut was telling me that it would be even worse than we'd imagined. After all, it was supposed to have been Viktor Kain's show. The only difference now being that the supernatural Armageddon had a different ringmaster.

Yasha pulled into a private parking garage on West Third Street a block from Washington Square Park, and began taking what I call the corkscrew route to the lowest level. Turn the steering wheel to the left and pretty much leave it there. It'd always made me queasy and unfortunately this time wasn't the exception.

At the bottom, Yasha pulled into a parking space near the back of the garage between two concrete columns and pushed a button on the dash. It was a hydraulic lift cleverly disguised as a parking space. The SUV was lowered into one of the city's many abandoned subway tunnels SPI had paved and converted to an access road to the headquarters complex.

Bob and Rob were waiting with what looked like a hospital laundry hamper. We tossed the trash bags in, and they headed for the freight elevator up to the office level. No one spoke. If we were a little less than four hours away from what we thought was going to happen, none of us were in the mood to exchange chitchat.

Me, Ian, and Yasha took the passenger elevator up to the bull pen. Normally, Yasha would stay with his vehicle to oversee it being prepped to go back out, but the rules had been thrown out the window. Your priorities changed when you might only have a few hours to live. Yasha wasn't going down without a fight.

We weren't going to let Yasha down.

————— **18**

JUST as Vivienne Sagadraco rarely left the executive suite, Kenji Hayashi simply felt better about the world and his place in it when he stayed as close to his beloved computers as possible. He was only a keystroke away from every agent at SPI New York, and another few clicks from every SPI agency office around the world. While each office had a chief technology agent—Kenji's official title—no one had anyone like him.

He was what every other SPI CTA wanted to be when they grew up.

Kenji wasn't at what I called his computer command center when the elevator doors opened.

He was waiting for us at the elevator doors.

"That it?" The elf indicated the messenger bag Ian wore across his chest because he wasn't letting it out of his sight.

Ian slipped the bag's strap over his head and handed it over without a word.

Kenji accepted it with a sharp nod and a fierce grin

directed at Yasha. "Want to watch me wring data out of this thing until is squeals for its motherboard?"

For the first time since we broke into Eddie's apartment, Yasha Kazakov smiled.

There was one thing Eddie's laptop refused to squeal—the name of the thief.

"There should be e-mails between Eddie and this white-cat-petting evil genius," Kenji spat. The fierce grin was history once he'd scored a big goose egg tracking down the identity of the baby gorgon's keeper. "What'd they do, write letters?"

We'd pulled up chairs around Kenji's main workstation, taking what time we could to sit down.

"Some people don't trust e-mail when they're trying to destroy the world," Ian said. "Apparently the last stupid thing Eddie did was piss off a gorgon. He's gotten a little smarter since then."

"He left his laptop and a ton of printouts in his apartment," I pointed out.

"I said a little."

"Could there be another computer?" Yasha asked.

"There could be," Kenji said, "but I doubt it. Other than missing e-mail between Eddie and the cat-petting Bond villain, this laptop's got everything you'd expect a guy to have, including links to some truly twisted porn sites. Good thing Eddie's a gorgon now; I wouldn't want to look him in the eye again. What we *do* have is an extensive search for boat rentals along the lower section of the East River. It looks like Eddie decided on one place in particular. There's also orders for a generator, work lights, search for wholesale meat distributors, and order confirmations on camping gear, including water purification tablets."

I grimaced at the thing that stood out to me. "Meat?"

"Wherever they are, they're feeding something that likes raw meat and a lot of it, and I don't think it's the kitty cat."

"That would be harpies," Ian said. "They're carrion feeders."

Kenji referenced the screen. "Ten sides of beef worth of carrion?"

I whistled.

"It just means that there's probably more than harpies guarding those diamonds and Ben," Ian said, "or at least more than three harpies."

"We couldn't handle the three that came at us this morning," I said. Jeez, had it only been this morning?

Ian leaned forward, scanning the screen. "All of that adds up to someplace you can only get to by boat, or it would be faster and have less chance of being seen, with no electricity, questionable or no shelter, iffy water—"

"And no Chinese takeout for harpies," Yasha said.

We all looked at him.

The Russian werewolf gave us a weak grin. "I try for laughs, too. It is best medicine, no?"

Screw the workplace hands-off policy; this guy was getting a hug. I stood up, used both arms, and I still couldn't get around the big guy's shoulders. "We're gonna stop this," I said against the top of his head. "It's not going to happen."

"Damn right it's not," Ian said. "The guy with the cat is gonna pay for even thinking about doing this."

"It'd stand to reason that Eddie would have gotten a boat from a rental place that was close to his destination," Kenji said, "but it doesn't mean that the closest potential location would be the lair."

"Lair?" I asked.

"We've got an evil mastermind bent on supernatural world domination or destruction, right?"

"Pretty much."

"IMO, that warrants the use of 'lair.'"

I couldn't argue with that logic.

Ian leaned forward. "Where's the boat rental place he used?"

"Near South Street Seaport," Kenji said while calling it up on Google Maps.

"Give me a broader view."

Kenji did and the East River came into view, along with a chunk of Brooklyn and Queens.

"I'm still pretty new in town," I said. "Are we seeing any likely lair candidates?"

"Entirely too many candidates," Ian said. "There are a lot of abandoned buildings, big and small, all up and down the Brooklyn waterfront, starting with the Red Hook Grain Terminal. Fifty-four circular grain silos and more for your hiding and lairing pleasure, closed since 1965. Then there's the ironic candidate. The Red Hook Warehouses on Imlay Street. Built in 1913; closed 1983. There're two of them. Christie's bought one and turned it into a high-tech, high-security art storage facility. The other is still empty."

"Ben's employer," I said.

"Uh-huh. And there are a couple of islands about twelve miles to the north. You've got Riker's, which I think we can safely eliminate due to the prison. Then there's North and South Brother Islands. South Brother doesn't have any buildings, meaning it also doesn't have anywhere to hide. North Brother was uninhabited until 1885, when a hospital was built there for people with contagious diseases."

"That one's got a big ol' dose of irony, too."

Ian nodded. "Typhoid Mary was an unwilling guest there for twenty years. Some people say between the patients who died there and the steamship fire victims, the island is haunted."

"Steamship fire?"

"In 1904, the *General Slocum* caught fire in the East River near there. Over a thousand people, mostly women and children on their way to a church picnic, died either by fire or drowning. The ship's fire hoses were rotten, the lifeboats tied in place, and the life jackets were rotted cork and canvas. I read somewhere that the manufacturer brought the jackets up to the minimum weight requirements by putting iron bars inside. Mothers were strapping their children in and throwing them overboard only to have them sink, not float. The *General Slocum* beached on North Brother, and a lot of the bodies washed up there. Said to be the largest loss of life in New York until 9/11."

Holy crap.

"The hospital was used for various purposes over the years, the last being a youth heroin treatment facility that closed in 1963 due to abuses and corruption. The island's been off-limits to the public ever since."

Kenji's phone rang. He picked it up and answered. "Yes, sir. They're here. I'll tell them."

"That was Moreau," he said. "Meeting, right now, main conference room. All of us."

19

SPI'S big conference room looked like a miniature version of the Security Council Room at the UN. There was even a big, U-shaped table in the center.

Bob Fitzwilliam and Rob Stanton were the codirectors of SPI New York's Research department. They were the go-to guys for esoteric, obscure, and occult knowledge, legends, and myths, which SPI calls history—all the lowdown on creatures of the night and critters of the day.

Bob and Rob were the kind of guys who believed in hitting you with the bad news first, then presenting options or solutions to make it not seem like the end of the world. This time the bad news actually was the end of the world, and there wasn't any way the boys could spin that to make it sound better.

Their team of analysts hadn't needed to go through all of Eddie's papers with a fine-toothed comb. A quick review had confirmed the theory they'd come up with in their own research into the diamonds that made up the Dragon Eggs.

I'd really hoped my and Ian's theory would be so far out there that it'd give you a nosebleed. No such luck. We were right on the money—for the basics.

There was more.

Yes, it was worse.

And it had started almost a hundred years ago.

Rob shared my love of history. He'd already told Vivienne Sagadraco the shortened version of what he'd discovered in the letters we'd found at Eddie's apartment. While the boss agreed that it was of monumental historical significance, our meeting needed to stick to what the Dragon Eggs could do, not how far Viktor Kain had been willing to go to get his hands on them.

So right before the meeting, Rob told me what he'd found.

In the early morning hours of July 17, 1918, the Romanov family was murdered.

And Viktor Kain was responsible.

In Imperial Russia under the tsars, real power was bestowed on the few and the favored.

Viktor Kain wasn't one of the few, and he'd never been anyone's favorite, so he joined the many who were sowing the seeds of revolution. His flair for intimidation and ruthlessness, and his total hatred for the ruling class, gained the admiration of a young revolutionary—Vladimir Lenin.

As Lenin's star rose, so did Viktor Kain, though the dragon used an alias and was careful to keep his involvement deep in the shadows. He'd learned about the existence of the Dragon Eggs directly from a drunkenly boasting Grigori Rasputin—and when Viktor Kain had learned, he'd coveted.

When Rasputin had failed to cure Alexei with the Dragon Eggs, and after the mad monk's death, the Empress Alexandra had planned to put the diamonds into the royal treasury, but when it became apparent that their days of freedom were numbered and they would be taken from the capital, she kept the diamonds on her person at all times.

When the royal family was taken into Bolshevik custody and removed from St. Petersburg, Viktor Kain knew that the empress had to have taken the Dragon Eggs with her. At this time, rescue by White Russian troops sympathetic to the tsar was a real possibility. Kain couldn't risk the Romanovs being rescued and taken from Russia—and the Dragon Eggs along with them. He goaded Lenin into ordering the family executed, also telling him that the empress had taken some of the royal jewels with her. Kain offered to go to Ipatiev House in Yekaterinburg to personally ensure that the execution orders were carried out, reclaim the "property of the people" in Lenin's name, and return to Moscow with the Romanov jewels.

During their imprisonment, Alexandra and her four daughters—the Grand Duchesses Olga, Tatiana, Maria, and Anastasia—had sewn the family diamonds and jewels into their corsets, thinking that their persons would not be searched; and should they be rescued, they would need the money to fund their life in exile.

Viktor Kain had thought out his plan and considered every contingency. What he hadn't factored in was White Russian troops getting entirely too close to Yekaterinburg. The possibility of the city being taken and the royal family rescued was too much to risk. The timetable for the executions was moved up.

In the early morning hours of July 17, 1918—before Viktor Kain could get there—the Romanovs and their few servants were awakened and taken down to the cramped basement of Ipatiev House. The men on the firing squad were drunk, having been drinking vodka all night in an attempt to find the courage to kill the royal family. As a result, when the first shot was fired, any discipline they might have had went to hell and what was supposed to be an execution turned into a bloody slaughter.

The bullets ricocheted off the diamond-lined corsets like

modern bulletproof vests. The empress had been killed by a single bullet to the left side of her head, but her daughters survived the initial volley, and were finished off with dull bayonets, rifle butts, and bullets to the head.

The superintendent of Ipatiev House, Yakov Yurovsky, was a jeweler and watchmaker by trade and on the night of the executions he was determined to find the Romanov diamonds—especially the Dragon Eggs.

When the bodies were taken to the shallow mineshaft outside the city where they were to be stripped and buried, it became apparent why the daughters had been so difficult to kill. There were seventeen pounds of diamonds and other jewelry sewn into their corsets. Yurovsky caught his men pilfering the bodies, but had made them hand over what they'd stolen, telling them that they would be shot immediately if they failed to comply.

The men handed over what they had stolen.

No diamonds matching the description of the Dragon Eggs were ever found.

It would take Viktor Kain nearly a hundred years to track down and gather them all again.

"The elven Eye of Destiny neutralizes magic in all forms in the affected area," Bob was telling those of us called to the meeting, which, in addition to the boss and Moreau, not surprisingly included the SPI's monster hunter/commando commanders Sandra Niles and Roy Benoit. The combat boots were about to hit the pavement, or boat deck as the case might be.

"This would include stripping the glamours from those supernaturals who use them to hide what they are from humans," Bob continued.

"How long will the effect last?" Vivienne Sagadraco asked.

"Unknown. Elven gem mages are closely bonded with

their stones, and have the stamina to prolong the effects as needed. It's the same for the size of the affected area. Under normal circumstances, this could be anywhere from just a few feet away, to the length and width of a battlefield. The gem mage puts a little or a lot into the activation depending on how far they need the influence to extend." Bob looked to Caera Filarion. "I understand Ben Sadler has been tested at a level ten."

"With no experience," Caera said. "And even less control. He runs wide-open. The most accurate comparison would be one of the city's water mains versus a tsunami—one controlled; the other a raw and deadly force of nature. As strong as Mr. Sadler's gift is, he would only need to touch the diamonds. It's possible that the thief wouldn't even need to have his cooperation; he simply needs to be conscious. Clenched fingers can be opened, then forced closed again."

Roy Benoit swore under his breath. "The boy could even be hog-tied and fire up those rocks."

"From the Dragon Eggs' reaction at the museum, we have no reason to believe otherwise."

"So our job is to separate Ben Sadler from those eggs and keep him that way."

"Yes."

"What if we can't physically reach Mr. Sadler in time?" Sandra Niles addressed her question directly to Vivienne Sagadraco and no one else.

The room was silent.

Sandra was asking for permission to kill Ben Sadler.

I found myself holding my breath even though I knew what the answer was; what it had to be. The life of one sacrificed for so many others. There was no choice, no question. I knew Sandra and Roy would give that order only as a last resort, but Sandra needed that command to come from the top.

"Mr. Sadler is not an enemy combatant in this situation," Vivienne Sagadraco said. "He is a captive. Our goal is and will always be the preservation and protection of innocent lives." She paused. "That being said, we must prevent the activation of the Dragon Eggs by *any* means necessary. You have your orders."

"Yes, ma'am."

There it was.

Vivienne Sagadraco didn't need to say neutralize, eliminate, kill, sacrifice, or any number of ways to say put a bullet through Ben Sadler's head if his hands come close to those diamonds. She didn't have to. We all knew. Only a few of us had even met Ben, but the silence was for him—and the knowledge that it could be any agent in SPI who was being forced to use a lethal talent against their will. Kill orders were not given lightly, but when they had to be given, Vivienne Sagadraco would not flinch—at least not outwardly.

"Mr. Fitzsimmons," the boss said, breaking the silence. "Your report on the goblin diamond?"

Bob had to drink some water before he could continue. "Both diamonds work for any and all supernaturals or humans infected by supernaturals. The Queen of Dreams will return humans infected by supernatural beings back to their human state. This includes vampirism, gorgonism, and those bitten by werewolves. As far as we know, there are no exceptions. And once enacted, the effects are irreversible."

Silence.

Supernaturals stripped of their ability to hide what they were from their human neighbors; the undead instantly returned to mortal humans, but keeping all of the years, decades, or centuries that their mortal bodies would have aged—turning them instantly into extreme old age, bones, or dust.

Half of the people in this room would die at midnight.

"And the five diamonds from this realm?" the boss asked.

Bob cleared his throat. "Right. The other five diamonds do nothing."

"Nothing?"

"Well, not exactly nothing. They are stones of power, but unlike the other two, they lack a focus. Gems like these tend to be called cursed by humans because unfocused power is naturally destructive. Tonight the barriers between the dimensions will be at their thinnest, and the goblin and elven diamonds will be at their strongest. When activated, those five diamonds will act as power boosters or amplifiers for the goblin and elven diamonds. Based on what our colleagues from the goblin and elven courts have told us, one amplifying diamond would be enough of a boost to cover a ten-mile radius."

"Ten?" Roy Benoit said, dumbfounded.

Bob took a little breath. It was clear he didn't want to say what he had to say next. "Five diamonds would extend that influence to fifty miles."

Stunned didn't even begin to describe the expressions I saw around that table.

"I sincerely wish I could tell you that was all, but . . ."

"Go on, Robert." Vivienne Sagadraco was the very picture of calm. A woman who, like a sea captain, was prepared to go down with her ship.

"There are ley lines involved. For those unfamiliar, a quick explanation. Ley lines are narrow, intersecting 'streams' that magnify magical and paranormal energies. There are a few in our immediate area." Bob nodded to Rob, who touched the screen of the tablet on the table in front of him. A map of Manhattan and the surrounding area was projected on the wall. Bright blue laser-looking lines ran through the five boroughs every which way. Two lines were thicker than the others.

Bob indicated the two thick lines. "One ley line runs north and south roughly along the East River. Another runs more east to west. The east/west ley line runs directly beneath this complex. It was one of the reasons why this location was chosen. Correct, Ms. Sagadraco?"

"Yes."

"Those possessing earth magic can tap a microscopic amount of power from ley lines, but they are unable to use the lines to magnify and spread their magic." He paused. "Diamonds, like ley lines, are of and from the earth. Those rare diamonds that are imbued with power can tap directly into ley lines to carry and spread the power they contain like an underground river."

Rob touched the tablet again and a red dot appeared at a point along the north/south ley line. An instant later, it completely overspread the blue ley lines with pulsing red.

"Two locations—North Brother Island and the Red Hook Warehouse—have not one, but two ley lines: a major artery and a smaller capillary. The larger and more powerful runs north to south; the weaker one, though still of significant power, runs east to west. They intersect near these two locations. We believe that one of these is where the Dragon Eggs will be activated."

"We can't narrow it further?" the boss asked.

"Not with the information we have, ma'am."

"Then we'll cover both. How far will the effects travel once the ley lines pick up the diamonds' magic, channel, and carry it?"

"We conservatively estimate that the power of the combined diamonds, plus the strength of the ley lines, will extend the fallout, if you will, to roughly the entire tristate area, and perhaps a bit beyond."

Holy mother of God.

Tens of thousands of supernaturals.

"We will dispatch teams to both locations," Vivienne

Sagadraco said. "Again, prevent this event by any means necessary." She turned to Alain Moreau. "We need to evacuate every supernatural in the city and beyond."

Ian leaned over to me. "Those things aren't diamonds; they're time bombs."

20

SPI HQ was now running RTC.

Round the clock.

Problem was the clock wasn't going to make it around before what was going to happen happened. Not shit-hits-the-fan big. This was cataclysmic.

In less than three hours, the Dragon Eggs would cure the undead of New York right out of existence, and strip the secret identities off of every supernatural being to leave them as naked and vulnerable as the day they were born.

Supernaturals in New York, New Jersey, and Connecticut were being told to leave. Now.

Vivienne Sagadraco called a fast all-hands briefing.

Every agent, researcher, and lab tech was gathered in the bull pen, looking up at the second-story catwalk. I was on the edge of the bull pen, toward the front, Ian and Yasha on either side. Kenji was close along with the Dorgan twins. For once they weren't being creepy, and they weren't standing next to each other as they nearly always did. They were standing on either side of the elf tech, their faces set in grim determination.

The boss was there, Alain Moreau by her side.

We knew what was coming—the evacuation order, not only for every supernatural in the area, but for supernatural SPI agents as well.

Yasha had informed us that he wasn't going anywhere.

The silence had been absolute as Vivienne Sagadraco had told them what we faced.

"The alert has gone out on all communication channels in the supernatural community to leave the city if they can, and if they can't, to make themselves and their families secure where they are. Remaining in a secure place applies *only* to those who are using glamours to protect their identities. Those immortals who were turned from a human are being ordered to leave immediately. If the Dragon Eggs are not found before midnight, every vampire or were within the area of influence will become mortal again. If you were twenty years old when you were turned a century ago, at midnight you will be a one-hundred-and-twenty-year-old human. You will die and be reduced to bone within seconds. Those older will be reduced to dust."

Vivienne Sagadraco paused to let her words sink in.

"I founded SPI with the mission of protecting supernaturals. That mission has never been more in force than right now. This mission is even closer to my heart when it comes to you—each and every one of you. You have stood ready to put your lives on the line every day. I will not see you remain here and forfeit your lives should we fail in the task set before us tonight. I want every agent in this room who was once mortal to leave the city. Now. I am determined not to fail, and will do everything in my power to prevent this. But should the worst come to pass, I will know that you are safe. As you have never disobeyed me before, do not disobey me now. Leave the city. I do not know when—or if—it will be safe to return. Regardless, we will regroup, and we will continue in our mission until those who brought this night upon us are brought to justice."

Naturally, she wouldn't say one word to indicate that she was in worse danger than almost any of them.

"Are there any questions?"

Vivienne Sagadraco carefully surveyed her people, ostensibly looking for raised hands. I knew different. She had either handpicked or approved each and every one of them before they were hired, and was now memorizing their faces as if it were the last time she would ever see them, either because they would be dead, or she would be forced to flee or be hunted down.

We were her family.

Family wasn't only people you shared DNA with. You couldn't pick those; and God knows sometimes you wanted to unpick rotten fruit from your family tree. Vivienne Sagadraco knew about that, too. She'd shared a nest with Tiamat.

Family was who you shared a mission and a goal with; who you shared life and faced death with. For many of the men and women gathered here, SPI was the only family they had who knew what their job truly was, a job they could never reveal to others.

SPI was created to protect and to serve, and at no time in its history would that be more true than during the next three hours.

The two commando teams, made up of a dozen men and women, a mix of human, supernatural, and immortal, were lined along the back walls, closest to the stairs that would take them down to their transport.

Since some of their numbers were immortals, Roy and Sandra had recruited extra agents to take their places if the Dragon Eggs were activated. The mission wouldn't end after that happened. The ultimate goal would not change—get those diamonds.

Or kill Ben Sadler.

Ian had put us within quick access to an exit. The instant the last word passed the boss's lips, he opened the door and pulled me through, Yasha on our heels.

The fastest way for the teams to get to the Red Hook Warehouse or North Brother Island would be to fly over and rappel out. But since 9/11, heavily armed men and women rappelling out of helicopters, or zipping around the city's waterways in high-speed boats, would get the same chilly reception—everything the NYPD and Coast Guard could throw at them, soon followed by federal reinforcements.

They had to get in and they couldn't be seen. Speed was critical, but so was stealth.

Roy Benoit's team would be going out from the South Street Seaport area. Party boats were always going out from there. Tonight was Halloween; they'd be just another two-boats-load of partiers going out for a midnight cruise.

The boss had arranged for Sandra Niles and her team to have a private charter from a marina on the Upper East Side.

Since masks tended to raise suspicion, even on Halloween, our teams were going with a couples cruise theme. The team members would pair off in any configuration they saw fit to complete a disguise. They couldn't travel as fast as they wanted to; zipping up or across the East River at the speed they needed to go would just get them pulled over. When you were carrying body armor and enough munitions to start and finish your own war, you tended not to get off with a slap on the wrist.

Once, I'd been allowed to go on a mission with the monster hunter teams. They'd taken me with them into the city's sewer and abandoned subway tunnels because as a seer I could tell ghoul from human and see grendels rendered invisible by an amulet that had been created with some science, but mostly magic. They'd needed me, so I had gone with them. Ian had been there, too—as the new seer's bodyguard.

They didn't need a seer this time, so Ian and I had been shut out, but hopefully we were about to get an assignment that'd be more productive than watching the clock.

Alain Moreau wanted to see us.

He'd asked us to meet him in the small conference room on the second floor.

Ian and I came up the stairs and stopped. There were two people having what wasn't exactly a fight, more like a polite disagreement.

Alain Moreau and Vivienne Sagadraco.

Moreau was only partially visible, standing in the hallway with his back half toward us. The boss must have been in the conference room.

". . . feared what I said would cause other agents of my age and condition to feel pressured to remain. Mine is a personal decision."

"You're staying." Ms. Sagadraco didn't ask it as a question.

"I am."

"And if I order you to leave?"

"Then I will disobey your order."

"What if I ask you as a friend?"

"As a friend, I would refuse you."

"You've never disobeyed me before."

"There is a first time for everything, Madame." I could hear the smile in his voice. "I can better serve you, SPI, and the community we protect from here—and here I will remain, by your side, where I belong."

"Regardless of the consequences?"

"I'm counting on you—and our people—being as good as I know you are."

We then witnessed an act we'd never seen before and were unlikely to witness again.

Vivienne Sagadraco stepped forward into the hallway, wrapped her arms around Alain Moreau, enfolding him in a hug. She then pulled back and kissed the French vampire on both cheeks.

"My dear and faithful friend," she whispered.

"Always at your service, Madame," Moreau replied quietly.

Vivienne Sagadraco smiled in a baring of teeth. "Let's get to work."

They had to have known we were just around the corner, but they didn't acknowledge us, so we did the same, preserving our plausible deniability of seeing my manager and boss show emotion.

Vivienne Sagadraco took the stairs at the other end of the hall.

"Be careful this evening, Agent Fraser," came the soft echo of her voice in my head. *"Tell Agent Byrne the same."*

So much for deniability. *"I will, ma'am. Please take care of yourself."* It was good that I wasn't talking out loud; I didn't think I could have gotten the words past the lump in my throat.

"Agents Byrne and Fraser," Moreau said without turning.

Busted again.

We showed ourselves in. Ian didn't acknowledge to Alain Moreau that we'd overheard anything, so I wisely followed the lead of my senior agent.

"I've received a call from the agents watching Viktor Kain," Moreau said. "His assistant has notified the hotel management that they will be checking out within the hour. He could be going to the airport."

"Not without his diamonds, he won't," Ian said.

One corner of Moreau's mouth quirked upward. "That is what we're counting on. I want you and Agents Fraser and Kazakov to follow him. Viktor Kain has had his people out looking for the Dragon Eggs, and one of them may have discovered their location. If he has made arrangements to travel to North Brother Island or to the Red Hook Warehouse, that would allow us to reroute one of our teams to reinforce the other. They will need it, because that will likely indicate that Viktor Kain means to fight to be the one to activate the Dragon Eggs."

I spoke up. "Sir, if he stays here, won't Viktor Kain get his magic and glamour zapped at midnight, too?"

"Unfortunately not. Kain's a multi-millennia-old gem mage. If he's the one to activate the diamonds, his proximity to them will actually act in his favor."

"The rocks won't bite the hand that unleashes them."

"Essentially." Moreau smiled, and his eyes glittered. "Though if Kain can't get to the diamonds, he'd better turn dragon and fly as far out over the Atlantic as he can." The vampire chuckled darkly. "In fact, if he values his life, he should keep going."

"Why's that?"

"If they haven't yet left the city, the sorcerers Kain lured here with the chance of buying the Dragon Eggs will have all of their considerable powers negated at midnight."

Ian whistled. I winced.

"Madame Sagadraco believes that was the true reason Viktor Kain said he would be selling the diamonds, to lure some of the most powerful sorcerers in this dimension and beyond out into the open."

"Kain is after more than revenge against Ms. Sagadraco," I said.

Moreau gave a single nod. "If we succeed this evening, our next order of business is to discover what Viktor Kain truly wants."

Ian grinned evilly. "If we succeed this evening, and the sorcerers on our most-wanted list catch up with him, Viktor Kain won't be a problem for anyone ever again."

21

IAN and I were in the backseat of one of New York's sixty gazillion yellow cabs.

Except this one was clean, with the latest communications equipment, some serious horses under the hood, and was being driven by an increasingly hairy Russian.

SPI had cabs. Who knew?

I'd learned something new tonight, though it made perfect sense. What better way to follow someone around the city than in a yellow cab.

Viktor Kain's dark sedan had left the Mandarin Oriental and we'd flowed into traffic soon after. When his driver turned left on Lexington Avenue, we were five car lengths away from doing the same.

"Time to change it up," Ian told Yasha.

The Russian pushed a button on the steering wheel.

Nothing happened—at least nothing that I could see.

"What was that?" I asked.

"It changes the roof lights. Kain or his driver will be checking for tails. We can't have them make us."

Yasha was doing his best impersonation of a New York cabdriver, meaning he was making an effort to dial back his aggression. For death-defying maneuvers, New York cabbies had nothing on the werewolf, whom SPI's other drivers called Kamakazi Kazakov.

I always carried chewable, orange-flavored Dramamine in my purse. I probably should eat one right now. If Kain's driver thought he was being followed and started doing vehicular acrobatics, I'd be wishing I had because there was no way in heaven, hell, or Hoboken that Yasha—or me or Ian—was going to let Viktor Kain get away.

"He has to know our people will follow him," I said to Ian.

"He does. We haven't been spotted, but he'll still take precautions. He's due for a car change anytime now."

I sat up straighter. "Then how are we going to stay with him?"

Yasha rolled down his window. "Big dragons stink. I can smell them a mile away."

Huh?

I'd been close enough to the boss on numerous occasions to get a good whiff. I thought she smelled nice, but maybe werewolves thought—

"He means male dragons," Ian clarified, at my apparently obvious confusion. "If Kain's going to the airport, he won't change cars or give a damn that he's being followed." My partner's smile was a flash of white in the dark backseat. "If he changes cars, the bastard is up to something and we're going to find out what and where it is."

Viktor Kain's driver pulled the sedan into a parking garage off East Twenty-third Street.

"Change number one, coming up. Looks like our boy's not leaving town."

Yasha calmly pulled over half a block from the entrance.

I started to get nervous. "Is there another exit?"

"Not for this garage," Yasha said. "We wait. He will come out. When he does, I will smell him."

The Russian werewolf's eyes were glittering gold in the rearview mirror. Tomorrow night was the full moon. Yasha wasn't old for a werewolf, but he was old enough to be able to control himself.

Mostly.

He and the other werewolves who worked for SPI usually made themselves scarce twenty-four hours before the full moon—which was right now. Normally, Yasha still being on duty would bother me, or at least be a concern. Tonight there was no one else, aside from Ian, who I wanted by my side.

Minutes passed. A blue sedan came out; no sniffs from the front seat. Then a white SUV emerged. No reaction. Next came a tiny Smart car. Yasha chuckled. When a dark green Land Rover came out, Yasha inhaled and nearly gagged.

"We have a winner," Ian announced. He put his hand on Yasha's shoulder. "Give him space, buddy. You won't lose him."

Yasha gave the Land Rover and its thankfully-smelly-to-werewolves passenger a few extra seconds and then pulled into traffic and followed him.

"We've got plenty of yellow camouflage now," I said, "but what about when he gets close to the docks?"

"Won't matter," Ian said. "Once he's in a boat and on the water, we've got other contacts waiting to track him from there, if necessary."

"What do you mean, if necessary?"

Ian almost smiled. "All we need to know is whether he's going north to North Brother, or south to Red Hook. Then we can have Kenji send Sandy to back up Roy, or vice versa."

Then there'd be *two* expert snipers available to kill Ben Sadler.

"The more backup they have and the quicker they get it," Ian said, "the better the chances of ending this thing without any of our people getting killed."

Ian was including Ben as one of ours.

I smiled. "I don't know why I bother to talk at all; you always know what I'm thinking."

"You're always obvious, though the quiet would be nice."

"You're out of luck there. You sure you don't read minds?"

"I just read you."

My eyes went to the cab's dash clock.

Nine forty-five.

Two hours and fifteen minutes.

Two faster car changes later, a Lexus sedan pulled up to a dock just off Wall Street, confirming that we'd at least gotten the East River right.

Yasha drove past where Kain's driver had pulled in, stopped as soon as he was out of their sight, and engaged in some highly creative and definitely illegal parking.

"What now?" I asked quietly after we'd gotten out of the car.

Ian pulled binoculars out of a bag he'd brought with him. I assumed they had night vision. "I take a quick look. You and Yasha stay here."

Yasha and I exchanged "screw that" glances.

Ian stopped short of rolling his eyes. "Yasha, you're not the only one with a sensitive sniffer. Kain's a dragon and the closer it gets to a full moon, the stronger you smell."

"I do not st—"

"I said smell, not stink. Me? I'm just one human passing by. No threat. And with the way the wind's blowing, plus the 'aroma' coming off the East River, Kain probably won't even notice me."

Ian went, we stayed, but we were not happy about it.

"Will you be able to hear if something goes wrong?" I asked in the barest whisper.

Yasha gave me one solemn nod. His golden eyes narrowed, telling me what I needed to know: that if the crap did hit the fan, we were going after Ian.

After the longest five minutes in recorded history, Ian came back.

"They've cast off, and they're headed north. No one's left in the Lexus; they're all on the boat. There's some kind of maintenance building that'll give us a better look and more cover."

Ian led and we followed.

The view of the East River was a lot prettier at night. The dark hid many things—best of all, us.

The water lapped up against a concrete barrier that wasn't concrete colored any longer. It was high tide, so what little shoreline existed was underwater. Ian removed something on a long chain from under his shirt and around his neck, squatted on the edge of the barrier, and dropped whatever was on the end into the water.

Yasha and I waited, staring intently at the place where the chain had entered the water.

Ian was calling something. Was there a scene like this in *Jaws*? I never got into any body of water at night other than a bathtub, hot tub, or swimming pool, and only then if they were lit. Nothing good ever came up out of the water at night.

A head broke the surface a few feet from where Ian crouched. Long hair flowed over slender shoulders and disappeared into the water. The features indicated that it was female, and all of the above seemed to be more or less human.

The skin, however, was green.

Or at least it looked green from what I could see.

Her large eyes were solid, dark orbs. Orbs that stared over Ian's shoulder to where Yasha loomed.

I glanced at the Russian. Dang, had he gotten taller and hairier? Maybe it was the shadows playing tricks. The mermaid—or whatever she was—clearly didn't like what she saw.

"Yasha, will you step back, please?" Ian kept his eyes on hers, and his voice quiet and calm.

I stepped back with him in case I was scary, too. Hey, it could happen.

The mermaid submerged completely.

Seconds later, she surfaced right under where Ian's hand held the chain and pendant stretched out over and into the water. My partner didn't move as a long-fingered, webbed hand reached up to him. Ian lowered his hand and she closed her definitely green, webbed fingers around his.

She gazed up into his eyes and they stayed like that for a good half minute. Then she simply released his hand and sank back into the dark river without leaving even a ripple as a sign she'd ever been there.

A little scary? Yes.

Amazingly cool? You bet.

Ian stood. "Kain's heading north. There are five men on the boat with him. Another boat launched from a dock north of here with ten men on board. All are armed."

"When did Sandra's team leave?" I asked.

"About twenty minutes ago."

"She either has company or is about to get it."

Two boats of armed Russians, one in front, another behind.

Ian called Kenji to give Sandra a heads-up.

I looked down at my watch. Ten o'clock. Nothing to do now but wait. Waiting sucked big—

The river exploded and a fireball lit the night sky.

To the north.

22

THE dock shook violently beneath our feet.

The first explosion was closely followed by a second and then a third, both from farther up the river.

In the direction of North Brother Island.

Flaming debris from the first blast fell from the night sky like comets, still burning after they hit the water.

Three explosions.

Three boats with men, women, ammunition, and full gas tanks.

Under the dying echo of the last blast, I heard it, heard *her*. We all did.

A shriek like a giant bird of prey.

"Fucking harpies!" Ian snarled.

"That had to be Kain's boat," I said of the first explosion and visible debris.

Ian had his phone out again. "Yes."

That was good, great even.

Then my heart dropped to my feet.

The source of the other two blasts had to have been the boats carrying Kain's men—and Sandra and her team.

Illuminated for an instant against the orange blaze was a harpy. One claw-tipped hand went to her chest, and came away clutching something small. Hovering above the flaming wreck, she reached over with her other hand and pulled . . .

Harpies with *hand grenades*?

Unholy hell.

Helena Thanos had said they could follow simple orders. Find target, pull pin, drop grenade. No rocket science required there.

"Now," said Yasha from right behind me, his voice oddly distorted, "I have seen everything."

I turned and looked up—and kept looking.

Oh boy.

In the minute since I'd last looked at him, Yasha had grown at least half a foot, and his teeth had grown too large and pointy for his mouth. A mouth that was elongating, even as I watched, into a muzzle to accommodate some impressive dental work.

Uh-oh.

"I am changing," he managed to say.

"I am noticing."

"Is early."

"Uh-huh. Uh . . . could it be stress?"

Yasha nodded in agreement. "That can happen."

Most folks break out in hives. Yasha might die in an hour and a half, and his only hope of salvation had just gone up in flames. His response? Break out in fur and fangs.

The harpy shrieked again, beating her giant, bat-like wings to gain altitude, turning toward—

"Holy shit," I said, "she's going south."

Ian paused on the phone. "Kenji, warn Roy. Somehow these bitches know which boats to torch."

An hour and a half until midnight, one of our commando units had their boat blown out from under them, and the other was being hunted by a harpy wearing a bandoleer of hand grenades.

I forced myself to look away from the wreckage. "If Roy can't make it—"

Ian held up his hand for quiet, and ran down the dock, talking furiously to Kenji.

Sirens started wailing all up and down the river as the first responders began what was going to be a swarm of cops, Coast Guard, and feds. They'd shut down traffic on the river and no one would be able to reach the island, period, let alone before midnight. Midnight would come and go. The human population of New York wouldn't notice a thing. Just another Halloween night.

I screamed in helpless rage.

There had to be some way we could get there. There weren't any boats here. Kain must have chosen it because no one else would be here, no witnesses.

"Dammit!" Ian paced the dock. Three steps down, three steps back, the stomping of his boots making the dock shake almost as much as the explosions had.

Kenji's news must have been even worse than ours.

Ian stopped and glared down at his phone, jaw clenched. "Dammit."

Patience was in short enough supply on my end. *"What?"*

Ian looked at me, closed his eyes, took a breath, and blew it out. He opened his eyes and looked back down at his phone. "We don't have a choice," he said, maybe to me, maybe to himself. "We don't have a fucking choice." He saw Yasha and froze.

"Um, buddy? You okay?"

"He's stressed," I said for him.

"I can see that."

As long as Yasha was half out of one form and half in

the other, the glamour SPI's werewolves used to disguise themselves during the full moon—known in the agency as "that time of the month"—wouldn't work. Yasha was stuck until he completed his change, standing before God and anyone else who wandered by, looming and lisping.

"What choice don't we have?" I asked Ian.

"I have to make a call," Ian said, scrolling down what I assumed was his contact list. "A call I do *not* want to make, but there's no other way."

He didn't seem inclined to elaborate further, so I stood and listened.

"This is Ian Byrne, and I . . . I need your help." My partner had to force those last four words out.

He moved the phone around to his other ear and continued to talk, but I didn't hear a word.

I'd caught a glimpse of the name on the screen. The name of who Ian was talking to, and I was in shock. My mouth might have fallen open and still been hanging open, for all I knew.

Satan must be serving sno-cones in Hell.

Ian Byrne had just called Rake Danescu for help.

23

ONLY ten minutes later, a low, sleek, black speedboat glided to a near silent stop at the end of the dock. At the wheel, dressed all in black like an honest-to-God—or in his case dishonest-to-God—cat burglar, was Rake Danescu.

Then again, his boat may not have been all that silent. Who the hell could hear anything over the sirens wailing up and down the river? And don't even get me started on the flashing lights. For some bizarre eye/brain agreement reason, looking at flashing lights made me dizzy. Being on a boat just made me flat-out barf. Now I was going to get on a goblin dark mage's speedboat on Halloween near midnight, then he'd elude police, Coast Guard, Harbor Patrol, and fireboats to take me to a haunted island that was guarded by monsters to find seven possessed diamonds and keep them from making New York's undead really dead.

I was gonna be popping Dramamine like freakin' Tic Tacs.

I felt like Velma about to board a seriously upgraded Mystery Machine. I glanced back at Yasha.

Yeesh.

That much hair officially qualified as fur.

I crunched down on my first Dramamine of the night. "Come on, Scooby."

Ian had called the boss to let her know we'd caught a ride to North Brother Island—and with whom. This evening was already chock-full of surreality; I'm sure hearing that Ian, Yasha, and I were going on a midnight cruise with Rake Danescu didn't even make her bat an eye.

"You got here fast," Ian was saying to Rake.

"I sensed your desperation and yearned to be of assistance."

"Cut the crap, Danescu. This isn't exactly your side of town. The yacht clubs are on the Hudson."

"Like yourself, I have business this evening that brings me here."

"Dressed like a cat burglar," I said. "Or a jewel thief."

"Touché, lovely Makenna. I don't suppose you'd believe I was going to a midnight Halloween party across the river?"

I just looked at him.

Rake laughed softly. "I didn't think you would. You and your organization aren't the only ones who have deduced what will happen at midnight. While some are fleeing the city, others are taking matters into their own hands."

"We had two teams of commandos," Ian said. "Who are you teaming up with?"

"I prefer to work alone, and was not going to change my preferences tonight."

"Just you against whatever's over there," Ian said, helping me on board.

"Often one can succeed where many will fail. I do not lack experience in such situations. Though I am surprised you set aside your dislike of me to request my assistance."

Desperate times called for desperate measures, I thought.

"It's not a matter of like or dislike," Ian said.

Rake's smile was wicked. "Disapproval, perhaps?"

"I don't trust you."

"That makes two of us. I don't trust me, either. I do not take offense, Agent Byrne. Goblins get a lot of practice with distrust. If anyone ever does trust me, I must be doing something very wrong."

Yasha stepped down into the boat, tipping it sharply to one side.

In addition to hairier and taller, the Russian had become heavier.

"No werewolves," Rake said flatly.

"He's on our side," Ian said.

"Define 'our.'"

Yasha's eyes were now bright gold and were boring into the goblin, like he was wondering what side dish would go best with him.

I hated to admit it but Rake might have a point; it'd be counterproductive to have our car driver eat our boat captain.

"'Our' as in he's going with us." The intensity of Ian's green eyes easily matched Yasha's I-could-go-moon-crazy-any-moment peepers. "He's ninety-six . . . and he's a friend."

In other words, the man/wolf was going to die in a little over an hour. Don't be a heartless putz; give him a chance to save thousands of lives—and his own.

Rake sighed and regarded Yasha solemnly. "If he goes fully wolf on my boat, he leaves."

Ian chuckled darkly. "If he goes wolf on your boat, you're welcome to tell him."

Rake Danescu's dark eyes flashed in the dim light of the boat's dash lights. "There will be no telling. I have not survived so much for this long to be torn apart by an overgrown barbarian mongrel."

Yasha growled, Ian came out of his seat, and Rake took one hand off the wheel. It was glowing.

"Boys." I said it like I'd heard my grandma say it many times—long, drawn out, and low with warning. Grandma Fraser had always been ready and willing to back up that word with a switch, the business end of a broom, or the flat of a cast-iron skillet. Grandma said that a skillet's good for three things: frying chicken, baking corn bread, and going upside an obstinate man's head.

I didn't have a switch, broom, or skillet. I only had an appeal to their good sense; hopefully at least one of them still had some. My money was on the werewolf.

"Let's see, we're going to an island with a criminal mastermind, a gorgon, harpies with hand grenades, and who the hell knows what else? We need everyone on this boat, *especially* the werewolf. I can vouch for him," I told Rake. "Unless you act like a royal jackass, he won't rip your face off."

I would have asked Yasha to actually promise Rake he wouldn't rip his face off, but Yasha's muzzle had grown a little long for small talk.

"But our problem right now is getting through that flashing light show out there to even reach the island."

Rake gave me a smug little smile. "That, darling Makenna, is not a problem."

With that, both of his hands began to glow. The goblin placed them firmly on the boat's steering wheel and the glow spread, completely enveloping the boat in seconds.

"So now we're glowing so brightly all the cops and feds won't be able to look directly at us, right?"

"We're not glowing. We're invisible, and cloaked for sound."

"I can still see—"

"If we couldn't see the boat, it would be most challenging to operate her, wouldn't it?"

I could see that, too.

We'd find out in the next minute because an NYPD launch was going to pass three boat lengths off our . . . starboard side. Left was port, and they both had four letters. Right was the one that was left, I mean remaining, which was starboard. Though to be on the safe side, I simply wouldn't say any of them out loud and risk humiliating myself.

"Good evening, gentlemen," Rake called out across the water.

I squeaked and hit the deck. I definitely knew what that part of a boat was called.

Rake Danescu was laughing; even Ian was fighting back a grin.

I turned on my traitorous partner. "You knew it'd work and you didn't say anything?"

"He's a mage, Mac."

"That still didn't mean it'd work."

"I can assure you," Rake said, "I am exceptionally good at many things; magic is merely one."

I sat in my seat and tried to ignore the way the police launch's wake was making our boat feel like it was riding on a Slinky.

"Can the harpies see us?" I asked.

Rake pushed the throttle forward, and we moved smoothly away from the dock. "Let's find out, shall we?"

Within ten minutes, we'd reached where the boat carrying Sandra and her team had been grenade bombed by a harpy.

Ian had called Kenji, who had spoken with Sandra, who was presently wrapped in blankets along with, thankfully, the rest of her team. There were injuries, some serious, but nothing fatal.

Fortunately by the time the first boatload of law enforcement types had arrived, everything that could have blown up on Sandra's boat had blown up, and their body armor had the consideration to sink to the bottom of the East River.

For now, the authorities didn't see them as anything more than a boat full of partiers who had been randomly targeted by New York's newest terrorist—some maniac on a boat with a grenade launcher, according to the chatter on Rake's radio.

Apparently the harpies' instructions had included staying out of sight, so at least flying harpies wearing bandoleers of grenades wouldn't be going into the police reports.

That was the good news. The bad news was that the police were stopping any and every boat on the water. If the harpies hadn't already blasted Roy and his folks out of the water, the cops' search and seizure would apply to them as well.

The boat jerked sharply to the side. Rake swore in goblin.

"What is it?" It occurred to me I didn't know where the life jackets were, or if Rake even had the things. Then I remembered the *General Slocum* and had a moment of panic. Though if Rake had life jackets, at least they wouldn't be loaded down with lead bars. The goblin had money and from what I'd seen of his sex club, penthouse, and this boat, he didn't mind spending it.

The goblin hissed air out from between his teeth and, with a firm grip on the wheel and slight throttle adjustment, guided us back into smoother water. Though right now, smooth was relative; it had also become nonexistent.

"We're in the Hell Gate." Ian came up from the back of the boat where he'd been talking to Yasha to sit beside me. "It's an area of converging tide-driven currents. It's not the safest place to take a boat. There's been a lot of shipwrecks through here."

"Oh lovely. To get to the haunted island, we have to go through the Hell Gate?"

"Actually, it extends to and surrounds North Brother Island."

A Coast Guard patrol boat was also battling the currents where the second boat carrying Kain's men had gone down. There were bodies covered with tarps on the deck of a Coast Guard patrol boat.

"All our folks live," I said. "Kain's men drown like rats."

"SPI has friends in watery places," Ian reminded me.

The mermaid and her merfriends had been busy—both saving and drowning.

"I suppose it's too much to hope for that Viktor Kain is under one of those tarps."

"Dragons can hold their breath for prolonged periods," Rake said. "And they are most proficient swimmers."

I slid over to a seat away from the sides of the boat.

"He's turned dragon and he's . . ." I made a slithering, swimming motion with my hand and arm.

"He'd want to get to the island quickly," Ian said. "To do that—and to keep from being attacked by the merfolk—he would have to turn dragon. Can we go any faster?"

"I take it, then, that you're through seeing the sights." The goblin indicated the drowned Russians. "We're now in more open water." He pushed the throttle up farther and the boat leapt forward, taking my stomach with it. "Let's annoy Mr. Kain by arriving at the party first."

24

NORTH Brother Island wasn't my idea of a party spot. However, if you were looking for a haunted island on Halloween night, I had to admit it rocked.

North Brother Island was between the Bronx and Riker's Island, home of the New York City Department of Correction main jail complex. Riverside Hospital had operated here until 1963, when it was closed and the island abandoned and officially declared off-limits to the public.

Tonight, for one night only, the hospital was again open for business.

Only this time, the cure would kill. Permanently.

The rest of the ride over was spent doing a quick review of the island's layout, what buildings were where, and which one was the most likely candidate to hide and activate death-dealing diamonds. At one hour until midnight, we didn't have time for a tour.

We went with the hospital's tuberculosis pavilion. It was the largest building on the island, the most recently built—if you could say 1941 was recent—and since it was the newest, it was also the best preserved.

Its preservation was the main reason we chose it as the winner of our most likely lair location. I'd think that it'd take some of the stress out of hatching an evil master plan to kill thousands if you didn't have to worry about the roof caving in on top of you.

There was an old dock on the west side of the island. We didn't go there. Instead, Rake fought the currents and piloted his boat around the east side of the island to the north shore, beaching his boat in a tiny cove. It was also the closest access point to the tuberculosis pavilion. In addition, the goblin had deemed this the landing site least likely to be guarded by whatever we were going to encounter.

I could see why.

Mama Nature had constructed a defensive barrier all by her lonesome.

The water extended right into the undergrowth—and overgrowth. Sleeping Beauty's prince wouldn't have been able to hack his way through this. Rake had assured us on our approach that it wouldn't be a problem. I could see right now that I was going to have a problem with Rake's assurances.

"Did you bring a chain saw with you?" I asked Rake. "With a silencer?"

"I will not need one."

"Then you're going to politely ask the plants to move?"

"Actually, I was going to command them." The goblin finished shutting down the boat and its lights. Suddenly, the only sound was water lapping against its sides, and the only light came from the reflection of the high-powered lights on the water from Riker's Island. Let me tell you, when the city lit a prison island, they didn't mess around. I almost felt like they had a spotlight on us.

"Sense any wards?" Ian asked.

"No," Rake and I said together.

"I was unaware you could sense wards, Makenna." Rake's intense yet pleased scrutiny was uncomfortable to say the least.

"A little," I said. "Enough to keep me from stumbling into things. I'm sure it's nowhere near what you've got up your sleeves."

"If we're dealing with someone who can put harpies into suspended animation," Ian said, "you'd think they would have wards, especially since they had to know we'd be coming after them."

"They could be saving their strength for securing the hospital," Rake said. His dark eyes carefully surveyed the trees beyond the nest of brambles at the shore. "They could be using more primitive security measures out here to prevent interruptions from reaching their doorstep."

"Primitive such as?" I asked.

"Harpies with hand grenades," Ian said. "Though whoever is in charge of this tropical paradise would want to keep it quiet. They want to destroy supernaturals, not attract the NYPD by staging their own mini war."

As we had witnessed out on the river, New York's mortal authorities reacted swiftly to anything that went boom. Ian was right; the harpies would keep their grenades to themselves. However, harpies could dispense death just fine without explosives.

That was only one of the surprises that people sneaking around a spooky island at midnight on Halloween didn't need. Eddie the gorgon was another one. And since he was a gorgon, we'd only be surprised once.

Ian checked what weapons he had. We'd been expecting to tail a car, not storm a building that looked like a castle. Rake appeared to be going with the "my body is a weapon" approach. I spotted a couple of knives on him, but his clothing was so tight, there was no way he was hiding anything else.

"We don't have any way of knowing if we're dealing with Eddie," Ian was saying, "the thief, three harpies, or if they have other friends playing bouncer."

"So it won't be a cakewalk," I said. "Check."

The boat rocked violently as Yasha the almost-werewolf went over the side. The water was only up to his knees—his bare knees.

Yasha was naked.

Though when your body was now covered with that much fur, clothes were redundant.

It appeared that Yasha had decided that like the Hulk, clothes were just going to get in the way of completing his transformation. From what I could tell, he was danged near there.

The Russian raised his muzzle and inhaled like he was trying to suck all the air out of our little cove of horrors. Then with a fang-filled, wolfy grin, Yasha threw his head back.

"No howling!" Ian whisper-yelled.

Yasha's grin flowed into a lip-rippling snarl. He didn't like being told no, but he didn't howl, either.

I felt myself smile. "Unless they've got a Hulk, they've got a problem." I was suddenly feeling a little better about our chances of actually surviving this thing, or at least reaching the hospital in one piece. "We have a werewolf. A werewolf who's decided that he *will* live past midnight."

25

SINCE Yasha was naked and therefore not wearing shoes, he offered to carry me to shore. I gratefully accepted. October in New York wasn't that cold, but slogging around an island in wet shoes? No, thank you.

The instant my feet touched solid ground I felt it.

Two massive ley lines running deep beneath the island.

We had ley lines running under the mountains in North Carolina where I grew up, but nothing like this. Maybe the thief had made some kind of magical preparations, or the presence of the Dragon Eggs on the island had gotten the ley lines riled up. Whatever had done it, there was no denying that these ley lines were awake; it felt strange saying this about something that existed only as energy—but they felt angry. I didn't know how raw energy could be pissed, but that was the literal vibe I was getting. The ground under my feet was vibrating. I glanced up at the sky. No planes, either coming or going from LaGuardia, though I would have felt and heard them if they'd been there.

I glanced over at Ian. My partner had taken off his shoes and was wading to shore. Yasha hadn't offered to carry him. Maybe he was still miffed at Ian telling him not to howl. Regardless, he didn't look like a man whose feet were vibrating.

Rake had gotten to the beach by going to the end of his boat's bow and leaping like a big kitty cat. It was easily ten feet to the nearest dry and undergrowth-free spot. Not surprisingly, the goblin nailed the landing.

I pointed toward the ground. "You feel anything funky?"

"If by 'funky' you mean the nexus of the ley lines, then yes."

Ian went still. "You can feel it?" he asked me.

"Oh yeah." I stepped from one foot to the other. "It feels like a seriously ticked-off nexus."

"It's the diamonds," Rake said. "Their mere presence calls to the energies below this island."

"They're not going to call on it to cause an earthquake, are they?"

"I'd much prefer an earthquake over those diamonds being activated."

Ian finished putting his boots back on. "Let's see what we can do about preventing both."

Rake had told us that the machete-worthy vegetation wasn't going to be a problem.

I'd taken that assurance with a grain of salt.

However, once again, the goblin had delivered as promised.

He'd commanded, and the plants had moved. Literally. Parted like the Red Sea. And if the branches couldn't bend far enough to clear our path, the plants had committed hari-kari by ripping themselves out of the ground by their roots.

The path stayed clear behind us. While I liked having an escape route I could take at full speed, if we left this much destruction, whatever guards the thief had dragging their knuckles around the island would find our boat. Nothing said disappointment like running for your life only to find your boat under the water rather than on top of it.

Ian was having similar concerns. "You got a ward for your boat?"

Rake's laugh from ahead of us was soft and low. "She can take care of herself."

"How about us?" I asked. "Yasha has wolf-vision going, and you can see in the dark like a cat." I jerked a thumb at Ian. "Mere mortals like us are at a distinct disadvantage. Yeah, we've got a full moon going, but with those clouds, it's not doing us a bit of good."

"I can shield us from sight and sound, though we will need to stay close."

"I was kinda planning on doing that anyway."

The goblin glanced at Yasha with obvious distaste. "However, there is nothing I can do to mask scent. Air must flow in and out, and that includes smell. You may use a small flashlight, but please keep it as dim as possible so as not to disrupt my own vision. Even with light to see by, my night vision is infinitely superior to yours."

Well, la-di-da.

"Good," Ian said. "Because Yasha's sniffer can smell Viktor Kain. And since right now we're downwind from the rest of the island, he'll know about Kain before Kain smells him. Do it."

Rake did. After a few words and a couple of gestures, the goblin simply turned and headed off into the forest.

I didn't feel any different.

"I'd advise that you keep up, agents of SPI," Rake called back. "The shield only extends to a radius of three meters."

Ian and I both had penlights, but they didn't do much to keep us—okay, me—from tripping over roots, rocks, and building debris that seemed to be everywhere.

The island was only thirteen acres, which wasn't very large when you thought about it, but add in near pitch dark and what appeared to be a forest primeval looming around us, and it made a perfect obstacle course, which I felt like I was doing while blindfolded. It also turned every building, tree, and kudzu-covered, crumbling wall into an ambush waiting to happen.

Before we'd landed, I'd distracted myself from the high potential for drowning by scanning some of the web pages about North Brother on my phone. One guy had been right on target by describing it as what you'd get if the world suddenly ended and nature took back what was hers, growing around and through the trappings of civilization. And to add to the island's vacation destination potential, there was an actual morgue in a building that used to be the chapel. It was across from the island's physical plant and coal house, and next to the main dock. I guess it was practical to have any dead bodies close to the place where they could be loaded up and taken off quickly and quietly.

The wind had picked up, pushing the clouds off to the east that had obscured the nearly full moon for the entire night until now, filling the open spaces between trees and buildings with light, making the shadows even darker by contrast. Now even Ian and I could see.

My eyes went from the moon, following the bright white light down to what once must have been a road leading to the front of the pavilion but was now covered in kudzu that carpeted the pavement and climbed the trees growing up on either side. Instead of a yellow brick road, we had a green kudzu road; and instead of ending at the gates of Oz, it ended at an abandoned hospital's tuberculosis pavilion. The one-story-high, rectangular entryway reminded me of the entry into the Dendur Temple at the museum. A rectangle of pale gray that looked almost white with the moon, surrounding the stairs leading up to the recessed doorway—all concealed where the moon didn't shine. Pitch-black.

The kudzu continued up the side of the pavilion. In the

center of the building, its elaborate brickwork and broken windows half covered in ivy or kudzu, was a four-story . . . "Tower" was the only word I could think of to describe it. And along the top, the brick masons had constructed what looked like battlements. Heck, they even had . . .

I stopped. Ian was forced to either do the same or run into me. Ahead of us, Rake and Yasha stood motionless; Yasha's muzzle was raised, analyzing the air.

Thankfully, we were still in the shadows.

Four harpies crouched unmoving on the edge of the tuberculosis pavilion like gargoyles on a castle tower.

Four, not three.

The triplets we'd been dealing with were now quadruplets.

They were perched four stories directly above the main door into the building.

"Is there another way in?" I asked Ian in the barest whisper.

He shook his head.

That wasn't the direction I wanted to see his head go.

Yasha looked back at us and nodded once.

Ben was in there; Yasha's nose said so. Unlike Rake Danescu's assurances or ulterior motives, I believed everything Yasha's nose told him the same way I believed the sun was going to rise tomorrow. That sun was going to come up. Though the way things were going, I might not be alive to see it.

Rake glanced up and signed in weary resignation, as if the Amazon-sized, and so far unkillable, harpies were nothing but an annoying influx of mosquitoes at a pig pickin'. As if all we needed to do was light some citronellas, fire up the bug zapper, and we'd be done.

And even if Yasha's nose hadn't led us here, I would have known that this was the place, and so would have Rake. The two massive ley lines met under the tuberculosis pavilion.

Ian and I had no more weapons than we'd had the last two times we'd tangled with these girls, and now there were more of them. Yeah, we had a highly-motivated-to-survive werewolf, and a goblin who was reputed to be deadly in a fight. Yes, he'd done everything he'd bragged he could do so far, but I'd rather not bet the farm—and my life—that he was as good as he thought he was.

The clouds moved all the way away from the moon, showing us what none of us wanted to see.

The entire length of the building's flat roof, not just the pavilion tower, was dotted about every fifteen feet or so with its very own harpy. And the trees I thought were simply shorter than the others, in actuality had their top branches weighted down by yet more harpies.

I didn't bother to count them; one was too many. When that one snapped me in half when we tried to make a break for the pavilion doors, thirty more piling on top wouldn't make me any deader than I already was.

Numbers didn't matter. Screwed was screwed.

"You got any tips on how to kill these things?" Ian asked Rake. "We're zero and two."

"These are exclusive to your dimension. We have a similar creature, and have found the joints to be vulnerable—once they have sustained enough direct hits."

"How many is enough?"

"Half a dozen has been known to be effective— occasionally."

Yasha made a snatching motion with one of his clawed hands, then the other.

Ian interpreted. "Yasha's just going to rip their arms off."

"That would work, too."

A tremor shook the ground beneath my feet, sending a vibration up into my legs. Two seconds later it happened again, the tremor more intense, going all the way up into my spine this time.

The guys felt it, too.

So did the girls.

The harpies shifted uneasily, looking around for the source.

They didn't have long to wait.

We looked up . . . and up . . . and up.

Viktor Kain in his true form was making an entrance Godzilla would have been proud of, right down the middle of the road, his massive body and tail twisting sinuously side to side with every step.

I'd seen a lizard move like that before on one of those animal or nature channels—a Komodo dragon, multiplied in size and temper by a hundred or so. Kain breathed out, and the fire he had banked inside glowed out of his nostrils.

I hadn't seen *that* on Animal Planet.

Kain had his wings tucked close to his body. Like Vivienne Sagadraco, he could have walked upright on two legs, but that would probably put his head above the tree line. With the East River full of police, he didn't want to draw attention to the island or himself.

Viktor Kain was in stealth mode, and the impact of his clawed feed tippy-toeing on the ground still felt like an earthquake.

Our all-powerful, badass, goblin dark mage spoke for all of us.

"Oh shit."

26

VIKTOR Kain could have taken the building apart with one claw tied behind his back. But then he'd have a pile of rubble to sift through to find seven diamonds. It'd be like looking for hypodermic needles in a hospital haystack made of bricks.

He didn't have time for that.

And we didn't want to end up squashed inside that brick haystack.

The booming we heard was the asphalt being crushed to pebbly dust beneath the weight and pressure of those four feet.

I got ready to make a run for the door.

Ian blocked me with his arm.

"But he's almost here," I protested. "Get there while the gettin's good."

"Wait." Ian was calm and sure.

I'd have been satisfied to share just one of those emotions. I was terrified. Big, crashing waves of terror, in fact. My fight-or-flight response was in full adrenaline overload, with my body and mind voting unanimously for flight—through those doors and into the pavilion. I didn't know what was waiting in there, but I sure as hell knew what I had out here. The prize I wanted was whatever waited beyond door number one; be it trick or treat, I didn't care. I'd deal with it when it jumped out and started killing me.

But Ian had been doing this for SPI, the NYPD, and the military before that for about a dozen years.

Coworkers still called me a newbie.

Ian said stay. I stayed.

There must have been some kind of unspoken signal, or one only harpies could hear. Almost as one, they dove from their perches, covered the four stories in an instant, and swarmed Viktor Kain.

"Go!"

Ian added a shove to his verbal order that put me a good ten feet in front of where I'd been standing, so that when my feet found the ground, I was actually keeping up with him and Rake.

Yasha had shot across the kudzu-choked street and through the pavilion doors before we'd even stepped off the curb. If anything had been waiting to jump us, it'd just been flattened by a werewolf who took his self-appointed job of clearing the way for us very seriously.

We covered the distance to the pavilion entrance without being shredded or even dive-bombed. Yasha had obligingly destroyed the doors, and was glaring into the darkness beyond, daring anything inside to have a problem with that.

Rake was the first to look our gift horse in the mouth. "I don't like it. I don't like it at all."

"You don't have to like it," Ian fired back. "You're still breathing, aren't you?"

The goblin didn't snap "For how long?" The look he shot at Ian said it for him.

In this kind of situation, I'd usually be the pessimist. But at this moment, a Russian mafia boss, who was a fifty-foot-tall, bloodred dragon that could tear through the trees out there like a can of pick-up sticks, was being attacked by a flock of harpies that made the playground scene in *The Birds* look like a Disney movie. Plus, they were out there; we were in here. That made me seven kinds of happy right now. I knew it wouldn't last, but I'd enjoy it while I had it.

Yasha had long shattered the hospital's quiet rule. Anything down the corridors that stretched into darkness to either side of us knew we were here. So while I asked my question quietly, I still asked it.

"Why didn't some of those harpies follow us in here? Not that I mind."

Maybe the harpies had been told to expect many heavily armed men, not two humans, a goblin, and a werewolf. If so, thank God for simple minds.

"Either Kain's the bigger threat," Ian said, "or their job is to defend the outside, and something else is inside with us."

Or some*one* we had yet to see hide or hair of.

Eddie the Gorgon.

No one had to say that out loud; we knew it.

In unison, we all put on our anti-gorgon-glare glasses.

Oh crap. Yasha had glasses, but they'd only fit his human face.

"The boss said dragons are immune to gorgons," I said. "How about werewolves?"

"I don't think so," Ian said. "Yasha?"

The Russian werewolf did something that on a human could be a shrug; then he flashed some teeth and flipped his thumb upward through his closed fist—like he was popping the cap off a bottle of beer.

Rake Danescu chuckled darkly.

Ian didn't need to translate that one; we all got it.

Well, Helena Thanos had said that the only way to kill a

gorgon would be to decapitate them. Popping Eddie's head off his neck like a bottle cap would discourage him from looking at us or anyone else ever again.

Ian got out his flashlight and turned it on. I did the same. Everyone and everything knew we were here, or at least knew Viktor Kain was here. Through all the screeching and hell-raising ruckus going on outside, we could pretty much make all the noise we wanted. No one would ever hear us.

Who would have ever thought that Viktor Kain would be helpful to SPI?

My inner pessimist did remind me that the world as we knew it was going to end in less than an hour unless we moved our asses and did something about it.

"Okay, buddy," Ian was telling Yasha. "Find Ben."

Damn, I'd completely forgotten about that. Ben had not only been inside of Yasha's beloved Suburban, but he'd bled there while Yasha had been in werewolf form kicking that harpy's butt. He'd told me before that once his wolf form smelled a person's blood, he could track them to the ends of the earth.

I slammed the door on my pessimist, and invited hope to come on in the house.

Dust was falling everywhere from Yasha essentially obliterating the front doors, which now hung in splintered ruin from one hinge each. He was now fully transformed. The excitement and sprint across the moon-drenched street must have topped off his tank. The Russian werewolf stood perfectly still, letting the air flow across his nose. He abruptly turned to the right, stalking with long and deter-mined strides into the dark.

27

THE last thing we saw was one of Viktor Kain's Smart car–sized front feet coming down hard on a harpy, reminding me of what happens when you step on one of those ketchup packets, but infinitely worse, at least for the harpy.

The adrenaline hadn't stopped, and considering that I hadn't slept since the night before last, the fear of imminent death was all that was keeping me upright and moving. So fear was good.

The walls of the tuberculosis pavilion were covered in sky blue subway tile, and someone long ago had the bright idea to paint the walls to match while they were at it. Probably had to do with being cheerful and soothing to patients. It wasn't doing a danged thing for me.

Chairs, charts, and miscellaneous papers were strewn down the hall along with chunks of the ceiling and wall plaster, doors stood open or rotted from their hinges revealing rusted examining tables; and beyond one door, a huge tiled bathtub with a small set of stairs going up the side sat in what must have been a treatment room.

One thing was missing.

Graffiti.

In the city, if there was a blank surface, it was a canvas to people with paint cans. Heck, I'd read recently that a dead whale had washed up in Jersey and had suffered the further indignity of getting tagged with graffiti.

Not here. It appeared as if the hospital employees had left at the end of their shift and simply never came back. At night, it was spooky. In the light of day, it would just be sad.

When we reached the main stairwell, the tile changed from blue to a pale yellow tile. Sections of the round metal railing actually gleamed in the beams of our flashlights.

Yasha didn't even pause, but took the stairs five at a time in complete silence. When I'd reached the second-floor landing, Yasha had stopped, sniffing in one direction, then the other.

This time he went left. The moonlight washed out the yellow tile to near white. There was only one nurses' station on the left side of the hall. The right side was lined with reinforced metal-covered doors with a single slit at eye level, and a big slide bolt—on the outside. They were the leftovers from the early 1960s when this place had been used as a rehab facility for young heroin addicts.

"The isolation rooms," Ian murmured. He shone his light down the line of doors: two were about to fall off their hinges; others were standing slightly open.

Yasha made a beeline for the one directly across from the nurses' station midway down the hall. We quickly followed.

"And it has one thing the others don't," Ian said with satisfaction, aiming his light on a brand-new, shiny lock on the door.

Bingo.

Yasha had gone into the room to confirm Ben's scent. He came out and nodded once.

"Stand guard while we take a look," Ian said. "And find which direction they took him."

Ian and I went in. Rake stepped into the room far enough to see.

The window was covered with a heavy mesh screen—the better to keep addicts in the throes of withdrawal from escaping. Along a side wall was a cast-iron radiator. Like the door, it was sporting new hardware.

Chains.

The heavy, steel links had been wrapped around the radiator and secured in place with another lock identical to the one on the door. What we didn't see were the handcuffs—or actual manacles—that the chain had been looped through, meaning that wherever he'd been taken, Ben was still wearing them.

There were scratches in the plaster next to the radiator. I knelt down and shone my flashlight on it. These weren't random marks on the wall. They were letters, and from the small pile of plaster dust on the floor directly beneath, they'd been done recently.

Today.

"What does it say?" Ian asked.

We were so focused on deciphering what Ben had scratched into the wall that we hadn't noticed the hole in the ceiling . . . until the harpy dropped through, landing on top of Rake Danescu and knocking him out cold.

"Perhaps I can be of service," said a cultured voice from the man framed in the doorway.

Instantly, Ian had his gun aimed at the man's head.

"Would the name be Sebastian du Beckett?" the man continued smoothly. "Or perhaps simply Beckett? My first name is rather lengthy, and young Ben wasn't left alone for very long during his short stay. He would have had minimal time for artistic endeavors."

28

HOLY. Crap.

A quick glance at Ian's face told me I wasn't the only one struggling to regain my mental footing.

"But . . . but," I stammered, "you were . . ."

"Dead?" du Beckett offered helpfully. "Petrified? I needed to buy time, and I located a gentleman who could have been my twin brother."

So he could have Eddie Laughlin turn him to stone. Bastard.

Rake groaned while the harpy quickly handcuffed him. The steel had a faint green glow with rune-like etchings.

Magic-sapping manacles.

Sebastian du Beckett had been prepared for everything, including magically talented opposition.

Where the hell was Yasha?

Ian's eyes flicked past du Beckett and out into the hall.

"Your werewolf friend is indisposed." He raised a pallid hand as he pulled his glove back on. "A light touch merely paralyzes. I haven't turned him to stone—at least not yet. That depends on how little trouble you give me."

Whoa . . . wait. *Two* gorgons?

"Yes, I am afflicted with that malady. If you doubt my word, I can demonstrate on your goblin companion."

The harpy roughly pulled the now semiconscious Rake to his feet.

"Lord Danescu, this is a surprise," du Beckett said.

I slowly stood, my mind trying to wrap itself around this one.

"Even though bullets will cause me no more than a momentary inconvenience," the gorgon continued, "I can ill afford any additional delays. Please holster your weapon, Agent Byrne."

The eyes behind the glasses that were as thick as the bottom of a Coke bottle turned on me. I flinched even though I had on my anti-gorgon-glare glasses.

"Agent Fraser, I presume."

I didn't answer.

He didn't care.

A second and third harpy came into the isolation room, one through the door, the other through the hole in the ceiling. Du Beckett said something short and sharp to them in a language that sounded to me like Greek, and they came toward us.

"They will not harm you," he said, "unless you resist. I've asked them to remove all of your weapons. You may keep your glasses for now. Disobey and . . . well, I will let the state of your werewolf friend act as a deterrent."

Then it started to make sense—at least some of it did.

I wore contacts. Without them, I couldn't see well enough to get out of my own way.

Judging from the thickness of the glasses that'd been on the dead man in his office, Sebastian du Beckett made Mr. Magoo look like the poster child for 20/20 vision.

"Your glasses," I said. "The dead man in your office was wearing glasses with a cracked lens, an old pair that was broken. You obviously need your glasses to see, but you needed to convince us that was you in your office chair, so you had whoever the dead man was sit in your office chair. Then you paralyzed him, put the broken glasses on him, then you turned him to stone, killing him."

"Bravo, Agent Fraser," du Beckett said blandly. "Vivienne has always hired clever agents. You're simply the most recent."

"Who was in your office chair?"

"A homeless gentleman I made the acquaintance of who, unfortunately for him, met my physical parameters."

"But Ms. Sagadraco likes you. Why would—"

"I assure you the feeling is far from mutual."

Rake's laugh was more of a dry rasp as he raised his head. One side of his face was cut and bruised, and a thin trickle of blood ran down over his chin from the cut on his bottom lip. That harpy had rung his bell but good when she'd flattened him.

"I had the chance to slit your throat three months ago, Bastian," the goblin said. "I could have done the world such a favor. An opportunity passed is a chance lost."

Something rattled in the hands of the harpy that had relieved me of my gun and knife.

Manacles, not handcuffs.

They were huge. The ones for Ian were similarly large. They'd fit around my ankles, but they'd fall right off my scrawny wrists, so I didn't struggle a bit as she clipped one around my left wrist and the other on my right. I hoped they weren't so loose that they fell off of me and Ian and spoiled the surprise we'd be giving them later. Helena Thanos had been right; harpies were *not* bright.

Okay, maybe we should have struggled.

The instant the second manacle closed around my wrist, both shrank, tightening around my wrists like a vise.

Ian swore and twisted sharply when his wrists got the same treatment. In an instant the harpy had her arm around his neck, cutting off his air.

"I would strongly advise that you not struggle further, Agent Byrne. Those manacles are of goblin manufacture. Shrinking to fit is not the only surprise they have. Too much resistance and they will add electric shock to their repertoire."

Ian glared at Rake Danescu.

"He said *goblin* manufacture," Rake snapped. "*I* didn't make them."

Ian always carried handcuff keys in his back pocket, but these were shrink-to-fit goblin creations; NYPD-issued handcuff keys wouldn't do us a bit of good.

Sebastian du Beckett turned and left the isolation room. The harpies with the three of us firmly in hand followed.

29

YASHA had slid down the wall and was sprawled there like a puppet whose strings had been cut. He was unblinking, unmoving.

Paralyzed.

A sound escaped his closed muzzle like the whine of a hurt dog.

"No!" Ian roared.

As one, we both lunged for Sebastian du Beckett. My harpy guard stopped me cold, but Ian made it, his shoulder slamming into the gorgon's midsection, taking him to the ground. His manacles ignited with a sharp zap, turning the roar to a guttural scream and putting him on his back writhing in pain.

Neither one of us had thought; we'd just attacked. If Ian's bare head or neck had come into contact with even the smallest patch of bare skin on Sebastian du Beckett . . . he'd have either been paralyzed like Yasha or turned to stone.

Yasha could hear us. He could think, feel, but he couldn't move or speak. He was trapped in a paralyzed body, completely helpless. I was a self-admitted control freak. This went above and beyond my worst nightmare.

The harpy reached down and clamped her hand around the back of Ian's neck, seizing his throat in her claws and lifting him off the floor, drawing blood.

Du Beckett snapped something in Greek and the winged monster loosened her grip a little as blood streamed in rivulets down Ian's neck. She set him back on his feet, but didn't release him.

Rake Danescu remained immobile, his face impassive.

Du Beckett sat up slowly, wiping blood from his nose. "If I die, he begins to turn to stone within hours. Are you prepared to be responsible for that, Agent Byrne?"

Ian didn't, couldn't, answer.

My vision blurred. Twelve hours. According to what Helena Thanos had told me, after twelve hours, the paralysis would be irreversible and Yasha would begin to turn to stone. During every second of the few hours he would have left, Yasha would feel his body turning to stone from the outside in, until the process reached his internal organs, finally killing him.

Using the wall for support, the gorgon got to his feet. "We have little time left." He said something to the harpies, and we were forced down the hall back toward the stairs, leaving Yasha alone and helpless on the floor in the dark.

I swore to myself and spoke silently to Yasha, willing him to hear my thoughts, my promise that he would not die alone in the dark. We would stop this, and we would force Sebastian du Beckett by any means necessary to undo the torment that he had inflicted.

Then Ian could finish what he'd started.

We were Yasha's only chance. He was depending on us. We would not let him down.

"We're not leaving you," Ian called back, his voice ragged. "We'll be back. Hang on!"

"You would do well to follow Lord Danescu's example," du Beckett said.

"I can assure you my intentions toward you make the humans' thoughts like those of innocent children," Rake told him. "They want to make you pay. I *will* see you suffer. I'm merely saving myself for a risk worth taking."

"You think I haven't suffered, goblin?" Du Beckett spat the last word as if he couldn't get it out of his mouth and away from him fast enough. "You and monsters like you are responsible for what I am. 'Get this for me, Bastian.' And 'There is only one left in the world, and I want it.' The last one of those trips had me crossing paths with a gorgon. I became a prisoner in my own home. The monsters that used me to satisfy their greed would have turned on me and killed me in an instant if they'd known what I'd become. I'd have been put down like a rabid dog. I was a base human servant, a dog used to fetch, suitable for association only when you desired something, but scorned and ignored when you had no use for me."

"I've seen you at social gatherings, Bastian," Rake drawled, "and you've never been the life of any party. If anyone avoided your company, you can find their reason by looking in the closest mirror. You overcharged, you swindled, you cheated. I'll admit you did it very well; I almost admire your painstaking deviousness. At times, you nearly approached my level of skill. The human saying is quite true in your case: It takes one to know one."

The gorgon made a derisive sound. "And now you won't be able to tell anyone. Pity."

"You mistake my intent, Bastian. I won't tell anyone what transpires this night."

Du Beckett gave a short laugh. "And you think this will secure your release?"

"I sincerely hope not. My intent is not to tell; my intent is to kill. And I can't kill you if I'm not here, so I'm right where I want to be. And if I don't get the pleasure of your death at my hands this night, another will. You have more enemies than you can imagine."

"And all of them believe me dead."

Rake smiled slowly. "Are you quite confident of that?"

Faster than you'd expect a man of his age could move, Sebastian du Beckett spun and backhanded Rake across the face. The harpy gripping the goblin's upper arm was all that kept him from slamming into the wall. That the gorgon's hand was in a glove was all that had kept him from being paralyzed or turned to stone.

"And *you*," du Beckett snarled, "always the most clever."

"You have yet to prove me wrong."

"Enjoy your false superiority, goblin; you won't have your arrogant and deluded fantasy for much longer."

Rake's smile simply broadened and he spit a mouthful of blood to the side, his dark eyes never moving from du Beckett's face, as if the gorgon was going right along with his master plan.

For all I knew, du Beckett was. I couldn't imagine any sane plan requiring that Rake be knocked flat by a harpy, bound with magic-sapping manacles, and backhanded bloody by a gorgon whose glove was all that had kept him from turning into garden statuary.

But I wasn't a crazy goblin, so what did I know?

The harpies took us up another three flights.

Judging from his glasses, Sebastian du Beckett couldn't see for crap in the daylight; at night he might as well have been tapping his way up the stairs with a white cane. Since he didn't want to mar the archvillain vibe he had going by falling flat on his face, he granted me my third fondest wish—enough light to actually see where we were going. My first and second wishes were Ian with freed hands, and holding the gorgon-beheading weapon of his choice. With the way du Beckett had been ordering the harpies around, the girls probably didn't like him much more than we did. If I'd known Greek, I'd have told them that slaves had been freed a long time ago in this country, and they should indulge themselves in an uprising.

When it had first been built, the top floor of the hospital must have been a favorite spot for anyone who came up here. The curved wall was ringed with windows. Some of them were broken and I was more than fine with that. The air coming through was cold, but compared to what the stale air, mildew, and decay that the rest of the building had going for it, at least it was fresh.

The only light in the room was from a Coleman lamp that Eddie had ordered, according to the invoice Kenji had found on the baby gorgon's laptop, and it showed us the room's sole occupant.

Ben Sadler was sitting chained hand and foot to a huge radiator against the far wall, beneath a series of broken windows. His broken forearm hung in a sling, though that was the only concession to mercy. Since that wrist couldn't be bound, Ben's torso had been chained to the radiator instead.

A blindfold hung around his neck.

It took me a moment to realize why he had one.

No anti-gorgon-glare glasses.

What better way to terrify a prisoner into cooperating than to have him kidnapped by harpies, taken to an island hospital that'd been abandoned for fifty years, and chained in a room where they tossed heroin addicts to dry out. And once Ben had soaked in the ambience, he'd been blindfolded to keep his former client from accidentally turning him to stone before he could force Ben to use a terrifying ability he didn't know he had the day before to cure du Beckett's sorry ass while killing thousands of people.

Eddie Laughlin was standing guard from a few feet away.

Wait, Ben didn't have glasses and his blindfold was off. How could he . . .

"Eddie must have outlived his usefulness to you," Ian noted, his voice tight.

"On the contrary, he's providing continuous instruction to Mr. Sadler."

Ben was doing everything he could not to look at Eddie, but his haunted blue eyes inevitably glanced back at the gorgon, then quickly away, his breath coming faster.

We were still outside the room, so he hadn't seen us yet.

Looking at a statue wouldn't scare anyone that badly, even if you'd been forced to watch while it was done. Unless . . .

I went very still. "He's still alive."

"There is another human saying that applies here," du Beckett said. "If you can't be an example, serve as a warning. Mr. Sadler required a warning, and Mr. Laughlin had made one mistake too many."

"Let me guess," Ian said. "Killing Denny Sykes and getting his apartment searched. And let me also guess: you were the one who infected him."

"Eddie's greed was his downfall. To be quite honest, this is the most useful purpose he's ever served. I require Ben's cooperation at midnight. Once Eddie returned earlier this evening and regaled me with his latest ill-considered activities, I realized that he would be infinitely more useful serving as both an example and a warning to young Ben."

"So did you enjoy telling Ben that you never wanted him for his diamond appraising, and planned to use him to commit mass murder all along?"

"I have received no pleasure from threatening Mr. Sadler. If I choose, I can reverse the process with Eddie—and your friend downstairs."

"Helena Thanos said that the paralysis is reversible for up to twelve hours," I told Ian. I didn't say that petrification would then set in, and Yasha would live in agony for hours after that as he turned to stone from the outside in until the petrification reached and consumed his major organs.

Sebastian du Beckett knew all of that. He knew and he'd still paralyzed Yasha, and Eddie Laughlin, as well—after the bastard had infected him with gorgonism. Satan had special rooms set aside for men like that. Rake Danescu had already said he wanted to send du Beckett there; I'd never wanted to murder anyone in my life, but as of that moment, I'd do anything I could to put Sebastian du Beckett in the express lane to Hell.

"If you're cured at midnight," Ian was saying, "you won't be able to reverse the process." Then his eyes met mine and widened in realization.

And Yasha would die from old age and shock when he ceased to be a werewolf and became mortal again.

Sebastian du Beckett said in an utterly flat and dead voice, "If I'm *not* cured at midnight, I never will."

30

WITH my hands chained behind my back, I couldn't look at my watch, but Eddie's online shopping spree had taken care of that, too. On an old school desk was a digital clock with the time down to tenths of a second left until midnight.

11:51:21

Ben was Dorothy, du Beckett was the Wicked Witch, and instead of an hourglass, du Beckett had locked Ben in a tower with a state-of-the-art digital clock to let him know how long he had left.

And a paralyzed gorgon to remind him that there'd be a price to pay for defiance.

When we'd walked through that door, excitement, hope, and relief rushed over Ben's face in rapid succession, ending with hope being shoved out the broken window behind him when he saw our harpy guards and our hands chained behind our backs.

I could only imagine his devastation. Ian and I were the only people he knew who knew that monsters were real and that monsters had taken him. So we were the only people who he had any hope might come and save him.

Even then, he had to doubt. We'd only known him for two days. Why would we risk our lives for him? And a man he *did* know and trust was the very monster who'd ordered him taken.

My harpy escort released my arm, and crossed the room to Ben. He shrank from her touch when she grabbed his blindfold and pulled it back over his eyes. Shrinking was all he could do; whoever had chained him to the radiator had essentially lashed him there, so he'd have no choice but to look at Eddie Laughlin. Her job done, she returned to her station behind me. The hand on Ben's unbroken right arm had been bound in such a way that his wrist was held immobile with the palm facing up—ready for du Beckett to put those diamonds in his hand at midnight. Ben could close his fingers into a fist to keep from taking the diamonds, but fingers could be broken, just like that harpy had broken his arm. Sebastian du Beckett had left Ben with no choice.

Oh yeah, the thermostat in that special room in Hell had been raised to "Molten hot," and a plaque with Sebastian du Beckett's name on it had been put on the door. I wanted nothing more than to help him check in before midnight.

As if reading my mind, the gorgon took a small pouch from his coat pocket. He opened it and poured the seven sparkling diamonds into his open hand. "Have you changed your mind, Mr. Sadler?"

"Touch those diamonds and thousands die." Ian pushed the words out in a rush in case du Beckett had omitted that part.

The kid's mouth went slack. "What?" he breathed.

The gorgon hadn't shared his evil master plan. Surprise, surprise.

"You'll kill thousands of people to cure yourself," Ian continued.

"Not people, Agent Byrne. Monsters. Thousands upon thousands of monsters. Creatures that are mutations, abominations of nature, things that can only exist by feeding on humans. SPI kills monsters." He gave a tight smile. "Though when you have a monster in charge, exceptions are made."

"You just described yourself," I said. "Vivienne Sagadraco is not a monster. If you want to see a—"

"She's a *dragon*," du Beckett snapped. "Any human who's ever drawn breath would scream in horror at the very sight of her."

"She would not slaughter thousands of innocents," Ian said. "Elves, goblins, the fae, gnomes, beings who have never harmed a human. Yes, vampires feed from humans, but are forbidden under prosecution to feed from any human against their will, and will be put to permanent death if they kill. If there is a crime, there is a punishment. You have killed, not to survive, but premeditated murder, and you would kill thousands more merely to save yourself. You are your own definition of a monster, yet you expect mercy when you're willing to give none."

Du Beckett sighed in mocking disappointment. "You've spoiled my surprise for Mr. Sadler, Agent Byrne, even after I paralyzed your werewolf friend. Now you dare to lecture me on my moral failings. Apparently one warning wasn't enough."

The gorgon nodded to my personal harpy.

Aw crap.

Well, it wasn't like I was really expecting to walk out of this anyway.

Standing directly behind me, the harpy quickly crossed her arms through mine that were chained behind my back, locking me in place. Might as well have tied me to a steel column.

Sebastian du Beckett reached out to remove my glasses. I closed my eyes and in desperation slammed my head back into the chin of the harpy holding me to try to loosen her grip. I might as well have rammed my head against a steel column, too. Though maybe I was now seeing enough stars to not be able to focus on Sebastian du Beckett's gorgonism-infected eyes.

I heard shouts and struggling from Ian, and I think even from Rake.

The gorgon barked another command in Greek and the voices were silenced into muffled growls and hisses.

A second harpy grabbed my head to hold it still, and I squeezed my eyes shut even tighter.

Du Beckett sighed again. "Agent Fraser, don't make this any harder on yourself than it has to be."

I clenched my jaw and my teeth in addition to my eyelids. Hell, I think I even tried to pull my eyebrows down. The second harpy's other hand pried my right eyelid open. Maybe only one eye would get me only half paralyzed. The whimper that escaped my lips told me I didn't believe that.

"Wait!" Ben shouted.

I had one eye forced open, but I still refused to look at du Beckett.

"You're still wasting my time, Ben," the gorgon's voice was clipped with barely restrained rage. "You know what I require. The dimensional barriers are thinnest at midnight. Those diamonds *will* be in your hand and activated when that time arrives." He made an impatient sound. "Agent Fraser, my helpers cannot touch your actual eye; their claws would puncture it, blinding you and rendering this most tiresome exercise moot. If you will not turn your eye toward me, then I shall be forced to get quite close to you, so that regardless of where you look, I will be there."

He moved and I screamed. I couldn't help it.

"I'll do it!" Ben pleaded. "Just stop!"

Sebastian du Beckett took one step back, and the harpy released my eyelid.

Warm, stinging wetness flowed into and from my eye and down my cheek. It could have been tears, blood, or both. My breathing was ragged, and I think the harpy had punched holes in my skull with her claws. A couple of gasps later and my vision started to clear, and I had wind enough to speak.

"Ben . . . don't. He can't do this unless you let—"

The eyelid-grabbing harpy clamped her hand over my mouth.

"Open your hand, boy," du Beckett commanded. "Now."

I couldn't hear or see Ian and Rake, but I had to assume they were as helpless as I was to stop what was about to happen.

Ben did as he was told.

11:59:00

One minute until midnight.

"Now close your fingers around them."

Ben's wrist was bound so that he couldn't dump the diamonds on the floor. I think if it were possible, he would've cut off his own hand to have the Dragon Eggs away from him right now. His breath came in trembling gasps as he closed his shaking fingers around the diamonds as if he'd been ordered to grab onto a cobra.

The diamonds flashed in a prism of blinding color. All the brilliance they possessed flooded out into the room through his clenched fingers. Ben didn't—or couldn't—look away. His pale eyes reflected the colors, then absorbed and became part of them against his will, joining him to the Dragon Eggs, their strength becoming his strength.

I felt the power building.

Too much power, too fast, and with too little control. Raw power with no experience.

And the energy had been awakened, ley lines flowing under the island like rivers of energy, meeting and converging at the nexus like the churning of whitewater rapids far below us.

This was bad. Beyond bad.

Lethal.

11:59:10

31

YOU knew you were in deep doo-doo when dozens of harpies attacking a dragon like planes in an aerial dogfight had been relegated to insignificant background noise.

I suddenly remembered Viktor Kain because I heard another voice I recognized—or, to be more exact, another enraged dragon roar.

Vivienne Sagadraco.

We all knew the instant when the two behemoths locked literal horns.

The tuberculosis pavilion shook from its foundation on up to the roof over our heads. Chunks of plaster fell from the walls, and crashed down from the ceiling, and several more panes of glass lost their grip on their frames.

Suddenly I could do more than hear what was happening outside. I could hear what was going on inside Viktor Kain's mind.

At the museum, he'd used images of torment from his sick and twisted memory in an attempt to intimidate and

terrify me. Tiamat had used words on New Year's Eve.
Apparently Kain had used a light touch then so as not to
destroy my mind because there was nothing light about what
I felt now. I realized this wasn't meant for me. This was Kain
ranting against Vivienne Sagadraco. I didn't know if it was
the nexus or the activating Dragon Eggs, but I could see,
hear, feel, and smell the memories triggered in Kain's mind
by his words. When the first wave of images crashed into
my consciousness, I was completely unprepared, like being
hit and pulled under by a giant wave.

I lost all feeling in my legs, and my body crumpled. The
harpy didn't bother to hold me up and let me drop to the
floor. She probably thought I'd fainted. My body couldn't
handle the images being forced into my mind.

*A black dragon leveled out over a city that'd been
bombed and was burning, choking black smoke billowing
into the night sky, pockets of glowing orange where anything
flammable burned inside the shells of ruined buildings,
illuminating the jagged silhouettes of the brick and stone
walls that'd managed to remain standing. The humans had
taken refuge in a place they called the Underground when
the air-raid sirens had sounded.*

*The dragon leveled off, intently scanning the ground for
her next target. She could hear the terrified heartbeats of
thousands of humans huddling together beneath the city in
tunnels. They were not her concern. They did not hunt her
kind. The others did. They called themselves protectors of
the humans, the small immortals, and the fae races.*

SPI.

*Only the strong deserved to live, to thrive, to mate, to
hunt. If a creature was weak and couldn't defend itself, it
was food.*

*The traitor led those who protected the humans and
immortals that populated this island called England, the
island desired by those the dragon had allied herself with.*

Her allies were also human; but they recognized the value of master predators and offered her a portion of these lands as her own in which to hunt, mate, and raise her young.

She and others of her kind had agreed to use their fire breath by night to wear down the humans of this island until they would submit. It was a small and enjoyable task in return for land of her own with humans to feed her, her mate, and their future young.

She found the place where the protectors had gone to ground when she came at night among the flying machines of her allies.

The black dragon banked and turned, inhaling the thick, smoke-filled air, fanning the flames that lay waiting inside, gathering at the base of her long neck, to engulf, to consume, to destroy, cleansing the land for her future family.

The humans could only fly when seated inside their winged, metal shells. Rigid and clumsy, they could not maneuver as she could.

That night she sought out and destroyed the burrow of the humans called SPI. Her fire had gone deep and struck true.

The humans pursued her in their machines, firing at her what she had learned were called bullets. The dragon's skin was thick and strong, and in the past, the bullets had been no more than a momentary annoyance.

These were different. They penetrated her scales, entered her body, and burned as no fire had ever dared to burn her before.

The humans in the metal machines did not react in fear when they saw her. They knew of her and her kind. She brushed their minds and gathered their thoughts.

Silver.

She had objects forged from it in her hoard. It was what the humans had used to forge their bullets. Their minds contained images of fire, descending into tunnels and chambers. Burning. Consuming.

Her fire. Their burrow. The protectors. SPI.

The traitor of her kind had sent them. They were all that remained of the protectors.

They hunted her as she had hunted them. They burned her with their silver as she had burned them.

Her burning became pain.

The pain became torment.

The torment made her leave her beloved sky and seek out the ground.

They pursued her.

She called out for her mate, but he did not come. Her human allies had long since abandoned her.

The dragon met her end on the island her human allies desired, the island she had been promised.

Groaning against the waves of nausea from the flickering images, I rolled over on my side, blinking my eyes to clear them.

The clock swam into view.

11:59:40

Thirty seconds?

All of that in only thirty seconds of Viktor Kain's rage-fueled memories?

He'd been with his mate that night in mind, not body. The telepathic link of a mated pair. He'd known where she was, what she had done.

Vivienne Sagadraco's SPI agents had taken his life mate.

He had felt her death in England in 1940 from hundreds of miles away, and had vowed vengeance if it took an eternity.

Tonight, an ocean away, that vengeance would be his.

Viktor Kain roared in my mind. *"I will destroy you and everything you ever loved! I will see you hunted and butchered as my Katerina was. There were no eggs with my Katerina, no young to continue her line. I gathered the Dragon*

Eggs as the legacy we should have had together—and as the instruments of my revenge."

Then came an image. It didn't come from Viktor Kain's conscious thought; instead it emerged from his subconscious of private gloating, a triumph finally achieved.

Two people with a ball of white fire between them. Each reached out and put one of their hands into the fire. Both had pointed ears, one with pale skin, the other gray.

An elf and a goblin.

One goblin gem to heal, one elf gem to reveal.

Five cursed human stones to light the fire.

Once ignited, they can only be quenched by an elf and goblin united.

The staccato flashes of memory, rage, and gloating stopped.

It was like a whirly swoopy ride at the fair that stopped way too fast.

Then, in my mind, was blessed silence.

In the quiet, a familiar voice asked with unflappable British calm: "Did you get that, Makenna?"

With a groan, I rolled over; the broken ceramic tiles cool against the side of my face.

I couldn't answer. I couldn't think. Kain's memories swirled in endless, high-speed laps in my head.

The London Blitz. SPI's destruction. Katerina's death. Kain's obsession. An elf and a goblin.

An elf and a goblin?

What the hell?

I struggled to sit up.

Then I knew.

Viktor Kain hadn't been able to resist, at the moment of his ultimate triumph, to let an image cross his mind of how it all could have been stopped.

It would have taken a miracle.

Viktor Kain didn't believe in miracles.

A goblin and an elf, races separated by ages of hostility and distrust, joining together, risking their lives, reaching into the fire that was the activated Dragon Eggs to claim their people's stones of power.

"Agent Fraser, it just so happens that I've brought an elf," Vivienne Sagadraco said in my mind. *"Do tell Rake to behave and make himself useful."*

32

MEANWHILE, all hell had broken loose.

The chaos surrounding me would have been impressive any way you looked at it, but I discovered that being sprawled on the floor introduced the added danger of being trampled. I rolled so I was sitting on the floor, not sprawled on it, and quickly crab-walked myself into the closest thing a semi-round room had to a corner.

The door exploded off its hinges as Yasha burst in, followed by an even more unbelievable sight.

Helena Thanos.

I didn't know if Sebastian du Beckett knew who and what Helena was, or if he had even seen her.

11:59:50

Ten seconds.

Sebastian du Beckett quickly maneuvered to put himself directly in Yasha's line of sight.

Oh, hell, no.

My hands were chained but my feet were right where

they needed to be. The gorgon didn't even notice me on the floor.

But he sure noticed when I tripped him.

Du Beckett hit the floor hard, his glasses sliding across the broken tiles.

"You bitch!" Spit flecked the corners of his mouth as he scrabbled for me. I jerked my knees up to my chest, getting my legs between us a split second before he threw himself on top of me, one gloved hand at my throat, the other clawing at my tightly closed eyes.

"Look at me!" he screamed. With du Beckett's hand clutching my throat, his weight, plus the pressure of my legs folded against my chest, I was in danger of passing out.

Then he was gone.

I flopped over on my side, legs still drawn up in a fetal position, coughing and gasping for air.

I risked opening my eyes and saw Ian with one arm around du Beckett's neck, forcing him to look into Helena Thanos's glorious violet eyes.

The two gorgons were locked in a death stare.

Sebastian du Beckett's body went rigid, and I could actually see his neck and then his face harden into gray stone. Only when the process was complete did Ian release him. Without my partner to hold him up, the gorgon fell to the floor, his body shattering on impact.

Caera Filarion knelt in front of Ben, her hand hovering over his clenched fist. He was aware of her, tears streaming down his face as he fought to open his hand. He couldn't. The force of the nexus pulling the power of the activated diamonds downward to merge with it was too strong.

"Rake!" I croaked, my throat bruised from the gorgon's grip. I coughed and tried again. "Rake! Help her! A goblin and an elf. Both need to take . . ." My voice failed.

12:00:00

Midnight.

Oh no.

Rake dove for Ben.

Caera desperately tried to pry Ben's fingers open. Rake's hands covered both of theirs. The diamonds blazed, engulfing them all, pulsing faster and brighter. Rake bowed his head over their joined hands, his forehead touching them.

Seconds later, Rake raised his head, but didn't loosen his grip. He was talking fast to Caera and Ben, but the rest of us couldn't hear over the frenzied hum produced by the activated diamonds. Caera loosened her hands as Ben's face became taut with concentration and determination. He forced his hand to open by sheer will, Caera's hand maintaining contact on one side of Ben's hand, Rake's on the other, as the elf and the goblin reached into Ben's opening fingers for the diamonds of their people.

The world went white.

33

I'D heard that diamonds were virtually indestructible, but damn.

There were five smoking holes in the floor of the tower room where Rake had used the back of his hand to sweep the five diamonds from our dimension out of Ben's palm.

Rake held the goblin Queen of Dreams in his other hand.

Caera had the elven Eye of Destiny.

Five holes the size of my fist had been burned through the fourth floor, through to the third, the second, and the first. They might have gone clear down to the interior of the island, but we couldn't see that far. The cursed diamonds had left a blazing path of destruction in their wake.

And New York's newest level ten gem mage, Ben Sadler, didn't even have a blister.

Not bad for a newbie.

As an added bonus, his broken arm had been healed.

Contact with both a goblin mage and an elf had kept the power of the activated Dragon Eggs from reaching the nexus.

As sensitive as I was to the island's ley lines, I would have known if it had—and so would every supernatural in the tristate area. Though all that power had to go somewhere, and Ben and his broken arm couldn't have been any closer. The Dragon Eggs wouldn't heal humans, but I guessed being a level ten gem mage trumped being human.

Yasha was working off his pent-up rage at not getting to pop du Beckett's head off his neck like a bottle cap by taking it out on Ben's chains. We didn't know where the keys were, so the werewolf was crushing steel links in his hands like walnuts. It seemed to be making him feel better. Caera sitting close to Ben, holding his hand, and talking to him was making both of them feel better. She didn't know how she had helped to deactivate the diamonds since she didn't have any magical ability. I had news for her; sometimes the best magic of all was simply being there.

Chunks of stone that were once Sebastian du Beckett were scattered all over the floor. In fact, it was difficult to tell the difference between him and some of the cement and brick mortar that had fallen through the new hole in the roof from the tower's "battlements." One look out of a glassless window confirmed that the boss and Viktor Kain had done more than a little property damage. From what I could see, it'd been enough to disqualify the tuberculosis pavilion from being called the best preserved building on North Brother Island.

The damage could be explained by a report that the same "terrorists" who blew up those three boats in the East River did all the damage to the island and its buildings, which was true. Between the two of them, Vivienne Sagadraco and Viktor Kain had also taken care of the harpy infestation. Again, Viktor Kain unknowingly helped.

Their knock-down, drag-out dragon fight had another casualty.

Me.

Walking in a straight line, or really simply walking, was more of a challenge than I was up to yet. Yasha took care of our chains. Dramamine took care of dizziness and nausea due to boats, planes, trains, and cars, but it wasn't quite up to handling the effects of telepathic dragon communication on a human. I dimly wondered if I should send the manufacturer an e-mail suggesting an upgrade.

We were all out of the building now, waiting on the patrol boat that would be here in the next half hour. Before it got here, I should probably toss back another of my little orange, chewable friends.

A case of the woozies was a small price to pay; tiny, insignificant even. Though if I was going to be making this a habit, maybe I should see if the folks in the lab could work up something stronger and even more fast acting that I could carry around with me.

As a gem mage himself, Viktor Kain had sensed when the diamonds had been deactivated by exactly the means he'd gloated about. The boss believed that he sensed the Dragon Eggs' separation from each other, and the five human diamonds making like nuclear cooling rods and having five mini meltdowns. He'd decided to cut his losses by leaving the island the way he'd come. LaGuardia was just a few miles away by water. His jet was waiting there.

"He'll be back," Vivienne Sagadraco said. She was sitting next to me on a stone bench across the kudzu-covered street from the pavilion. Most things on North Brother Island had crumbled with age; others like this carved bench had stood the test of time just fine. It was nice to sit down on something that didn't move.

"Viktor's mate, Katerina, believed me to be a traitor for choosing to protect humans and immortals over my own kind," she said. "Katerina immolated one hundred and thirty-six of my agents in that London bunker that night. She was on her way north to Edinburgh to do the same to our Scottish headquarters there. I defended my people then, as I will always defend them. The pilots who pursued Katerina were RAF, but they were also SPI agents. My people gladly served and protected their country. Viktor was correct in one accusation; the orders that night were mine. As RAF or SPI, those pilots were charged with protecting Great Britain and its people from *all* threats. Whether from dragon or Luftwaffe, the deaths of British citizens—whether human or supernatural—would not be tolerated. For decades Viktor has plotted his revenge for the death of Katerina. He will go home and plan his next move."

"Hopefully it won't be as creative," I said. "Or as disorienting."

"My apologies, Agent Fraser. By remaining silent, I hoped that you would be able to hear Viktor clearly. Whether human or dragon, when one is consumed with a desire for revenge, when that moment finally arrives, emotion can override reason."

"And you can say—and show—things you shouldn't, even if you didn't mean to."

"His pain made him careless. During his long life, Viktor has caused untold pain and suffering, but it did not prevent him from feeling love for another. The loss of Katerina caused a wound so deep, that even if he had been successful and destroyed me as well as those I love and protect, his pain may have eased and his need for revenge may have been satisfied, but only for a short time. Wounds like that—the loss of the one who made you complete, who you looked forward to sharing your life with, to growing old with—such wounds do not heal; they merely become more bearable. I had hoped, and I still do, that Viktor would realize this." She shrugged, a simple and common human gesture, made by a small woman who half an hour ago had been a big dragon. "He has never listened to me."

I shook my head in wonder. "Viktor Kain comes here,

your enemy, a known murderer, with the intent of murdering and destroying even more people, and you feel sorry for him."

Vivienne Sagadraco looked across the street at the damage she and Viktor Kain had done. "I can feel sympathy for his loss and his pain without affecting who I am and my opposition to all that Viktor Kain is and stands for. When we lose our empathy for others and allow our enmity to spiral downward and twist into mindless hate, we are no better than the Viktor Kains of the world. Compassion is our strength, not our weakness." She paused. "And it is a treasure that is meant to be shared. Do you understand?"

I nodded slowly and let myself smile, truly smile, for the first time in two days. "I understand perfectly . . . Miss Vivienne."

Vivienne Sagadraco continued to look ahead, but now she smiled very slightly.

We watched as Helena Thanos and Alain Moreau emerged from the pavilion and walked slowly down the steps. Ian, wearing his protective glasses, met them at the bottom. He spoke briefly with Helena, reached down, took her hand, and kissed it, no doubt thanking her for coming to help, and especially for reversing Yasha's paralysis. Just as an older gorgon's stare could turn a younger one to stone, they could also reverse the paralysis inflicted by a younger gorgon. Helena leaned in and kissed Ian on the cheek.

However, du Beckett's touch on Eddie Laughlin had taken the paralysis too far. The petrification had entered his bloodstream and begun spreading from there to his organs. Helena said it was turning him to stone from the outside in, his internal organs slowly solidifying, and would eventually end with his brain and heart. And, as it happened, Eddie would continue to be aware, but paralyzed the entire time and helpless to do anything to stop it.

Helena had mercifully looked into his eyes, and done what needed to be done.

Helena Thanos and Alain Moreau, arm in arm, continued to the island's dock where a Coast Guard patrol boat, with a crew of clued-in humans and supernaturals, would be arriving shortly to take us back to the city. There wasn't anything that Kenji couldn't arrange.

Moreau had come over to check on me when Ian had first carried me out of the building since I hadn't been able to walk two steps without falling down. I'd been used to seeing my vampire manager in a suit. Tonight he was wearing what looked like biker leathers in midnight blue. He absolutely rocked that look, and it seemed that Helena Thanos agreed.

Vivienne Sagadraco had made use of the invisibility amulet she had used on New Year's Eve to defend Times Square against her sister Tiamat and her grendels. Tonight it had enabled her to fly herself, Moreau, Helena, and Caera to North Brother Island, sight unseen by the swarms of law enforcement boats patrolling the East River. Moreau had used a harness that the boss had had made long ago to enable her to carry her second in command. Helena and Caera had the stomach-dropping experience of being strapped into, essentially, a modified helicopter cockpit with a carrying bar. Ms. Sagadraco picked it up in her claws, and away they went.

"So older vampires are immune to older gorgons," I noted with a smile. "Nice."

"It was indeed a pleasant surprise. Both are equally rare, so it's not surprising that there is no record of immunity." She tilted her head back, gazing at the stars. "Many happy accidents have resulted from this evening's events."

I nodded in agreement. "The potential for vampire and gorgon romance. I'll bet he'll even be able to talk her out of the house."

"That is highly likely."

"Why did she agree to come? Especially traveling here the way she had to. If du Beckett had succeeded, she'd have been at ground zero."

"She believed that had she remained at home, she would have died a coward. By coming here, even if she became dust, she would have tried to stop Bastian, and her death would have served a purpose. If you can choose your death, it is always better if you die so that others have a chance to live."

"What about Caera?"

"When Agent Filarion asked to accompany us here, my first instinct was to refuse her. It wasn't safe. However, she is fond of Mr. Sadler, and was quite insistent. On a night like tonight when so many things might have ended, other things should be given a chance to begin."

The boss stood and walked over to where Ben and Caera were sitting against the base of a tree. Ben had seen her coming over and had attempted to stand. I smiled. My grandma Fraser always said that one of the true tests to tell if a man's been raised right and is a gentleman is whether he stands when a lady enters the room—or tonight, in Ben's case, when a woman walks under a tree. I wondered if our Mr. Sadler was a Southern boy. I hadn't heard an accent, but you never knew.

Ms. Sagadraco gestured for Ben to stay put, not that he was having more luck keeping his feet than I was. She knelt down next to them, and started to talk. I had a feeling Ben might eventually be getting a job offer that was better suited to his skill set than being a diamond appraiser at Christie's. Though I could see where the boss might find it valuable to have an agent on the inside in one of the world's top art auction houses. Sometimes art was more than it appeared, and in the wrong hands could cause a world of hurt. Yep, an agent on the inside would be good.

I took my third and last Dramamine out of my pocket. If the second one hadn't kept me from staggering like a drunken sailor, a third one—

Ian sat next to me on the bench. "Take that only if you want to pass out."

I snorted. "You say that like it's a bad thing. I haven't slept in two days." The fire hydrant standing perfectly preserved on the curb started tilting slowly to the right. "Oh boy." I put my hands down on the bench on either side of me, bracing for the next wave of the dizzies. It was getting better. The first time I'd fallen right off the bench and into the kudzu.

"Is it happening again?" Ian asked.

"Oh yeah."

His arm went around my shoulders, pulling me against him. "Don't worry, I've got you."

It didn't stop the dizziness, but it did wonders for everything else.

"That was entirely too close," I said quietly.

"Falling off the bench?"

"No. Tonight."

Ian sighed and gave my shoulder a squeeze.

I settled tiredly against him and looked back over at the pavilion.

Five of the world's most valuable diamonds were somewhere in or below that crumbling pile of bricks. If most New Yorkers knew that, the police, feds, Coast Guard, and the Hell Gate wouldn't keep them from swarming the place in the ultimate Easter egg hunt.

Vivienne Sagadraco had said she was perfectly fine with leaving them right where they were.

The goblin crossing the street to our little bench would probably be paying the island another visit, just for the challenge and the fun of it, if nothing else. If anyone could coax diamonds out of rubble, it'd be Rake Danescu.

Ian extended his right hand. "I'd stand, but I think I'm all that's holding her up."

Rake took my partner's hand and shook it. In his other hand was the Queen of Dreams.

I couldn't wait for some sleep and dreams of my own.

The diamond still had a residual glow from Ben's touch. The goblin met my eyes and winked. "I told you pink was evil."

"Hey, I never said I doubted you—on that."

I hadn't doubted that pink was evil, but I had doubted Rake Danescu—though not nearly as much as Ian. He'd had reason to; he knew the goblin better.

"We couldn't have done it without you," Ian told Rake. "Thank you."

To Ian's credit, he didn't choke on any of those words. Though he did pause a wee bit before the last two.

The goblin inclined his head in acknowledgment. "From what I understand, Makenna's eavesdropping on Viktor Kain sealed the deal."

We'd probably never know if Rake had agreed to help because he knew that if those diamonds weren't stopped, not only would he lose his human disguise, but everything he'd built here for himself.

Or had Rake had an actual moment of caring for someone else besides himself?

Or was it another reason entirely?

I didn't know, and Rake would never say. Not to mention, I was too tired to waste my breath asking. He'd just answer my question with another question until I forgot what I'd asked in the first place. I ran my hand over my face. Oh yeah, I was definitely too tired for that.

Not that Rake would mind taking credit for saving every supernatural in the tristate area—it'd just be more fun to keep us all guessing as to why he'd done it.

If the goblin was going to keep popping into my life, I'd have to learn to pick my battles or he'd drive me crazy. This time it meant being satisfied with knowing what he did, but not knowing why he did it. He was a riddle, wrapped in a mystery, inside an enigma, and that wasn't likely to change anytime soon. I'd be better off just accepting that and preserving my sanity.

We looked across to where Yasha had changed more or less back into human form, and was getting Ben Sadler on his feet. Ben was tall, Yasha was much taller, but they made it work. It was a big change from just this morning when the Russian had growled when Ben had gotten into his SUV.

As Vivienne Sagadraco came back over to us, Yasha and Caera started helping Ben to the dock; one on either side of him. The big Russian was doing all of the helping; Caera with her arm around Ben's waist was doing the holding. While I was sure Ben appreciated Yasha's efforts, all of his attention was on Caera.

Rake was formally thanking Ms. Sagadraco for keeping Viktor Kain occupied—thus preventing the Russian dragon from ripping the roof off the pavilion like opening a trick or treat bag and snapping us up like Halloween candy. My words, not his.

"I knew there were only the four of you," the boss said, "and that Viktor wouldn't have let anything keep him from getting to the island and his diamonds."

Including homicidal merpeople and the harpies with grenades.

"Also, the lab had the results of the DNA test on the remains from Bastian's office," she continued. "Of course, you already knew that the dead man wasn't Bastian. Given that the victim looked exactly like him, and that Bastian had been essentially refusing to leave his house for the past few months, concluding that he'd been infected with gorgonism was a logical assumption."

"Okay, I'm having a problem with part of this," I said.

Ian let out a short laugh. "Only part?"

"Yeah, good point. But this one's at the top of the list.

Sebastian du Beckett picked out, lured into his home, and killed a total stranger just to throw us off his trail, so he clearly didn't have a problem with murder. And from what I've heard the past few days, he wasn't exactly a social butterfly. Add willingness to murder and antisocial curmudgeon, and if anyone would be a natural as a gorgon, it would be Sebastian du Beckett. Yet to cure himself, he knocks out those harpies for six days, organizes a major jewel heist, and pisses off the likes of Viktor Kain. And if he wouldn't leave his house, how did he put those harpies into stasis? That was done at or around Heathrow, right?"

"All excellent points, dear Makenna," Rake said. "Though there is one more thing that bothers me, and it is not insignificant. I make it a point to know the magical capabilities of those who I may be forced to do business with. Sebastian du Beckett was a sorcerer of only moderate skill."

"Digging into Bastian's background, we found that his mother was a Greek sorceress who had a way with harpies," Ms. Sagadraco said.

"I did not know about his mother, Madame Sagadraco. While pertinent, it does not negate my hypothesis. I believe that Sebastian du Beckett did not act alone. Even if he despised the very ground upon which we trod—and I will admit to having given him ample reason on occasion—his motivations felt somewhat lacking. I know you may not—"

"I agree."

"You do?" Rake was taken aback, almost comically so.

Vivienne Sagadraco offered up an amused smile. "Is it that inconceivable that we would arrive at a similar conclusion from time to time?"

"No, it's merely that—"

Her eyes twinkled. "See? We agree again."

I wasn't sure which was more fun, watching the boss toy

with Rake Danescu, or seeing the goblin flustered. Nice thing was, I didn't have to choose; I sat back and enjoyed them both.

"While Bastian's mother was a sorceress," Ms. Sagadraco said, "and was probably qualified to put harpies into and bring them out of stasis, it doesn't necessarily mean that her son had the same skill."

"Is his mother still alive?" I paused and grimaced. "Or some kind of undead?"

"Neither, Agent Fraser. She is deceased—and has remained that way. In addition to the questions raised by Bastian being in his home in New York, and the harpies shipping from London, whoever brought those harpies out of stasis would have to have been present at the museum and in the Sackler Wing within sight of the 'statue.' Sebastian du Beckett was not at the Metropolitan Museum that night. He was at home at the time the harpies were awakened. He was receiving a package at that time from a courier service, and he came to the door and signed for it personally."

"Could it have been the homeless man who looked like him?" I asked.

Ms. Sagadraco shook her head. "The signature was Bastian's, and the courier service is used for delivering high-value items. Bastian dealt in antiquities, so his brownstone was a regular stop for them. The owner of the company is familiar with the supernatural community, and since his service occasionally handles objects of a paranormal nature, he is familiar with ways that fraud and theft during delivery could occur—namely shapeshifters hired to impersonate the recipient. The delivery agent wears a lapel camera which takes a photo of the recipient. That photo is subjected to a computerized fifteen-point identification verification. Within seconds, the recipient's identity is either confirmed or rejected. If approved, the package is retrieved from the armored vehicle and delivered."

I whistled. "So if they said it was du Beckett, it was du Beckett."

"They have never been wrong."

"I use the service myself," Rake said. "Even if Bastian had an identical twin, it wouldn't have been a match."

"So if du Beckett wasn't in London, and he wasn't at the museum," I asked, "then who was?"

"Of the sorcerers previously unknown to us who were recorded on the Metropolitan's surveillance cameras, four were known to be in the Sackler Wing when the theft occurred. All are accounted for except for one who has vanished, and who has a rather distinctive facial quality."

"Let me guess, the woman who was packing more magical mojo than anyone else there?"

"The very one."

"Have we found out anything else about her?"

"Nothing. It's as if she didn't exist before the night of the exhibition, and has ceased to exist now."

Ian cast a sideways glance at Rake Danescu, but addressed his statement to the boss. "In other words, it sounds like she's not from around here."

"We are leaning toward an extra-dimensional being," Ms. Sagadraco said. "Or at least one that is adept at concealing their identity by not remaining in any one dimension for too long. If she were still here, or had left, but used a mortal means of travel, there would have been some trace of a trail."

Ian regarded Rake with suspicion. "So, Danescu, do you know any high-powered ladies who would be interested in having New York wiped clean of supernaturals and most of SPI?"

"Off the top of my head, I don't—"

"I don't care about the top of your head," Ian said, his voice low and intense. "I want to hear what you *know*. You weren't expecting Sebastian du Beckett to be here any more than we were. So who did you think you *were* going to find when you got here? You were in your boat, on the East River, and heading this way when I called you, and don't say you were going to a Halloween party."

"Why don't you say what you're thinking? That I was dressed like I was up to no good."

"You haven't answered my question."

"And I don't intend to."

Ian went dangerously still. "It's all secrets and games with you. You're playing with lives, and you—"

Rake stepped in on him, putting them almost nose to nose. This was about to get ugly.

"My life was one of them. How dare—"

"Your life is all that matters, isn't it? If you could no longer hide what you are from humans, all you'd have to do is go home. You wouldn't be reduced to a pile of dust, or be on the run for the rest of your life. You risk noth—"

The goblin's eyes blazed. "I'm risking more than you'll ever kn—" Rake stopped and blew out his breath in a sharp hiss from between clenched teeth—and two very prominent fangs.

Vivienne Sagadraco stood.

That was all it took.

Both men immediately backed down. The top of her head barely reached their shoulders, but when you're a dragon—and a fire-breather—the size of your human form didn't mean a thing.

Though I think the main reason was respect.

They didn't like each other, but Ian and Rake respected Vivienne Sagadraco, and not because she could squash them flat with one clawed foot.

Ian took a calming breath. "I'm sorry, ma'am." His eyes stayed on Rake, but the fire was gone. "But you know how I feel abo—"

"Yes, Ian. I know."

"My apologies if I caused offense." Rake's words were for Ms. Sagadraco, but his eyes stayed right where they were, on my partner.

"Rake, for the protection and continued well-being of the city that I truly believe we both hold dear, I trust that you will tell me anything you know or may discover regarding this threat."

Rake finally looked away from Ian, turning solemn eyes on Vivienne Sagadraco. "On the honor of myself, my family, and my house, I swear."

I didn't know anything about goblin oaths, but that sounded impressive to me. I stole a glance at Ian. My partner looked taken aback. Another expression I'd never seen on him. Apparently that was one more serious goblin oath.

Then it was my turn to be shocked.

Ian extended his hand to Rake for the second time this evening.

Rake glanced down at Ian's hand and then up at my partner's face in surprise.

"I was out of line." Ian left "this time" unsaid, but we all knew what he meant. "I meant what I said earlier. We couldn't have done it without you—regardless of your reasons."

After only a brief hesitation, Rake extended his own hand and shook Ian's.

Disabling the Dragon Eggs, saving New York's supernaturals, Ian and Rake spending hours in each other's company without fists involved, then shaking hands twice and making nice—or at least polite. It'd been a night chock-full of miracles.

"So with du Beckett and Eddie both dead," I said quickly, before the boys could change their minds and turn hand-shaking into arm wrestling. "They can't tell us who they were working for or with, so we're right back where we started from."

"Far from it," Ms. Sagadraco said. "The person wanted the Dragon Eggs activated, and to destroy or force into hiding tens of thousands of supernaturals. SPI New York would have been decimated and rendered ineffective for an undetermined length of time. Once again we must ask ourselves who would benefit from such a scenario and how? New York has the greatest concentration of supernatural beings in this dimension. Those who would not have died outright would have been living in fear—and SPI would have been rendered powerless to help or to stop whatever this individual planned to do when that happened."

"They're setting the stage," I said. "For something they were ready to put into play immediately."

"That is what I believe."

"But what?"

"I'm certain we will be finding out. One doesn't plan the destruction of thousands of supernaturals, have those plans fail, and simply give up and walk away. They will be back— that is, if they ever left. That individual was in the Sackler Wing last night. We know that. We have surveillance camera footage; we have artists' sketches where the mortal technology failed." Her deep blue eyes burned with a fierce glare. "We only have a few names, but we have *every* face." Her words were clipped and deliberate. "We will start there, we will find who was responsible for this, we will learn what their next move will be, and *we will* stop them."

I looked out over the river to the lights of the city.

Our city.

"The unknown woman will be our starting point," Vivienne Sagadraco continued. "Though she may not be as unknown as we thought—or as well disguised as *she* believes. Our agent couldn't get a clear look at this individual's face. The features shifted and flowed—and the agent insisted that most of those features were male."

We only had the moon to see by, but I clearly saw the color drain right out of Ian's face. It was like he'd seen a ghost, but not the cold spot in a creepy old house variety; this ghost from Ian's past haunted him 24/7/365.

The "ghoul" that led the jewel thieves that had eaten Ian's NYPD partner and had put Ian in the hospital for a month wasn't really a ghoul, at least not all the time. The first time I'd seen him had been on a dark street last winter. I'd only seen the bottom half of his face; the rest was covered by the brim of a hat. Even though I'd only seen half, that was plenty enough to give me a lifetime of nightmares. I got the impression of multiple faces, each different from the one before, layered one on top of another, extending into the distance like looking into a wall of fun-house mirrors.

Years ago, on that night in the jewelry store, he'd promised Ian that he was next—next on the menu after he finished eating Ian's partner. Ten months ago, on New Year's Eve, Ian had come entirely too close to being this thing's midnight toast. It had been allied with Tiamat, Vivienne Sagadraco's sister.

I swallowed. "Did the agent say the different faces were layered on top of each other and looked like they kind of stretched into infinity?"

"Yes, she did."

The boss knew all about Ian's spectral friend. Well, she knew about each incident. What none of us knew or had been able to find out were any details about the creature itself. Heck, we didn't even know what it was. Logic would dictate that it was some kind of shapeshifter, but even shapeshifters were *something* to begin with.

"We don't know it's him," I told Ian.

"We don't know it's not." Any trace of fear was gone

from my partner's face, replaced with a slow smile that crept over his lips. Determined. Ferocious. Ian actually hoped that it was him; I could see it in his eyes. "But if it is him, this time I'm going to be ready."

Vivienne Sagadraco stared straight at Ian. "We *all* will."

MONDAY MORNING, SPI HEADQUARTERS

I'D slept for a good chunk of yesterday. I hadn't meant to, but my body clearly had other plans. Though I had to admit if I hadn't slept yesterday, I wouldn't be sitting upright in my office chair now.

From what I'd heard, this place was pretty much a ghost town yesterday. Supernatural bad guys didn't acknowledge weekends, so neither did we. SPI kept the same hours as the NYPD—which meant all of them. Some of the agents who'd stayed for the duration of the emergency were catching up on sleep. Sandra and her team were still recuperating; that meant Roy and his folks were on deck should anything hit the fan. The agents and civilians who had evacuated with their families were coming back into the city and getting resettled in their homes.

That was another thing that had made the news—New Yorkers suddenly turning Halloween weekend into a get-away holiday. News and lifestyle bloggers were debating whether it was the start of a new vacation trend.

I snorted. Not if we had anything to say about it.

I looked around the bull pen, and let my eyes wander to the upper floors. It looked like a regular Monday morning at SPI, but it was far from normal. My coworkers were either really chatty or unusually quiet. I guess we all handled near-death experiences in different ways.

Vivienne Sagadraco hired talented people, many with a lot of experience in their areas of expertise. New York had the largest concentration of supernaturals of anywhere in the world. SPI needed the best of the best working here. A lot of the time, experience came with age. When you were talking about supernaturals, age meant older—much, much older.

If the power of the Dragon Eggs had reached the energy of the ley lines' nexus, SPI's best and brightest would have been gone in an instant at midnight on Saturday.

Coworkers, mentors, and friends—they would have turned to dust, crumbled into bones, or died within minutes from extreme old age or the shock to their bodies of going from immortal back to mortal.

At least half of those talking, laughing, joking, or—as I was doing—just sitting quietly and watching, wouldn't have been here now.

I realized that it didn't matter how old you were, or even if you were a so-called immortal; your life could end at any time. If you were smart, you lived your life and treated the people who were in your life—those who were important to you, those you loved—as if every time you were with them might be the last time. Not in a morbid way, but joyfully, so that when that time did come, and it would, there would be no regrets.

I'd found out early this morning that the newfound urge to live life to the fullest, no regrets, carpe diem, and all that had also affected a certain goblin businessman. Though who was I kidding? Rake Danescu had found all of his urges a long time ago, and none of them were new.

He'd called this morning and invited me to lunch, offering to send a car to take me to that new restaurant in Tribeca with the superstar chef and a six-month waiting list that even Kylie hadn't been able to get into.

I admit to being tempted, but not necessarily by the restaurant. Rake Danescu had built a highly successful business based on temptation. Tempt and tantalize was what he did best.

I told myself there'd be plenty of other people in the restaurant. It'd be broad daylight, there'd be a table between us, and cutlery within reach in case I needed backup weapons to defend my virtue.

Though while I was admitting things and being honest with myself, I wasn't all that certain that if push came to shove, or grab came to grope, that I'd be all that enthusiastic about defending anything of mine from Rake Danescu, least of all my virtue.

And Rake knew it. He'd been in my head. He knew which buttons to push.

That was the biggest problem of all right there. My buttons hadn't had a good pushing in a long time.

Nearly being turned to stone by a gorgon had made me think about a lot of things.

I hadn't told Rake yes, but I hadn't told him no. I went with a time-honored stall that in my case was probably going to be true—I might have a meeting at lunchtime. We'd just dodged the tristate, supernatural Apocalypse; surely there were going to be meetings. I told Rake that I'd find out and get back to him. Naturally, Rake's countermove was to upgrade lunch to dinner.

Dinner with Rake Danescu was out of the question. I could see it now: dim lighting, candles, soft music, wine . . .

Uh-uh. No way, no how.

Lunch was better—or at least safer. And no car and driver. I could only imagine Rake's idea of a car and driver.

I'd get in and there wouldn't be any handles on the doors, but there'd be locks, and they'd only be controlled by the driver, who was actually Rake in a tight black chauffeur uniform. With boots.

Sweet mother of—

A grip, Mac. Get one.

I would definitely be taking a cab. If I even agreed to go. I glanced up to the fifth floor executive suite.

The floor-to-ceiling curtains on Vivienne Sagadraco's office were open. Usually that meant she was there, but I couldn't see any signs of lights being on. Though dragons didn't need light to—

Just ask her, Mac.

"Ma'am? Are you there?"

"Yes, Agent Fraser."

I could hear the slight smile in her voice as if she was sitting at her desk in the dark, musing like the rest of us on what had nearly happened, while waiting on me to ask what I was about to ask. I sensed that she hadn't been eavesdropping on my thoughts, she'd simply been aware of me.

"Um . . . ma'am? Rake Danescu just asked me out to lunch."

"I am not surprised."

"Come to think of it, I guess I'm not, either."

"Did you want to alert me of your meeting with Lord Danescu for safety purposes?"

"That wouldn't be a bad idea."

"It would be a prudent precaution." She paused. "But one that I believe is unnecessary."

"It's not?"

"What does your judgment tell you?"

"I think lunch would be fine. I would kind of like to go. It's just that—" He's so hot he might not be safe with me. I froze. Oh crap, did I think that out loud?

"Yes, you did, Agent Fraser." I could almost see a finger

with a newly manicured nail pressed to her lips, preventing the escape of something that might have resembled a laugh. *"Since I am a dragon, Lord Danescu is not . . . my type, as humans would say. However, dragons have a keen appreciation for beautiful things. In my opinion, Rake Danescu qualifies."*

"So it's okay if I go to lunch with him? Me being a SPI agent, and him being a . . . perpetual SPI suspect?"

"I believe no harm will come from it. And contrary to what your perception of me may be, I have always been in favor of personal enjoyment." There was a moment of silence. *"Go and have fun, Makenna."*

I smiled. "I'll try, ma'am. Thank you."

Then there was silence. The normal kind.

Vivienne Sagadraco had "hung up." That was good, because I had no idea how to hang up, sign off, or whatever was the right way to end telepathic human/dragon communication.

My phone beeped with an incoming text, and I glanced down at it.

Rake.

His message consisted of a single question mark.

I bit my bottom lip. I still wasn't sure about this.

I typed: Still checking.

Before sending, I proofed it to make sure auto correct didn't change it to something pornographic.

My phone beeped again almost immediately. I looked down.

Coward. ;)

Bastard. I thought it, and I was really tempted to type and send it.

With most people, emoticons didn't give you a visual, but I had no trouble seeing Rake's crooked grin—or as we called it back home, a shit-eatin' grin.

Fine. I'll go.

When's our reservation? I asked.

Noon.

If I was going to have lunch with him, I might as well throw caution to the wind as to how I was gonna get there.

Send your car, I typed. I'll be ready.

While I was contemplating safety precautions, I thought of the most important one of all: I might want to hold off on telling Ian that I was going to lunch with Rake Danescu.

Kylie O'Hara was making the rounds of the morning news shows.

Ian was standing with some other agents in front of one of the big TVs mounted on a section of wall. They were watching Kylie on *Good Morning America*. We'd all been through hell since Friday and Saturday, and most of us felt like it, and looked as bad as we felt.

I couldn't imagine Kylie slowing down, much less sleeping since Friday night. Sleep requirements must be different for dryads. Way different. In her dark slacks, ivory blouse— and yes, she was actually wearing a short *forest* green blazer—Kylie O'Hara looked like the fresh-as-a-daisy poster child for getting your beauty rest.

My partner stood with the other agents but slightly apart from them. Though a little bit of space wasn't all that separated Ian from the rest of the group.

He was wearing a jacket and tie. Very spiffy. I'd seen him in a tie before, though it'd always been when he was going out on a—

Date.

I grinned. My partner had a date.

I walked over and stood next to him, watching Kylie work her magic.

She sounded mentally sharp, confident, and articulate as all get-out while explaining the elaborate hoax at the

Metropolitan Museum of Art on Friday night. The robbery wasn't a hoax; that part was very real. But believing that the thieves were living, breathing, flying harpies?

"I'll leave finding the motive up to the experts—the men and women of the NYPD," Kylie was saying. "I've explained some strange events, but even I'm at a loss to explain why thieves would go to that much trouble, risking mechanical malfunction, and end up not getting the diamonds they went to such great lengths to steal."

I raised an eyebrow. "Mechanical malfunction?"

Ian raised a hand. "She's getting there. It's worth the wait."

Kylie grinned, and her trademark dimple briefly popped into view. "I'm no jewel thief, but surely there must be an easier way to—"

Ian leaned his head toward my ear. "Segue to the jewel thief turned author with his latest book . . ."

"You're kidding."

Ian chuckled. "Nope. He's up next."

"Smoke and mirrors at its finest."

"You ain't seen nothing yet."

Kylie launched into an explanation of animatronics, advances in robotics, and the latest in drone technology. She couldn't understand why someone would do it, but she admired the technological brilliance it had taken to carry out the robbery. The Dragon Eggs had not been found, but Kylie was more interested in finding the robotic harpies and getting at least one of them into a lab to analyze the technology.

The camera cut to a man in a chair next to her. A caption with his name and title appeared across the bottom of the screen, but Carl the ogre picked that moment to walk in front of the TV, so I missed it.

"Dang it, Carl," I muttered. "Who is he?" I asked Ian.

"The vice president of Research and Development for a

Japanese robotics company. He was on CNN last night. They're offering a twenty-million-dollar reward for the delivery of one of the harpy drones to their New York office."

My mouth dropped open. "Is that for real?"

Ian grinned. "As real as remote-controlled animatronic harpy drones."

"So this guy's a fake?"

"No, he's the real deal, and so is his company. But he's on our side."

I looked closer. I didn't see an aura to indicate that he was a supernatural.

Ian saw me squinting at the screen. "Not a supernatural. His lab is one of the many international corporations owned by Saga Partners Investments; that is, if you can dig down through the all the layers of holding companies."

Saga Partners Investments, the first letter of each, which happened to spell SPI, was owned by our very own Vivienne Sagadraco.

As soon as Kylie's segment wrapped, Ian reached up and adjusted his tie.

Oh yeah, my partner definitely had a date, and I now knew with whom.

I lowered my voice so only Ian could hear, but kept my tone casual. "So where are you and Kylie going for lunch?"

"Some new place . . ." He caught himself and stopped.

I did a little celebratory fist pump. "Gotcha, partner."

"Okay, you got me. I called Kylie yesterday and asked her out."

I grinned. "And she said yes. I told you she would."

"Actually, she said no."

"Huh?"

A mischievous smile flitted across his mouth. "She said she'd go out to dinner with me this week, if I let her take me to lunch today. Apparently it's one of those fancy places that's way above my pay grade."

My heart did a double thump, but I kept the smile on my face. "Fancy *and* new place? What's the name?"

"Kylie wouldn't say; she wants to surprise me. But I did some pre-lunch detective work and found out. All the publicity this weekend apparently bumped Kylie up to the local A-list, and into a lunch reservation at that new place in Tribeca. The one with the hotshot chef and the six-month waiting list."

Oh boy.

ABOUT THE AUTHOR

Lisa Shearin is the national bestselling author of the Raine Benares novels, a series of six comedic fantasy adventures. Lisa is a voracious collector of fountain pens both vintage and modern. She lives on a farm in North Carolina with her husband, three spoiled-rotten retired racing greyhounds, and enough deer and woodland creatures to fill a Disney movie.

For more information about Lisa and her books, visit her at lisashearin.com.

Explore the outer reaches
of imagination—don't miss these authors
of dark fantasy and urban noir who take you
to the edge and beyond . . .

Patricia Briggs	Anne Bishop
Simon R. Green	Marjorie M. Liu
Jim Butcher	Jeanne C. Stein
Kat Richardson	Christopher Golden
Karen Chance	Ilona Andrews
Rachel Caine	Anton Strout

penguin.com/scififantasy